Heads Deacon, Tails Devil

by P.J. McCalla

a P.J. McCalla novel

HEADS DEACON, TAILS DEVIL

Published by
The Elevator Group
Paoli, Pennsylvania

Library of Congress Control Number: 2009932535

Hardcover: ISBN 978-0-9819719-0-2
Trade Paperback: ISBN 978-0-9819719-9-5
E-book (e-pub): ISBN 978-0-9819719-1-9
E-book (e-pdf): ISBN 978-0-9819719-4-0

Jacket and interior design by Stephanie Vance-Patience

Published in the United States by The Elevator Group.

This book was printed in the United States.

To order additional copies of this book, contact:
The Elevator Group
PO Box 207
Paoli, PA 19301
www.TheElevatorGroup.com
610-296-4966
info@TheElevatorGroup.com

DEDICATED TO:

Mrs. Beatrice Harris

Mr. Jasper Fitzgerald

Mrs. Gwendolyn Young

Mrs. Phyllis Awkard

Ms. Marian Ricks

Mrs. Barbara Eunice

Mrs. Christine Norman

❖ ❖ ❖

INTRODUCTION

This book is fictional, but it is altered and loosely based on bits and pieces of true information. Some facts my mother told my sister and me when we were children. Some I learned or overheard when the "old folks" didn't know I was in the room.

Mom Maggie is the principal character in the book. My Irish great-grandmother, Margaret Turner, was her prototype. According to the family, her wisdom, fortitude and knowledge of herbs were legendary. She lived to be 103 years old.

Rachel, Mom Maggie's daughter, was fashioned after my grandmother, Rachel May White. Actually, she bore little resemblance to the weak, fictitious Rachel. She was strong willed and wise like her mother. She, too, understood the value of herbal medicine. She taught me how to read tea leaves, but she called it my gift.

Robert Grant, Rachel's husband, was loosely based on my grandfather, William White. He was a professor, composer, singer, deacon and tyrant. He ruled his family with an iron hand. He left home alone and migrated to Philadelphia, hoping to promote the hymns he'd composed. He became ill shortly after he arrived. Unlike Robert Grant in the book, he died an ordinary death. Someone stole the songs he'd written and kept in what he called his ballad box. He was never credited for his works, but they are still being sung today.

Rachel White, my grandmother, was the only one I knew. The others died before I was born, but I carry their genes, and that is exciting.

— *P.J. McCalla*

▼

CHAPTER 1

Rachel Grant sat in the third row pew at Nazarene Baptist Church. With her were her five children, Evelyn, Jim, Mary, Betty and Fran. Her husband, Robert, sat up front with the deacons. The Reverend Clyde Bacon was preaching one of his finest sermons. His closeness to God was evident by his facial expression and closed eyes. His text was "Church, Don't Go There."

The amens of the congregation pushed the pastor to even greater heights. The building seemed to rock on its foundation. With a flourish, the preacher wiped his face from time to time with a large, white handkerchief. He was perspiring profusely. The children no longer whispered. Every eye was on the man of God. He brought his sermon to a dramatic close amid thunderous clapping and amens. He wiped his brow once more and said, "Sing, choir!"

The choir took over where he left off. Amy Anderson, the soloist, was a large woman with a voice to match her girth. She belted out, "It's a Highway to Heaven". The rest of the choir accompanied her in the background. It was simply awesome! Five people joined the church that morning.

After the service, a sumptuous dinner was served to all. Tables were set up in the church yard, laden with chicken cooked in every style, potato salad, corn, peas, and greens. There were also hot biscuits, cornbread, and a variety of beverages.

This was before the turn of the century. People in the country traveled primarily by horse and buggy. Because of the distance, food was brought to the church. They ate there and remained for the afternoon service. It was the perfect time for people who hadn't seen each other for awhile to socialize.

After they'd eaten, Robert Grant rounded up his wife and children and they rode home in the buggy. They rode in silence because Robert both expected and demanded that they not talk without his permission. The children held hands, trying to draw comfort from each other. Robert maintained total control over his household. Rachel was a strong woman, but she was no match for him.

Rachel had a lot of time to think during the long, silent ride home. She earned extra money by working for the funeral director in town. She sewed the linings and fancy pillows for the coffins. In those days, the funeral director and his assistant handmade each coffin. Sometimes a carpenter was hired to make them, but she always sewed the linings.

Robert was super strict with all of them, but oddly enough, he never made her give the money she earned to him. Rachel couldn't accurately explain it, but she guessed that he merely hadn't thought of it. She swore that if that day ever came, she would stop helping the director.

While riding along, she thought about her mother, Mom Maggie, who lived a few country miles away. She was a tall, handsome woman with long, silver hair. She wore it braided and wound around her head. Often, she put on her bonnet and traveled on foot to see her family. All seven of her children were married and had families of their own.

Mom Maggie was a very special woman who had very special gifts. She could make predictions that always came true. Rachel smiled to herself when she thought about her mother's talents. She, too, had that same gift. They both used it quietly, but people knew and respected them because of it.

Rachel's thoughts shifted to her husband. He could be described as a man of average height, super-neat, highly intelligent, but very condescending. He had an extraordinary singing voice, and he composed religious music. Those two assets were the only thing that kept him from being a totally un-likeable human being. People came from far and near to hear him sing his music. He was always the main attraction at the annual camp meetings.

Few knew the real monster that lurked behind that glorious voice. Involuntarily, Rachel shook her head when she recalled how his singing attracted her to him. She was flattered when he pursued her. She was, at the time, envied by her friends. When he asked for her hand in marriage, she readily agreed.

Mom Maggie had reservations, and she wanted Rachel to turn him down. Rachel, too, didn't feel quite right about it, but she ignored the small voice inside. She married Robert in spite of everything. Tears stung her eyes when she remembered her wedding night. She knew immediately that she would regret marrying him for the rest of her life. That night he announced, "You are to see that I have a fresh white shirt every morning. My clothing is to be placed on the bed every day. I expect you to keep my shoes shined, and my meals served on time."

Rachel had been speechless! Where was the romance? This was not what she expected on her wedding night. It was too late to wish that she had listened to her mother. She was in it now for better or for worse. She would try to find a way to operate around him, she hoped. If things became too difficult, she would consider telling her brothers about him. They would have a little "talk" with him, she was sure.

She remembered one Sunday, in particular. They had attended church together. Robert seated her, and then he walked over to the deacon's bench. He shook hands with the others and took a seat. Rachel enjoyed the service so much that she joined in the singing. When it was over, she found herself still basking in the glow.

She and Robert rode home in almost complete silence. There had been no afternoon service, so she started supper. Robert came into the house later and stood in the kitchen watching her. She hummed as she moved about the room. When the meal was ready, they ate in silence.

Rachel had cleared the table before Robert spoke. "Rachel, did you join in the singing this morning?" She thought that it was an odd question, but she said she had. He grabbed her arm, and asked, "Did you sing every song?" Rachel nodded. He said, "If you did, you were singing a lie. You are not a child of the King. You are the devil's child!"

Rachel could not believe that he had actually said something so ridiculous. She exclaimed, "Oh, Robert! What is going on with you?" Instead of answering, he slapped her hard across the face. Before she could react, he began to beat her with his fists. Her screams brought no help as the houses were too far apart. When he stopped, finally, he yanked her to her feet. "Get in the bed and shut up!" She was weeping, but she did as she was told. She thought, "I've married a beast!"

They rode over a rocky place in the road, and she was jostled a bit. It interrupted her train of thoughts, briefly. Losing herself in thought was kind of a salvation for her. The road became smooth again, and she let her mind wander once more.

Now, she remembered when she became pregnant with their first child, Evelyn. He seemed pleased, oddly enough. He was almost kind to her. Her mother came over one evening, with a little bag that she had packed. She put her hands on her hips and said, "You're going to give birth tonight! That's why I'm here!"

Rachel remembered how surprised she was when Mom Maggie said that to her. She hadn't had the slightest twinge. What's more, if she'd counted right she had a few more weeks to go before anything happened. She'd smiled indulgently at her mother, but she said nothing.

Sure enough, just as Mom Maggie said, the pains began that very night. A few hours later, her mother delivered a baby girl. Mom Maggie stayed a few days to be sure that Rachel could properly care for the baby. Robert was gracious all of that time, and he even took her home in the buggy. Mom Maggie watched him, and she let him think that all was well, but he hadn't fooled her.

Rachel found that everything had just been put on hold. After the baby was born, the beatings resumed. She began hating him on her wedding night, and that would never change. She had four more children. Each was delivered by Mom Maggie. Having the children was the one good thing in her life. It was a good thing for Robert as well. Now, he had five more people to abuse. He beat them for the slightest reason. Baby Jim was so afraid of him that he wet his pants whenever Robert walked into the door.

Rachel was jarred out of her reverie when she heard Robert talk to the horse. They rode near the carriage house and got out of the buggy. While Robert was tending the horse and putting the buggy in the carriage house, the children washed their hands and faces. They laughed and chattered until they heard their father's footsteps on the porch. All laughing ceased, and they formed a line.

Robert started at the beginning of the line, asking that they recite numerous bible verses. No mistakes were permitted. Evelyn was the oldest, but the most sensitive. She feared him so much that the words would leave her memory. When she stammered, Robert said, "Step back!" When the quiz ended, sometimes one of the others had faltered also, and they would have to step back.

He made them wait while he played cat and mouse with them. Suddenly he would dismiss the ones who had not made error. To the offenders he said, "You haven't studied. I am not satisfied with your disobedience. Therefore, I must punish you." The children leaned across a chair and he beat them with his belt. Sometimes he drew blood. Rachel would step in when she could no longer stand such brutality. "Please, Robert! Don't hit her again!" Slowly, he would turn to her and say, "Do you want to take this for her?" If Rachel were feeling brave that day, she would say, "If it will make you stop!"

From Monday through Friday, the children got up early to help milk the three cows and feed the chickens and pigs. They ate a hearty breakfast, and then they walked to school. That walk was another chance to laugh and have a little fun with each other. They were joined by other children along the way.

Grades one through four were in one classroom. Jim, Mary and Betty were in that room, and Miss Addie was their teacher. Grades five to seven shared the back of the room. Grades eight through ten were the bigger children. Robert, their father, was the teacher. Their school time was not as carefree as it should have been, because their father had them closely monitored at all times.

Robert was an intolerant parent. As a teacher, he was very strict. He held every child to the same rigid standard. He was intolerant of slow learners, and he refused to give them special attention. Some of them really weren't slow at all. They were just deathly afraid of the teacher. Now and then a child would drop out of school and go to work on the farm. Robert's rage and abuse had become too much for the child to bear.

Study time was always after they'd eaten supper. Robert checked their homework and put them "through their paces." He demanded perfection from the children. They were well aware of the consequences if they fell short of his expectations. Evelyn knew the work and proved that she did when she was in the classroom. However, before her father's hostile stare she lost all that she had studied. He didn't care that she got excellent grades in school. His only concern was the answers she gave him. He gave her ten whacks with his belt and threatened to give her more if she continued to look him in the eye when he spoke to her. To him, that was considered rebellion.

The children slyly watched him like a hawk. He would reach for his belt for the slightest infraction. What's more, the rules changed whenever he saw fit and without warning. He seemed to thrive on the fear that he created in his house. He never paid his children a compliment or patted them on the head. Robert made demands, never requests. At one point and for some unknown reason, Robert decided that it was un-Christian to beat the children on Sundays. He adopted a new policy which was effective immediately. He would beat them on Saturday night for what they might do on Sunday! He informed his wife Rachel of his new rule. "From now on, there will be no punishments on Sunday. I have decided that to do so is wrong. Saturday is the best day. Therefore, I will beat them on Saturday for what they might do on Sunday. That covers everything. After all, I am a deacon in the church. My life has to be lived a certain way. God wants this change, and I am going to do His will."

Rachel had never met a madman, but she wondered if Robert was one. She wondered, "I don't know why I never thought to question his sanity before. His mind swings back and forth more that a pendulum in a clock. We're all kept off balance because of him." Other than in the classroom, he showed the world a different, gentler man. He had enough control to manage that.

She wondered, too, if there were other women in her predicament. "I never talk about my own private hell. Maybe there are other women who have rotten marriages, and like me, they're quiet about it. For some reason, I'm inclined to believe that Robert is in a class by himself. Marital breakups are, virtually unheard of, but how does one cope?"

Rachel began to pay more attention to other women. She was afraid to broach the subject with them, but she made subtle hints. Several times a few of the women began to fidget. She guessed that they understood her meaning, but they were reluctant to say anything to her. Their apparent nervousness tied her tongue, and she changed the subject. From that moment, she waited for an opportunity that never came.

Mom Maggie began showing up at unusual hours. Rachel believed that she was trying to catch Robert beating her. Because her mother had urged her to not marry Robert, she never said anything against him to her. He professed to not believe in Mom Maggie's gift. He thought that Rachel had talked about him, and he was careful when she was around. If he had not beaten her before the visit, he would be sure to beat her afterwards.

Mom Maggie was almost eighty-years-old, but she was still

strong, and she looked like a woman in her sixties. Robert was uncomfortable when she was around. He tried to avoid looking into her piercing brown eyes. Mom Maggie was aware of his discomfort, and she deliberately tried to make him even more uncomfortable. Always, she succeeded.

Sometimes, Mom Maggie spent the night, unexpectedly. Robert's explosive personality went underground when she was there. The next morning Robert would say, "I'll take you home, Miss Maggie." On the spot, she would change her mind and say, "I'm not going today. Do you mind?" Robert would die a little on the inside, but he would take on a wide-eyed look. "Of course not. Stay as long as you wish." Rachel would turn away so he couldn't see her broad grin. She loved seeing him squirm and so did her mother.

When her mother decided to leave, the house seemed to sag and die. Once more the children became quiet and withdrawn, and Rachel resumed her constant alert. The air became charged with tension, and gloom spread throughout the building. Robert's swagger returned along with his take charge attitude. The children didn't talk above a whisper, and they walked quietly so as to not disturb their father.

Rachel wished that her mother would close her place and move in with them. Robert would not dare to block the move because of his awe of her. She knew only too well that was just wishful thinking. Mom Maggie had a special love for the house where she had lived with her deceased husband and her children. Whenever Rachel asked her to come with her, she had her answer ready. "I don't want to give up. I have to be there!"

Unexpectedly, Robert received an offer to sing at a revival meeting in a nearby state. Rachel clasped her hands together. "Oh this is a blessing from the Lord! I'm going to get down on my knees right here, and pray that he'll accept that invitation!" At one point, he said, "I'll take the family with me. I can't control your wildness if I'm not here."

Rachel went down on her knees again. At the last minute, he packed a bag and left alone. One of the deacons at the church took him to the train station. When Rachel was really sure that he had gone, she danced a jig in the kitchen. She sang, "Lord, let him fall in love with somebody! Let him leave me for good!"

A million ideas popped into Rachel's head. She would make the most of the week of freedom. She would show her children another side of family living. "I will begin now!"

When the children came home from school, she had baked pies and cinnamon buns for their enjoyment. For the first time in their young lives, they were allowed to be children. Rachel put records on the phonograph, and they had a little party. Rachel loved seeing the smiles on their faces and hearing their spontaneous laughter. It was worth more than all of the tea in China.

They did their homework in peace for the first time in their lives. From force of habit they formed a line in the living room. Rachel cried when she saw them, and she tried to gather them all in her arms. "No lines, babies! Daddy won't be back until next week. This will be our secret." Little Jim said, "I don't like Daddy, do you?" She answered him by saying, "We are going to make our time together joyful. We won't mention Daddy's name. Okay?" Little Jim nodded his head and winked. That made all of them laugh.

When it was time for bed, Rachel turned it into a game. "The last one to say prayers and get into bed won't get a goodnight kiss." They laughed and scrambled to avoid being the last one. She giggled as she watched them trying to be the winner. To her amazement they all jumped into bed at nearly the same time. She said, "That was just too close to call. I declare everybody a winner and nobody a loser." She hugged and kissed each one.

She planned a special treat for them the next day. After school, Rachel hitched up the buggy and took her children to see their grandmother. When they arrived, Mom Maggie was baking a batch of her "secret recipe" cookies. She planned to bake enough for all of her children's families and deliver them personally. She was pleasantly surprised when Rachel and her children showed up at her door. The children hugged her knees and pulled her arms. They adored their Mom Maggie and she adored them. Separately she told them, "I love you a lot! Give Mom Maggie a big kiss!"

Little Jim made a mad dash to the barn to see the horse. It had been along time since he'd seen him. Mom Maggie reminded him that she had sold Old Ben. When he remembered, Little Jim was sad for a brief moment. His sorrow vanished rather quickly when he spied a swing in the tree. He let out a loud whoop as he ran towards it. Mom Maggie laughed until tears sprang up in her eyes. She said, "Well, so much for missing Old Ben."

The great lady finished baking cookies while she and Rachel talked. Robert's name wasn't mentioned, but he was certainly on their minds. The very mention of his name would have caused a blanket of gloom and doom to descend on them. The visit would have been ruined. By silent but mutual consent, they avoided his name like the plague.

The girls amused themselves and the adults by trying on some of their grandmother's bonnets. They modeled them for their mother and Mom Maggie. They took exaggerated bows while the grown-ups applauded. They almost succeeded in remembering that they had a father.

After the little show, Mom Maggie made thick sandwiches and Rachel made lemonade for their lunch. Little Jim tore himself away from the swing and joined his family.

It had been a splendid day and one that they would remember during the difficult days ahead. They had tried very hard to thrust their father's shadow aside, but it loomed in their midst in spite of their best efforts. Mom Maggie knew, and she cuddled each one on her lap and kissed them.

When they left her house, they climbed up into the buggy. Robert had no idea that she knew how to drive the buggy, and she would never tell him. She thought, "In this case, Robert's ignorance is truly bliss!"

The children slept until they rode up to the house. Rachel woke them up and sent them to the house. She then took care of the horse and buggy. She put them in the exact spot where Robert had left them.

The outing had worked wonders for all of them. They slept soundly all night. The days passed too quickly, but each day was full of great times and promise. Rachel had given them a bit of sunshine and something to remember. For awhile, they were able to live like children, not like robots.

Rachel had not deluded herself. She knew that all good things must come to an end sooner or later, and so it was with her and the children. Robert was due back the next day, so it was time for them to settle down. She told the children, "Your father is coming home tomorrow. We won't be able to do the things that we have done. I hope it was as special for you as it was for me." She didn't have to warn them to not tell him about the fun they had. They wouldn't!

CHAPTER 2

The next day, Robert strolled into the house as if he had never left. The shadow of despair walked in with him. His very first act was to summon all of the children. He lined them up and announced, "I'm sure you did something while I was away. Because I am so sure you did, you will be punished now!" The children flinched, and tears sprang up in their eyes. His eyes gleamed as he said, "Somebody get the chair!" Slowly he removed his belt, and Little Jim wet his pants.

To prolong their agony and to milk the situation, he slapped the belt against his leg. He looked at them to get their reaction. He moved back and forth, beating first one then another. He then doubled back to beat the same one again. This was something new! When he finished, they were on the floor in a heap. This was by far the most savage beating he had ever given them. They could barely move, but he ordered them to get up and go to bed.

After they had dragged their beaten bodies upstairs, he turned to Rachel. He had a strange gleam in his eyes that she couldn't see through her tears. He said, "You are unfit to be a parent of a dog." With that, he struck her on the side of her head with his fist. She staggered under the vicious blow, but he held her up with one hand and hit her with the other. When he let her go, she fell to the floor. He stepped over her and went to the desk to total the household expenses.

Rachel lay there silently begging God to kill him. "You see him! Why don't you kill him? Are You afraid of him? If You are, I will stop asking you to help me." Neither she nor the children could continue to survive such beatings. They were unreasonable, unwarranted, and sadistic! "Today, I saw the look of satisfaction on his face. I feel responsible for some of it. I should never have brought those innocent children in the world to be beaten and treated worse than animals. Surely, God won't permit this to go on! He can't!"

Rachel struggled to her feet. She stood there, looking at the man she had married. She tried to understand why she and the children had to suffer so at his hand. 'If I had a gun I would kill him and dance on his grave." She realized with a start that there was blood on her face and her eye was swelling.

Just then, without turning around, Robert said, "If you are still on the floor, get up and go to your room! If you are standing, go to your room immediately!" Rachel could feel the hysteria forming in her throat. She put her hand over her mouth and ran from the room.

With some effort, she regained control and slipped into the children's room. She had a jar of the ointment that Mom Maggie had taught her to make. She tended to their wounds, cooing softly all the while. Fran was covered with ugly marks from Robert's belt. Little Jim, Mary, Betty and Evelyn had massive wounds on their legs, stomach and back. She whispered, 'I'm sorry. I'm so sorry!"

They whimpered because they dared not cry aloud. Evelyn whispered, "Mama, why can't we live with Mom Maggie?" Rachel kissed her cheek. "I'll think of something, Evie. I know you are in pain, but try not to make noise. I have to go now. Nighty night!"

The next day the children were still in pain, but Robert would not allow them to stay home. The funeral director brought satin for her to sew. After everyone left the house, Rachel began her work. As she sewed the intricate quilting stitches, her mind drifted. She couldn't erase her daughter, Evie's, tearful plea from her mind.

She tried to remember where to find the poisonous berries that grew behind the house. She decided, "When I remember, I'll make jelly or a sauce especially for my dear husband. Robert's death is the only way out for us. I refuse to sit back any longer and watch that ogre beat my children. Sooner or later he will kill one of them. No, I have to get him first!"

Rachel worked on the lining a couple of hours, then laid it aside. She was too upset to continue. She went outside and walked to the area where she thought she would find the berries. She searched for an hour, but she couldn't find them. Knowing that she couldn't spend any more time looking, she went back home.

She started supper and picked up the material again. Today's search was a big disappointment for her. She didn't see how they could live another day with Robert. Rachel knew that she should have an alternative plan in case she couldn't find the berries at all. In the meantime, she would walk on eggs even more cautiously. She had to avoid another beating! Sadly, she realized that there was no way to save the children while she waited for the perfect plan. Even if they were as good as gold, he would beat them on Saturday routinely.

She thought, 'Mama is getting too old to take that long walk, but maybe I can get her on Friday, and she'll be here on Saturday. He won't beat the children if she's here. The more I think about it, the better it sounds." The thought grabbed her and wouldn't let her go. The problem would be getting her mother there.

Friday passed and Saturday was upon them. After the noon meal, Robert lined the children up and took off his belt. As usual, Little Jim wet his pants. This infuriated Robert. He grabbed the child and shook him until his eyes bulged! At that moment, the door opened, and Mom Maggie was standing there with fire in her eyes.

Robert took his hands from the boy. A sheepish look replaced the former look of fury. Mom Maggie said evenly, "I seem to be on time!" Rachel had under-estimated the "gift." Her mother had sensed that all was not well. She couldn't rest until she traveled the miles to check the feeling that she'd experienced.

She strolled across the room and stood before her son-in-law. "I know what you really are. You are a wolf in sheep's clothing. I'm prepared to stay here awhile. Try something while I'm here, if you dare!" Robert tried to muster up a bit of courage, but he failed miserably. Even at gun point, he could not explain why he was so intimidated by her. Robert only knew that he was. His fear of her could not be disguised. He was almost docile while Mom Maggie was there. He tried very hard to stay out of her way. He spent a lot of time away from home.

The children loosened up, and Rachel tasted sweet freedom. She smiled, and thought, "This is the way it will be when I kill Robert." Once more, the house took on new life and no longer served as a maximum security prison. This was all due to the presence of Mom Maggie. The children were enthralled by the tales she spun, and Rachel became young again.

Mom Maggie and Rachel made dresses for the girls, and a shirt and pants for Little Jimmy. They were busy as bees in a hive, but it was a labor of love and laughter. They almost forgot that there was a person called Robert.

The days sped by, and it was Sunday. Jimmy tugged at Mom Maggie's apron. "Please, Mom Maggie, will you stay with us forever?" She threw her head back and laughed! "I love all of you, but I can't leave my home. Your grand mom is older and weaker now, but I promise you, though, that I'll come when I can."

Jimmy wouldn't give up. "Daddy hates us, and he's mean to us. He's mean to Momma, too." Mom Maggie folded him in her arms and said, "I'll keep an eye on things!" Robert was in the yard hitching the buggy and didn't hear the things they said.

When it was time, they climbed in the buggy and Robert took them to church. Mom Maggie kept up a running conversation. Robert pretended not to notice, but he didn't approve. Riding in silence was his rule. He didn't dare make waves, as he wanted his mother-in-law to go home today.

He sang a solo during the service and almost shook the rafters. Some people fainted and others shouted. Rachel and her mother were unmoved and unimpressed. They knew the true spirit of the man. It took quite some time before Reverend Bacon could speak. When it was quiet, he said, "A man can only sing like that, if he has been touched by the hand of God!" The people responded noisily.

Mom Maggie looked toward the deacons' bench at Robert. She shook her head and snorted audibly. Robert wiped the satisfied look off his face and bowed his head. He thought, 'That old lady is trying to ruin my sterling reputation."

After service, the tables were set up. Robert moved comfortably from group to group in search of praise. Miss Addie, who was some of the children's teacher, was there. She beamed as Robert approached her chair. He took her hand, and they chatted five or ten minutes. Mom Maggie followed his every move. He was the star, and he was playing the part.

When the afternoon services ended, she let Robert take her home, first. As he helped her out of the buggy, she looked him in the eyes and said, "I'll be seeing you. Trust me!" She waved goodbye to her daughter and grandchildren, turned, and went in the house.

Robert breathed a sigh of relief and shook the reins. His shoulders straightened, and, he held his head back. His bone of contention had gone. He would take over the household again, as he had always done. Nothing had changed. Things had only been put on hold.

Mom Maggie took off her bonnet and her shoes. She relaxed in her favorite easy chair. She sighed as she put her feet up on a stool and closed her weary eyes. The weekend had been wild. There were more marks on her grandchildren and she didn't like it. Aloud she said, "Their father is a savage beast, and he is not fit to be with human beings."

She was sorry that she had sold her horse and buggy, but she thought her traveling days were over. 'The next time I go to Rachel's, I'll ask one of my neighbors to take me. Lately, the miles seem longer, and I'm forced to rest along the way. Growing old is a nuisance."

Mom Maggie knew that having to walk to her daughter's place, would never stop her. The bottle of sweetened water she carried did seem to help some. She smiled and thought, "Thanks for the ride, my dear son-in-law. It kept me from having to soak my feet when I got home."

Her eyes closed and she dozed a bit. Suddenly, she sat straight up in the chair! She'd had a mental picture of Robert with a lady, but she didn't see her face. She said, "That is very odd. Who is she?" Mom Maggie was certain that it wasn't Rachel, but who? She was not the sort of person that stewed over what she didn't know, so she put it to rest. "If I'm supposed to know, I'll see it."

She went to the kitchen, pumped a glass of water, then took the Bible to her bedroom. Mom Maggie knelt in prayer, and then she sat on the side of the bed to read a chapter. As she reached for the Bible, there it was as plain as day before her face! She saw Robert again. This time, though, she saw the lady's face. It was the children's teacher! The very one that she saw him talking to in the church yard. She said, "That man is rotten to the core!" Armed with those facts, she read the scriptures and then got ready for bed.

Rachel endured the silent ride home just as she usually did. There was a positive side to the silence. She didn't have to listen to her husband's voice. When he wasn't barking orders, or trying to belittle her or the children, he was always silent. He never talked about the weather or the children's progress. He treated her as if she didn't exist.

Today, as usual, she allowed her mind to roam. This time she thought about the splendid weekend they'd had with Mom Maggie. She smiled as she visualized Robert cowering before her mother. "That was priceless!" She looked back at the children. They were huddled together, not knowing what to expect when they got home. Rachel was going to live one moment at a time. Looking ahead was too depressing. Tomorrow she would search for the berries.

After what seemed like a flash, they reached the house. She and the children climbed out of the buggy. Usually Robert would ride towards the carriage house, but this time he didn't move. Rachel looked up at him, but he looked away. He said, in a very brusque manner, "I have an errand to run. Get in the house immediately!" He turned the buggy around, hitting the horse as he did so, and rode off.

He had never done that before, but his family was more glad than curious. They were not going to look a gift horse in the mouth. Rachel wished that he would drive off a cliff! She didn't know where he was headed, and she didn't care. She thought, "Wouldn't it be great if he was deserting us? Please, God, let it be that!"

They went into the house happier than they were when they left. She gave the children a piece of peppermint candy that she had hidden. They took turns kissing her on the cheek, and she hugged each one. She knew how starved they were for affection. They understood that their father didn't allow her to show love for them, but it hurt just the same. She hoped with all of her heart that they would use their life as a learning experience and have normal lives when they grew up. "I'm not at all sure they can. They don't know what normal life is!"

She said, "We're by ourselves. Let's have fun!" Rachel stood watch while they played games before bedtime. Their laughter was wonderful to hear. They were tired but happy when they called it a night. Rachel went to their room and told them a story that she made up. Before she finished, they were asleep. She tucked them in and then got ready for bed herself. Robert was still out, and that made her ecstatically happy. She wished that he would be struck blind like Paul on the road to Damascus and be unable to find the house!

She didn't wonder where he was, nor did she care even slightly. She said aloud, 'I hope this is the start of something new. I hope it becomes a habit. I'll do everything in my power to encourage it."

CHAPTER 3

Robert pushed the horse to its limit. Miss Addie's cottage was not too far away, now. He rounded the bend in the road, and her house came into view. Robert slowed the horse down a little and rode close to her cottage. As he dismounted, he could see her through the window moving about. His heart beat with anticipation. Robert knocked on the door and waited for her to appear.

Miss Addie answered the door wearing a smile. She invited him inside and told him that he could water his horse. Robert returned her smile and said, "Why, thank you very much, Miss Addie. I'll take advantage of your kindness. I'll be back in a few minutes. Stay sweet!" She covered her mouth with her hand and smiled shyly.

Robert tended his horse and then returned to Miss Addie. She patted the sofa, signaling him to sit beside her. They talked about school and church, then they talked about each other. She had a lot to share with him. He found her lady-like yet interesting. Miss Addie found him attractive and very stimulating. She hung onto every word that he spoke.

After awhile, Robert placed his hand on her knee, and she smiled at him. She leaned back against the settee, letting him know that she wanted to be kissed by him. He understood her body language, and he kissed her passionately. He found her exciting, and she thought he was charming. She was putty in his hands!

Robert said, "Miss Addie, I'm falling in love with you. You're what I want." She said, "I love you, too. I'm so glad we found each other. We teach in the same school, and we see each other every day! Who knew!" Robert cut off her words with a kiss and she wilted. Miss Addie knew he was married, but she didn't care. He didn't leave her until a little after midnight. He sang all the way home.

He unhitched the buggy and went into the house. It was quiet, and he knew everyone was asleep. "Maybe being with Miss Addie will help me to put up with Rachel." He undressed and lay on his side of the bed. Rachel knew when he came in, but she pretended to be asleep. She was grateful that he had gone out. She didn't care where he went or how long he stayed. She wished that he had stayed longer.

In the morning the children walked to school, and Robert rode as usual. Baby Jim, Mary and Betty saw Robert come into their class room two times. He whispered something to Miss Addie and left. Miss Addie appeared flustered and uncomfortable after his visit. She saw his children looking at her, and she had a short-lived attack of conscience.

Rachel continued to look for the berries. She felt that her husband was going to attack her at any time, and she wanted to beat him to the draw. Waiting for him to beat her was almost as bad as the beating itself. Her nerves were frazzled, and she had a constant headache. Robert was an expert at waging a war of nerves. "With a bit of luck, he'll lose the battle."

She looked for the berries as long as she could. She had to go home without finding them, in the end. The funeral director picked up the linings and pillows. She put half of her pay in a box that she had hidden. She had been saving for a long time. Knowing that she had a cushion was comforting to her. Having a man like Robert, it could turn out to be the smartest move she had ever made.

Rachel spent the day cooking, cleaning and worrying. Robert, she believed, was playing the waiting game, and he was winning. She jumped at the slightest sound. "Why didn't I even try to develop several plans? I have to do that, and I have to do it soon. I have relied too heavily on finding the berries. Suppose I don't find them? What then? Maybe I can set fire to the bed when I'm sure he's sleeping soundly. No! That's a bit too risky. It will only work if he doesn't wake up too soon."

Rachel tried to brush her headache aside so she could think clearly. "It's just a matter of time before he goes into one of his rages. Even the children seemed to be poised and waiting. I have to find something that I can use as a club. It should be heavy enough to kill him, but light enough for me to wield." She stored the idea in the back of her mind. "Maybe something better will come to me. I have to protect my children at all costs."

When the children came home, she sent them upstairs to put on the padded underwear she'd made for them. This was a precautionary move on her part. She finished cooking dinner when they started their homework. Robert came in as she was putting biscuits in the oven. Rachel put the food on the table immediately, as she was expected to do.

Robert took his seat at the head of the table, and the children followed. After a lengthy prayer, they ate in silence. Robert looked at Rachel with a gleam in his eyes. She noticed the way he was looking at her, but she couldn't figure it out. She had no way of knowing that he was comparing her to his new girlfriend.

Robert saw himself as a very clever man. He was handling an outside woman and a wife, both at the same time. He could very definitely have his cake and eat it too. "If Rachel does find out in some way, I will beat the living daylights out of her if she tries to interfere. I will live my life as I choose. I will conduct it as I see fit!"

Rachel cleared the table and washed the dishes while Robert sat there with a "cat that just ate the canary" look on his face. Rachel's back was to him, but she could feel his eyes on her. She thought, "He is taunting me before he beats me. I've never seen him in this mood. What could it mean?"

Rachel became more nervous as the tension mounted. Without meaning to, she dropped a platter on the floor. Her heart began to pound in her ears, and her hands shook visibly. Robert rose from the table, leaned over, and picked up the broken china. Deliberately, he put them into the trash can. Rachel was shocked beyond belief! He walked slowly over to her, and gently touched her shoulder. "Poor little Rachel. Why are you breaking dishes? Are you trying to put me in the poor house? Have you become so wealthy that you can order more? Are you clumsy as well as stupid?"

He hesitated a moment to let his words sink in, then he continued. "What do you think your punishment should be? Tell me!" He was toying with her – playing cat and mouse! Rachel didn't know if she should answer him or be silent. He leaned over and kissed her on the mouth. Her stomach heaved in revulsion. She knew it was all part of the game, and she loathed having his lips on hers. Robert looked at her mockingly, enjoying the game he was playing.

Over his shoulder he said, "All of you children, upstairs!" Rachel stood there, not daring to look directly at him, or to question his intent. He put his hands around her throat and squeezed tighter and tighter. Rachel clawed at his hands, trying to remove them, but she was losing ground. Bells began to ring loudly in her ears! She couldn't get air! Suddenly he let her go, and she fell to the floor.

Rachel lay there gasping. Robert had come very close to killing her! She heard him order her to get up, but she couldn't. He kicked her very hard on her back. He then knelt beside her and lifted her head. He spoke in a gentle voice. 'You thought you were going to die, didn't you? I hope you are ready to admit that I am your lord and master. Now, I am going to carry you upstairs, and you will fulfill my needs!" He swooped her up in his arms, and took her upstairs.

Miss Addie sat at her dressing table, looking in the mirror at herself. She was quite satisfied with her appearance. She said to her mirror image, "If you play your cards right, you can take Robert from his wife. He adores you! You are so lucky to attract a fine man like Robert. When he sings, the very gates of heaven seem to open up! I believe I would follow him almost to hell when he sings! He is so tender, yet at the same time he is manly and strong. Addie, old girl, I believe you are in love!" She combed her hair in a fashionable style, then surveyed herself with satisfaction. Before Robert came into her life, she had a problem with her self-esteem. His attention had given her the confidence that she'd lacked heretofore.

In that area, men of courting age were quite scarce. Until recently, Addie feared that she was doomed to die an old maid. Now, she has experienced a miracle. "This gentleman has come into my almost drab life. He's just in time to save me from that fate. I plan to pull out all of the stops to seal my future with him." Miss Addie didn't especially want to be a mother, although carrying Robert's child would be an added blessing. She just yearned to be somebody's wife.

She loved Robert, and she wanted him to be hers alone. She envied Rachel's position in his life. Miss Addie didn't know the type of life that Rachel actually lived because Robert withheld that information from her deliberately. Had she known, she would have warmly embraced the life of a spinster.

She had no idea that Robert could be a raving maniac. Robert was as fine an actor as any on the stage. Being able to portray himself as two very different people was part of this sickness. He was able to swing easily from one personality to the other. He saw himself as very clever, not sick. His ability to manipulate people, he thought, was a testament to his brilliance.

Miss Addie decided, "Today, I'll enjoy all that he offers. Tomorrow hasn't come yet!" Painstakingly she applied her makeup, and selected what she thought was a fetching outfit. Addie went downstairs and fluffed the pillows. She placed candles where she thought they would be most effective. Miss Addie was more than ready for Robert, but he didn't come. He didn't come because he was with Rachel.

Robert snored loudly, and Rachel wept. She felt degraded and worthless. She no longer prayed for a change because God wasn't listening. She was more than certain of that. Her throat felt raw, and her knees trembled. She couldn't bear to look over at Robert. Rachel hadn't known that it was possible to hate him more than she did, but the depth of her hatred was endless.

She wanted to get out of bed, but she didn't want to wake him. She tried to make her mind a blank, but she couldn't. She lay there, trying to come up with a workable solution. "If I didn't think that my children would be mistreated, I would end my life. Mom Maggie is too old to raise five children, and Robert wouldn't want them at all." Rachel tried to sleep, but she couldn't do that either. "If I could sleep, maybe it would erase my encounter with Robert."

She lay there looking up at the ceiling. She thought, "What would happen if I get my scissors and plunge them into Robert? I wonder if I can sink them into his chest or his head and get away with it. I have to be very sure when I hit him. I have to kill him, or I'll have to pay the consequences. I shouldn't have to entertain these thoughts. What have I done to make God turn his back on me?"

She closed her eyes and didn't open them until morning, but she had not slept. Her limbs were stiff and her voice was raspy. Robert would not permit her to stay in bed, so she got up. When everyone left the house, she crept back to bed. That is where Mom Maggie found her.

Rachel was feverish, so her mother made a poultice with bay leaves and put it on her forehead. She then brewed a tea with mint leaves and Rachel sipped it. Rachel felt better, but the soreness was still there. Mom Maggie took a jar of ointment from her bag, and rubbed her body. She said, "You stay in bed. I'll fix supper. I'm here, and you're safe!"

Robert would be in for a big surprise when he came home. Rachel wished that she could be downstairs when he entered the house. "The look on his face when he sees Mama will be worth a pot of gold!" Rachel knew that she was fortunate to have her mother. Whenever her back was against the wall, she sensed it and came through hell and high water to get to her.

Mom Maggie heated the mint tea again and took another large

cup to her child, her only daughter. She loved her sons, but Rachel was special to her. She'd longed for a baby girl, but she thought it was not to be. Just as her child-bearing days were ending, Rachel came along. Her prayers had been answered. She named her for her own mother.

Rachel sipped the tea and tried to talk. Her voice was hoarse, but her throat no longer hurt. "Mama, have I told you lately how much I love you. I pray that you out-live me. I couldn't stand to be in this world without you." The happiness that Rachel's words gave Mom Maggie showed on her face.

"Child, love is more than telling, 'though that's good. It's a touch at the right time. It's a look that we need. It's an act that brings comfort, and it's in the small sacrifices we make. Yes, love is more than telling." She reached out, took Rachel's hand. "This is love. Can't you feel it?" Rachel croaked, "Yes. Mama!" And she let the tears flow freely. Tears were standing in Mom Maggie's eyes as well.

Shortly, she went downstairs to see about supper. She made a big pot of vegetable soup complete with little dumplings. Her soup was hearty and definitely a one dish meal. She made the biscuit dough and cut them out. It was to be baked at the last minute. She made a peach cobbler especially for her grandchildren.

The wonderful aroma wafted through the house, and even Rachel was hungry when she smelled it. Rachel remembered that after her father died, Mom Maggie cooked for the men – mostly field hands. She and her children were able to survive off what she was paid for the meals and her pastries. Her mother saw that they were never hungry or without proper clothing. The men chopped wood for her, but she could be seen with an axe as well. The pot belly stove in the parlor and the wood stove in the kitchen kept them warm.

Mom Maggie was bustling about the kitchen when the door opened. The children were home from school. They shouted when they saw their grandmother. She sat down so they could climb all over her. She thought, "This is love, too." Fran said, "I hope you are moving in, Mom Maggie." Betty echoed her. Baby Jim said, "Daddy hates us. He's worse, Mom Maggie. We don't like him!" Evelyn added, "We hate him and he hates us more!"

Mom Maggie was angry because of what she was hearing. She thought, "These children are innocent. They shouldn't have to know such suffering as young as they are." To her grandchildren she said, "Try not to mess up your minds with hate. Your father will pay heavily for his sins. Mom Maggie is here, and I'm staying awhile." Little Jim did a somersault on the floor and brought down the house! They clasped and laughed a long time.

If Robert had been home, the house would have been as quiet as a tomb. Laughing or gaiety of any kind was not permitted. Now, they made up for lost time. Little Jim sang, 'Yes, Jesus Loves Me' for his grandmother. They clapped and he bowed over and over until Evelyn stopped him. They were having a wonderful time.

Upstairs, Rachel could hear their laughter. She thought "That's nice. Laughter is love, too!" It was music to her ears, and it made her feel warm, even to her toes. This was what she wanted so much for her children.

Soon the house became deathly still. Rachel knew that Robert was approaching the house. She heard the door open and Robert roar at the same time, "Line up!" Evidently, something had gone wrong at school, and he was upset. The children had to bear the brunt of this anger.

Downstairs the children formed a line as Robert whipped off his belt. He yelled, "Where's the whipping chair?" Mom Maggie entered the room at that moment and said, "I have it!" The belt fell from Robert's hand, and his jaw almost hit the floor. His mouth was open so long that he began to drool, but he didn't know it. Mom Maggie walked close to him, and said, "Do whatever you started to do! Go on, Robert!" he found his voice at last and stammered, "I – I was going to drill them." Mom Maggie raised her voice, "Then why did you take off your belt?" Robert's lips moved soundlessly. Her eyes were blazing, and her stance was threatening.

Robert forced his feet to move back from her space, but she

moved closer. He put his hand out, and his mouth opened. His eyes had the look of a trapped animal. Finally, he willed himself to turn and he stumbled from the room and from the presence of this great lady!

Mom Maggie's face relaxed, and she winked at the children. They cried and hugged her. Evelyn said, "Thanks, Mom Maggie. You saved us again." She shooed them into the dining room where the table had already been set. They hoped that their father would stay away from the table so they could eat their meal in peace.

Evelyn took a steaming bowl of soup upstairs to her mother. She whispered, "I know you'll enjoy this. Mama, you should have seen Mom Maggie! She is mighty!"

Rachel couldn't laugh with Evelyn because of her throat, but she smiled. She squeezed her daughter's hand and nodded. She wished that she could have been there for that, too.

The wonderful aroma was tantalizing, and Robert was hungry. He walked quietly into the dining room and took a seat. He bowed his head in preparation for one of his long prayers. Mom Maggie said, "The Lord only wants one grace. I already said it!" He kept his head bowed for a few more seconds because he didn't know what else to do. The children glanced at each other knowingly. They would have a lot to talk about tomorrow as they walked to school. As they ate, Mom Maggie engaged them in conversation. Robert disapproved of their speaking, but he knew to keep it to himself. One scorching looking from his dreaded mother-in-law was sufficient.

Robert wanted a second helping, but he didn't want Mom Maggie to know how much he enjoyed her cooking. He pushed his chair back, and got up with his stomach half satisfied. Everyone was glad when he left the room. He had a knack for depressing everyone around him. He went upstairs and looked at Rachel. Under different circumstances, he would have slapped her and ordered her downstairs, but not today. He knew that the slightest whimper from her would bring Mom Maggie.

Feeling like a stranger in his own house, he went outside. He wanted to ride over to see Miss Addie, but Mom Maggie might question his absence. He wouldn't want her to come up with the right answer. He pretended to not believe in her gift, but he did. Had he known that his mother-in-law already knew about his affair, he would have dug a hole and crawled into it.

CHAPTER 4

▼

Miss Addie was beginning to be confused about her place in her beau's heart. She saw him at school briefly, but he hadn't visited. All of her former self-doubt had begun to creep into her mind. She sat on the settee to ponder her position. Before long she was crying. "Robert led me to believe that he had no feelings for his wife. Was it all a lie? He knows that I'm waiting for him, but he chose to stay home with her."

She didn't understand what was going on, and she didn't want to be without him. "I need him to love me. Should I have waited longer to tell him how much I love him? Is that the problem? Is he now unsure of me?" Miss Addie reconstructed their relationship from beginning to end. She tried to see where she had gone wrong with Robert.

She said, "I tried everything I knew, to be exciting to him. I thought I held his interest. I haven't had the opportunity to know many men, but Robert is, by far, the most exciting and the most interesting man I've ever known. I can't lose him so quickly. I really love this man with all of my being."

She wondered if Robert and his wife had made-up with each other. He had told her that their marriage was no more than a sham, but maybe that wasn't true. "Maybe it was true then, but no longer." She was sure of just one thing. He no longer came to see her, and she didn't know why.

Miss Addie wiped her eyes and sat up straight. "I have to keep my wits about me. I will do almost anything to make him love me again. All of my future lies with my Robert. My hope for tomorrow is in his hands." It was important for her that she continue to trust in their love. He, too, had declared his undying love for her. She would cling to that a little while longer.

She went to the window and looked out. She thought she heard Robert's horse and buggy approaching, but she was wrong. Twice more, she looked out when she imagined she heard him coming. Each time she was wrong.

Miss Addie started crying again. "Will this be my life? Looking out of the window for a phantom man?" She leaned back in the chair and closed her weary eyes. The tears ran from under the closed lids and trickled down her face. Robert had to be trying to come! "He loves me too much to stay away."

She put a pillow and a blanket on the sofa, then she made a pot of tea. She took the tea back to the parlor to drink. She tried to be calm and so sure of herself, but it was a dismal failure. She drank a cup of tea, and propped herself up on the pillow. Miss Addie didn't want to, but she positioned herself where she could watch for Robert. Dawn came, but Robert didn't!

The next day Rachel felt better, but her mother insisted that she spend another day in bed to make sure. Her fever was gone, and her throat felt fine. There was a little soreness in her back where Robert had kicked her. She was ashamed to tell her mother about that, but she had a feeling Mom Maggie knew. Very little was hidden from her mother.

Robert almost ran from the house to get away from Mom Maggie. He was glad that it wasn't the weekend. He would be trapped there with no reason whatsoever to leave. He wanted to be with his love, Miss Addie, but he couldn't get away without arousing suspicion. It wasn't possible to talk to her at school. Jim, Mary, or Betty might mention it to their grandmother, and it would be doomsday for him! "I don't really care if Rachel finds out, but it would be dangerous information in her mother's hands. Anything might happen!"

He entered the school building hoping that he would bump into Miss Addie. He wanted to hold her close and kiss her sweet lips. Only his mother-in-law stood in their way. He thought, "Maybe, I should have really killed Rachel when I choked her. She certainly deserved it. I need a woman like Miss Addie. She knows how to please me. Very soon, if the old lady ever leaves, I might consider letting Rachel meet Miss Addie. Either that, or I will really kill Rachel. That would be the one sure way to get rid of her mother."

Robert realized that he was passing Miss Addie's room. He took a couple of steps backward and looked inside. She was sitting at her desk with her head lowered. He wanted to kiss her, but he didn't dare. Her pupils were due at any moment. Robert moved quickly to his own classroom. He placed three books, three pieces of paper, and a pencil on each desk. He checked the ink wells to make sure they were filled with ink. After he did that, he sat at his desk to await his students.

Suddenly, the door opened, and Miss Addie slipped into the room. She said, "Robert, are you angry with me?" Have I failed to please you in some way? Why haven't you come to see me?" Robert opened his mouth to answer her, but his pupils began to arrive. He waved her off, and she left in haste. She was sure now that he was displeased with her.

Miss Addie couldn't know, but Robert was flattered that she would practically throw herself at him. He thought, "She's as different from Rachel as night is from day. I could definitely love that woman!" He wondered if his pupils heard what she was saying. "She should have been more careful. When I'm free to see her, I'll discuss that with her. We'll have to be more discreet. I'll remind her when I see her." All of Robert's students were there, so he called roll. His day had begun.

Miss Addie was somewhat distraught when she went back to her classroom. The children were there and seated. It was difficult for her to go about her business as usual when her heart was breaking. Her heart told her to leave school and go home. Her dedication to her children was the only thing that kept her there. "It would have been better for me if Robert had never seemed to be interested in me. I fell for him hook, line and sinker, but I have to set aside my feelings and concentrate on my pupils. They need me, even if Robert doesn't."

She called the roll, got out the workbooks, and asked one of the girls to pass them around. After she explained the lesson, the children tackled their assignment. Miss Addie, in spite of her best efforts, could not concentrate on the work because her mind was on Robert. She sat at her desk struggling with her problems with her one true love, Robert. She sat there battling her feelings until she felt like screaming aloud! She stood up and went quickly to the cloak room.

She made it just in time before the dam broke. She buried her face in a jacket that hung there and cried. When she was a tad more settled, Miss Addie emerged red-eyed but composed. The children hadn't heard her crying, but they knew something was wrong with their teacher. They looked up when she came back into the room, then continued their work. She thought, "I owe my best to the children. My problems aren't theirs." She would complete the day.

Mom Maggie sat in the room talking with her daughter. They cherished the few times that they were able to "just talk." Rachel said, "Mama, you never complain. Do you feel all right?" Her mother answered. "I think the good Lord gave all of my pains to another old lady. I'm as sound as a gold piece." Rachel was relieved to hear her say that. She didn't want her problems to pull her mother down. These should be her best days.

Out of the blue her mother said, "You know, I think I'll stay for a couple of weeks. That bit of news should send Mr. Monster off his rocker!" She threw her head back and laughed at the thought. Rachel tried not to, but she laughed, too. Imagining the shocked look on Robert's face was very funny. They needed to enjoy life, if only for two weeks.

Rachel didn't have to wonder how the children would receive the news. They loved their grandmother more than anyone in the world, with the exception of their mother. They would pay after she left, but nobody could erase the wonderful time they would have.

Mom Maggie would take over most of the cooking to relieve Rachel. "You'll do enough of that when I leave." Mom Maggie had already wrung the necks of two chickens and plucked the feathers. She washed them, then she put them in salted water to draw out any remaining blood. The children would be ecstatically happy when they saw fried chicken on the platter. That was usually a Sunday treat.

The school day was over, and Robert gathered all of the things he needed for the next day's lesson plan. As he walked to his buggy, he saw someone standing nearby. It was Miss Addie! She tried to get his attention, but he had to pretend he didn't see her. Most of the students were leaving the building, along with his own children.

Upset, but emboldened, she walked over to him, ignoring the students. She stood on tip-toe and kissed him. He wanted to respond, but he could not. He thought, "I love her fire, but can't she see that this is too risky?" He pushed her away and turned his attention towards his horse. Robert was excited by her daring, and he wanted to hold her close. He battled with his feelings and climbed into the buggy.

Miss Addie stood there, crushed by his seeming indifference to her. She watched him ride off in a small cloud of dust, then she sank to the ground sobbing soundlessly. She raised herself to her knees and put one hand over her heart. She screamed loudly, as if she were in agony.

Miss Moore, the other teacher, came out of the building at that time. She saw Miss Addie kneeling on the ground, obviously in distress. She rushed over and assisted her to her feet. Miss Addie clung to her, as she lost the battle she was waging for control. Miss Moore ordered the students to leave at once. She led her co-worker back to the building.

Miss Addie cried even harder when she went inside. Miss Moore was patient with her and waited quietly for her to settle down. She wiped her eyes after a bit, and she seemed ready to talk. She said, "I'm in love with a magnificent man, but he's no longer in love with me. I put my whole life and my future in his hands, and now he's gone! Death, for me, is far better than trying to live my life without him. I threw myself at him, and he pushed me away. He seemed disgusted." Miss Moore wiped her face and held her hands. "I don't know who this man is, but he can't be worth this! When you've had a good nights rest and time to think, you'll know I'm right. Someone who deserves you will walk into your life. Be there for him!"

Miss Moore gave her good advice, but the words merely bounced off Miss Addie. She was sure that her co-worker didn't understand the depth of her love for Robert. She couldn't know how much she wanted to be with him. There was no other man after Robert.

Miss Addie brushed her skirt with her hand and thanked her friend for being there for her. She was too washed out to feel shame. "I think I can make it home, now. I love you for your kindness to me. I'll be all right, and I'll see you tomorrow." She walked out unassisted and climbed into her carriage. In a moment or so, she was off and headed for home.

The ride home was filled with the memory of Robert brushing her aside, as if she were a pesky mosquito. He couldn't have made it more plain that he was through with her. Her eyes were dry, but she continued to sniffle. "If I could make him love me again, I would! There must be something lacking in me. I'm disposable."

The drive seemed to go on forever, but she did finally reach her house. When she entered the parlor, her eyes rested on the settee. "That's where Robert and I declared our undying love. The memory of that was enough to cause more tears. "To be cast aside so callously is unbearable! Not to mention falling apart in front of students!" She drank a cup of tea, trying to calm herself, but it didn't work.

Miss Addie sat on the settee and lay back against the pillows.

She tried to visualize and recapture the love they had shared. Instead of beautiful memories, it brought hopelessness and rejection. She tried to look beyond her present state to a brighter day. That proved to be an exercise in futility. Her life, as she saw it, had become a tangled mess, and there was no way for her to extract herself from it all. "How can I endure this terrible pain? How can I ever hold my head up when I'm around my students! How can I see Robert everyday and know I disgust him? Oh, God, I can't!"

Miss Addie stopped crying now. She'd chosen the only course of action that was visible to her. There was only one answer to the overwhelming predicament, she felt. Her mind was made up. She stopped slouching and sat straighter. She began to feel better, now that she had made the biggest decision of her life. Very calmly she bathed in scented water, then she put on the dress she'd worn the first time Robert visited her. She combed her hair the way he liked it. Next, she touched her bosom and ear lobes with the toilet water that Robert had given her. Miss Addie smiled sadly, but she was pleased with her image in the mirror.

She took out pen and paper and composed a letter to Robert. She sealed it and placed it on the cushion. Next, she doubled a length of clothes line and tied it around a beam in the ceiling. She was standing on a stool as she did this. The other ends of the doubled line she tied around her neck, and she stepped off the chair into space!

Almost instantly, the rope tightened around her neck. Saliva oozed out of the side of her mouth, and she gasped Robert's name. Her feet kicked in the air for a second, but it was a reflex. Her eyes began to bulge, and she wet herself! Her body went limp and still. She had not panicked, but remained resolute to the end. It was all over for Miss Addie. Her spirit left her body in search of a resting place!

CHAPTER 5

Mom Maggie was taking a pan of rolls out of the oven when Robert came home. He wasn't going to speak, but Mom Maggie forced him to acknowledge her presence. "Well, hello to you, too!" Robert said, sheepishly, "Good afternoon, Miss Maggie." She turned her back to him, dismissing him in the process, and put the rolls in the bread basket. The children set the table, and they beamed when she complimented them.

Rachel joined them in the dining room. Under her mother's fine care, she looked and felt very well. Robert came to the table first and looked around. Mom Maggie knew what his fidgeting was all about. She said, "You can say grace, but don't tire God with all of your empty words!" Robert was both furious and embarrassed, but he had the good sense to hide his displeasure. He bowed his head and said, "Father, we're blessed and we thank Thee for this food. Amen!" Rachel and her children couldn't believe he finished so quickly. Mom Maggie laughed and passed the chicken.

As usual, the food was delicious. Robert was tempted to suck the chicken bones, but he restrained himself. He thought, "That old bear would like to see me do that. She'll never know that I enjoy her cooking. I hate to admit it, but she could boil a stone and make it taste like steak!" Midway through the meal, Mom Maggie said, "Children, I have good news for you. I've decided to stay at least two more weeks!" The children felt like dancing on the table! Little Jimmy said, "Great, Grandmama Maggie! We love it when you're here!"

Robert nearly choked on a chicken bone when she made the announcement. He wondered what she was trying to pull. "If I didn't know better, I would think that she is trying to ruin my romance with Miss Addie. But of course, that is impossible. She doesn't know anything about it."

Robert was furious. He would be forced to ignore Miss Addie two more weeks? "How can I be without her that long? She'll never understand!" He felt that his mother-in-law had gone too far. Robert now had yet another reason to dislike her. Robert said, under his breath, "Big Mama, you're being shrewd now, but your precious Rachel will pay when you do leave!"

Mom Maggie looked at Robert. She could see that her decision to stay was very disturbing to him. She asked, "Robert, do you mind my being here?" He swallowed the potatoes in his mouth, along with his pride. He answered, "I don't mind." Mom Maggie said, "Then it's all settled. If I like it, I might move in!"

She added that just to give Robert a "heart attack." She almost succeeded! Robert cleaned his plate and got up quickly from the table. His mother-in-law wasn't looking at him, so he felt brave enough to glare at her. He moved away before she did see him.

The children did their homework and Rachel did the dishes. Robert had gone to the parlor. Earlier, Fran and Evelyn told their grandmother about Miss Addie kissing Robert. She had put her finger to her mouth and said, "Hush! Don't tell your mother about this. I'll take care of it."

Mom Maggie went to the parlor, following Robert. She sat in a chair directly across from him. She watched him intently with her piercing eyes. He looked up from his book, and their eyes locked. Robert was glad that he wasn't standing, as he felt very weak. He wondered, "Why did she come in here? Is this a preview of the weeks to come? What is she up to?" Mom Maggie's eyes seemed to probe his very soul.

When she knew she had him on the ropes, she moved in for a knockout. "Anything interesting happen this week?" Her eyes never left his as she spoke. Robert was glad once more that he was sitting down. He wondered, "What has she heard? What has she sensed? Is she alluding to Miss Addie, or not?" He hadn't fig-ured out a way to answer her. She persisted. "Cat got your tongue, Robert?" He knew, for sure, that she was on to something. He found his voice, finally, and answered. "Almost routine. Noth-ing worthy of discussion."

He looked down at the book, but the words meant nothing. He was too rattled to focus! Mom Maggie put her feet up on a stool. She was sending him a message that he read clearly. She was in the par-lor with him, and she would stay as long as he did. She mused, "Just a few more seconds, and he'll have to leave the room." There was perspiration on his forehead, and his face was ashen. He felt the penetrating eyes boring holes into his bowed head. He wiped his brow, and Mom Maggie knew she had him pinned against the wall.

After two tries, Robert lifted himself out of the chair to his feet and he fled! Mom Maggie leaned back in the chair and closed her eyes. She was exhausted from pitting her will against Robert's. The fact that he feared her worked to her advantage. She said aloud, but to herself, "Robert has just begun to pay. There is more." Mom Mag-gie saw the face of death, but she didn't know who was marked. She prayed, 'Let it be anybody, but my Rachel."

She got up after a few minutes and joined the rest of the family. They were so carefree and at ease that it would be doubly hard on them when the great lady went home. Her neighbor was kind enough to bring her. The long walk had become impossible for her. She was strongly considering buying another horse and buggy. That is, if she could find a good bargain. Mom Maggie's family was her life. Her sons brought their families to see her, but Rachel could-n't do that. She had always said, "As long as there's breath in my body, I'll take care of my family.

The next day, school started as usual, but Miss Addie wasn't there. She just did not show up. This wasn't like her at all. Miss Moore attributed her absence to yesterday's incident. "She probably needed the day to re-group." Her class was left without a teacher. Miss Moore divided her time between the two classes.

Robert knew she wasn't there and blamed himself for her state of mind. He couldn't go by her house because Mom Maggie was on to something. Who knew what she would do? Robert agonized over Miss Addie's absence all morning. His pupils were grateful for whatever kept them from being yelled at.

He didn't know how, but he had to find a way to let her know what his problem was. Maybe he would walk away from Rachel after all, and live with her. He wanted to be with her. Memories were not enough for a man like Robert. He thought of every angle, but it all boiled down to Mom Maggie. She was the root of his problems.

Finally, he thought of the obvious. "Perhaps, I can get a letter to her. That might be the solution, at least temporarily. I believe it is worth the risk." When he went to school the next day, he would slip it to her. Having decided a course of action, he turned his attention to his class. He was sorry that he hadn't thought of that in the beginning. "Well, better late than never."

Mr. Barney, Rachel's neighbor, had gone fishing and caught an abundance of trout. He gave her six large ones. She and her mother spread papers on the ground and scaled them. They took them inside and washed them clean. They then dipped them into Mom Maggie's "secret ingredient" batter. Now they were ready for the frying pan.

When Robert sat at the table and tasted the fish, he shook his head without realizing that he had. If he didn't hate "the old bear" so much, he would beg her to stay on bended knee. Her cooking was that good."

The family talked to each other at the table and ignored him. Silence was his rule, not theirs. Mom Maggie noticed that Robert was reaching for this second piece of corn bread. She asked, "Robert, is the food to your liking?" He grumbled, "It's all right." She said, "By the way, I hope you had a good day."

His hand trembled with helpless rage. Robert would not look at her or answer. If he was unsure before, he was aware now that she knew all about him and Miss Addie. That was the real purpose for her extended visit. Without lifting a finger, Mom Maggie would force them apart. She could hurt him in other ways, too. If Reverend Bacon ever heard about it, he would be taken off the deacon board. The pressure would be too much for him and for Miss Addie.

Without meaning to, he said aloud, "I want her out of my life!" His mother-in-law said, "Excuse me. What did you say?" Robert realized what he had done. He said, "Uh, I said I need another knife. This one is dull." She knew what he said the first time, and she was amused.

Rachel and the children were in the dining room during all of it, but they were totally unaware of the sparring match that was occurring. That was the way Mom Maggie wanted it.

The following day, he rode to school with the letter he'd written to Miss Addie. Hopefully, the letter would clear up things for her, but it would not enable them to be together. She was a resourceful person. Maybe, she would have some ideas. Robert looked, but he didn't see her carriage. He thought he might be a little too early.

He went inside to prepare the day's lesson, and to distribute the books and paper. Robert patted the letter in his pocket and smiled. Casually, he walked past Miss Addie's door. He would go inside and give the letter to her. She wasn't there, and he was disappointed. "Oh well, I'll try later."

Miss Addie didn't come to school at all. Miss Moore, once again, took over her class. This was totally unlike her. What was going on with her? Miss Moore began to cry. She was, now, worried about her friend and co-worker. She tried to explain to Miss Addie's pupils. "Your teacher isn't here today, but I'm going to see her after school today. She's probably sick, but we'll see. I'll tell her that you miss her."

When Robert realized that Miss Addie hadn't shown up again, he became very upset. He wondered if she had moved away. "If she has left town, I'll find her somehow." Not being able to be with her made him realize how very dear she had become. He made it through the day, then he went home.

The very last person he wanted to see was Mom Maggie, but she was the first. She was taking clothes off the line. She was singing, "Nearer My God to Thee", as she worked. Grudgingly, Robert observed that she had a stirring voice. It seemed to penetrate his being. He felt a deep sadness as she sang, and he tried to shake it off.

When he'd put the buggy in the carriage house, he headed towards the house. Mom Maggie said, "It's a nice day Robert." He mumbled something and went inside. Rachel was in the kitchen. He looked at her with hatred in his eyes. "She's smug since her mother came to visit. I'll humble her in due time."

Miss Moore went to her own home first. She fixed a little basket of fruit to take to her friend, Miss Addie. She hoped that she would be able to convince her to return to school. She liked Miss Addie, and she didn't want another teacher to take her place. She tied a pretty bow on the basket and left her house.

Miss Moore flipped the reins and started out on her mission. She rehearsed a little speech as she rode. "She simply can't allow her heart to rule her head. She has a lot of common sense, and I hope she'll use it now. A broken heart can be stressful as well as painful, but a broken heart can mend." She was confident that she would listen to her.

Soon, she arrived at Miss Addie's cottage. She stopped the horse and walked to the door. Miss Moore knocked repeatedly, but there was no response. She walked over to Miss Addie's carriage house to see if she'd gone away. No, the carriage was there, and the horse was in the stall. Miss Moore decided, "I'll go back to the house. Maybe she was indisposed and couldn't answer the door."

She returned to the house. This time, she banged on the door. On impulse, she tried the door, and it opened. She called her name, then she stepped into the foyer. The stillness was overpowering! She called her and waited a few moments. Miss Moore moved on into the house, calling Miss Addie as she went. The back of her neck chilled suddenly!

She closed her eyes a minute, then she walked towards the parlor. As she entered the parlor, she saw Miss Addie hanging from a ceiling beam! Time seemed to stand still! Miss Moore screamed until she was faint! She staggered outside, and then she vomited. She knew the picture of Miss Addie dangling from the ceiling would be forever etched in her memory. When she was able, she wiped her face, climbed back into her carriage, and rode to the nearest neighbor's house. She tried to tell the man and his son what happened, but she was incoherent. They gave her a cup of cool water, and that seemed to help.

As soon as she was able, she told them what she'd witnessed at Miss Addie's house. She offered to take them there, and they climbed into her carriage. When they arrived at Miss Addie's house, she couldn't go in with them. She waited outside while they went in to investigate.

When the men stumbled out of the house, disbelief was etched on their faces. The older man shook his head, as if to clear it of the awful sight he'd seen. He said over and over, "Awful sight! Awful sight!" His son was trying to be brave, but he was obviously moved.

They asked Miss Moore to take them home. They would ride into town and report the hanging to the constable. She tried to help by writing down all that she knew about Miss Addie for them. She dropped them at their house and headed for home. She had to stop several times along the way because her vision was blurred by her tears.

She saw Reverend Bacon's house up the road and decided to tell him what she'd found. After stopping, she managed to tell Reverend Bacon about the untimely death. He said, "May God have mercy on her soul! I'll ride out to Robert Grant's house, later. He's one of our deacons, and I'll want him to sing a solo at the funeral." He thanked her for informing him. Miss Moore rode home to nurse her sorrow herself.

Reverend Bacon was eating supper when Miss Moore stopped with the shocking news. He went back to the table to finish and told his wife about the young teacher. His wife pushed her plate away. "I can't eat another bite after hearing such news. I mourn for the soul of that dear sister. Too bad! Too bad!"

Reverend Bacon was in total agreement with his wife. "For the moment, I'll have to set aside my feelings and assume the task of contacting relatives. I believe they're sprinkled throughout the various counties. They'll arrange to have the funeral on Sunday at church."

He worked out a few details, kissed Mrs. Bacon's cheek, and started on his way. This was the side of his job that he really didn't enjoy. "The up side is, I can always depend on my good deacon to lend a hand."

The Grant family and Mom Maggie had finished dinner. The children were doing their homework, and Rachel and her mother were sewing in the kitchen. Robert was in the parlor correcting papers. He was totally unaware of the drama that was unfolding.

CHAPTER 6

Robert heard the carriage as it approached the house and wondered who it was. Folks didn't travel after dusk very often, except on the weekend. Usually, it was to bring bad news or exceptionally good tidings. There was a gnawing feeling in the pit of his stomach, and he didn't know why.

He waited for the knock, then went to the door. He was very surprised to see Reverend Bacon standing there. Robert stepped aside and asked him to come inside. He took a seat in the parlor. Rachel and Mom Maggie recognized the pastor's voice, and they went to the parlor to show their manners. Mom Maggie said, "I hope this is a social call." She and Rachel took their seats.

Reverend Bacon's face was somber, and he said in sorrowful tones, "I'm afraid my mission is a serious one, Miss Maggie. I came over to ask Robert if he'll prepare a solo for a funeral that will be held on Sunday. I'm reasonably sure of that." With all of the humility that Robert could muster, he said, "Of course I'll be available, Reverend. May I ask who died?" The preacher cleared his throat. "Yes. You're familiar with her. She's a teacher at your school. Miss Addie! She hanged herself in her home."

Mom Maggie looked at Robert. He had bent over as if he had been hit in the stomach. He knew he was reacting badly, but he couldn't stop himself. It would have been easier for him to make his heart skip every other beat, or to hold back the dawn! His world had just come crashing down around him.

When he was able to straighten up, he fought like a tiger for control. Reverend Bacon said, "I know you must be upset. It's only natural that you would be. After all, she was one of your co-workers." Rachel said, "This is very sad. My children liked her."

Mom Maggie looked at Robert again, and said, "I wonder what caused her to do such a thing? She must have been under a lot of pressure."

Robert knew how it must have looked, but he couldn't restrain himself any longer. If he stayed in that room, he didn't know what he might have done. He thought, "I can't take it another minute!" He opened the door, and stepped outside to get some much needed air. He wondered if he would be able to stand up under this terrible shock. He walked deep into the wooded area behind his house. There, he was free to vent the overwhelming feeling of despair. He raised his arms to heavens, and screamed out of guilt, hopelessness, and frustration. Robert fell to the ground, and he lay there sobbing as if his heart had been seared.

He moaned, "Miss Addie, I love you! I love you! Why didn't you wait for my letter? It's my fault! How can I live without you?" He lay there questioning and weeping, until he was drained of all energy. He reached in his pocket for a handkerchief, and his fingers touched the letter. That dreaded letter! The letter that could have saved her life! He tore it into many pieces and let the wind scatter it in many directions.

When he was able to stand, he knew that he had to go to his sweet Miss Addie's cottage. He didn't care about anything at that moment but being where she had spent her last hours. He had to go to the place where they had laughed and loved together. Robert walked back to the house and hitched the buggy. In a daze, he rode to Miss Addie's place.

He had to push himself to get out of the buggy when he arrived. Each step he took seemed like a mile. He looked up at the window, and for a brief moment, he thought he saw her smiling face. His feet turned to lead as he entered the house and looked around. The house was very still, as if it, too, was in mourning. He expected her to run into his arms, the way she always did. His eyes misted when it didn't happen. As Robert walked through the house, he could feel her presence everywhere. There was a faint odor of the toilet water that he had given her. He remembered how her face lit up when she opened the package. She asked him to put a dab on her bosom.

Looking back, he saw that as a wonderful moment. The memory of that was almost too much for Robert to bear. When he looked at the settee, he had to fight the tears. "How can I ever forget sitting there with her in my arms?" His legs felt weak, and he was forced to sit on the settee.

He picked up a pillow to cover his face as he sobbed. He said, "I'll try to find comfort in her scent!" That's when his eyes fell on the letter. It was propped on a pillow, and it was addressed to him. He recognized her beautiful handwriting. Feverishly, he opened the letter. His heart bled as he read the pitiful words.

My Dearest Robert,

I don't know what I have done to displease you, and you won't tell me. How can you not know the depth of my love for you? After you, I cannot love another. I believed with all of my heart that we were born just for each other. I don't want you to feel guilty. It's not your fault that you did not love me back. Remember, that in heaven or in hell, I'll always love you.

All of my love,
Addie

Robert pressed the letter to his heart and sobbed. "She never knew how much I loved her and wanted her in my life!" He wanted to throw the letter away, but he couldn't. He folded it carefully and put it in his pocket. He wet a face cloth and washed his face. Robert looked around the room for the last time, and whispered, "Bye, my love. I know you're still with me!"

He'd done what he'd felt the need to do. Robert left Miss Addie's cottage and traveled home. "Where else can I go? I hope they're in bed. I don't want to see, hear, or talk to anybody! Miss Maggie won that round! Will she be satisfied with less than my blood, or my head on a stick?" He was too exhausted to give it a lot of thought. The light in his life had gone out!

Robert left the house early the next morning. He couldn't sit across from Rachel and Mom Maggie at breakfast. He was more than certain that Mom Maggie would be gloating in her own way. "Yes, and stupid Rachel would be talking about the sad event. Going to school is the last thing on my list, but it's better than staying home." He approached Miss Addie's room, and his heart pounded wildly! Robert looked at the desk, and fought the urge to go inside and throw himself across it.

When Robert made it to his room, he breathed a big sigh of relief. Automatically, he took out books for the day. To avoid speaking, he wrote instructions on the blackboard. Being there and doing that was second choice. He would get through the day, anyway he could.

Miss Moore knew that the day for her would be a struggle. She had to burn a lamp all night! She couldn't stop thinking about Miss Addie. Whenever she closed her eyes, the image of her suspended from the ceiling was before her. Each time she prayed, "Heavenly Father, please free me from that horrible scene!"

The children arrived and rescued her from her own thoughts. A substitute teacher had come to replace Miss Addie until a permanent person could be found. That was a good thing for Miss Moore, handling that many children wasn't easy. She gave her pupils the lesson for the day and returned to her desk.

Miss Moore tried to not think about her co-worker, but it wasn't possible. She remembered Miss Addie's shame when she helped her from the ground. "It must be awful to love someone who wants no part of you." That is what she had gathered from the things Miss Addie told her. "But," she thought, 'Where is the logic or the balance? How do you decide that unrequited love plus death, equals anything but waste?"

Miss Moore regretted that she hadn't come up with the words that would have turned her around. "Whoever the man was, he could not have been worth dying for. Why couldn't she see that? Why could she not see that what she did would affect many people? Her family! Her co-workers! Her students! Perhaps after the funeral, I'll be able to put this uneasiness on the shelf. I'll try to move away from my fears and anxieties. In the meantime, I will devote my time and energy to the pupils. They need me, and I love them a lot."

Rachel was mildly surprised to learn that Robert left the house so early without breakfast. It was something he had never done before. She couldn't figure out what was going on with him, but she was glad he wasn't there. There was something very different about him now. Evidently, he'd sneaked in the house last night, and sneaked out again in the morning. Rachel knew that her mother was the one he was avoiding. "I want my mother to stay with us forever!"

Mom Maggie knew about everything that was going on, and she was determined to protect her daughter from Robert's sordid affair. Fortunately, Miss Addie wasn't the kind of woman who bragged about her conquests. That was in Robert's favor, and indirectly in Rachel's also.

The children had seen the lady kiss Robert in the school yard. "They seemed to have forgotten that. I hope they've forgotten for all of eternity. It's obvious to me, that Robert is in deep mourning for his dead love. I see it as a slap in Rachel's face."

Rachel was so glad that she wasn't being beaten, that she paid very little attention to Robert's unusual behavior. Had she known about her husband's love life, she would have tried to help it along. Every hour that he spent with someone else, was an hour of peace for her and her children.

Robert appeared in time for supper. The children talked to their mother and grandmother, but Robert was silent. Actually, this time it was what he wanted. By talking to each other, he felt that they wouldn't pay attention to him. Mom Maggie looked at him from time to time. Somehow, he could feel her stare, and his hands shook. When he could take it no longer, he stood up. As he was leaving the table, his mother-in-law spoke. "Oh, Robert, have you chosen a song for the funeral?" Robert froze for a minute. He was fully aware that she was needling him and trying to drive him over the brink. When he was able to move, he said over his shoulder, "I will!" Privately, Robert wasn't sure what he should sing, or even if he should try to sing at all. In all honesty, he wasn't looking forward to it.

Rachel finished sewing the lining and pillow for Miss Addie's coffin. Shortly, the funeral director would pick it up and pay her. She had used a different stitch this time. She was pleased that it turned out so well. She'd thought, "After all, Miss Addie was three of my children's teacher. I want this lining to be special." Rachel had only seen her a few times at church, but Miss Addie had made a favorable impression.

Miss Addie's relatives stayed at her house when they arrived in town. One of her sisters looked remarkably like her. She, too, was a teacher. Reverend Bacon was there to console them and to iron out a few snags. He outlined the order of service for them and answered their questions. Dolly, the sister who looked like Miss Addie, was the most vocal. The soloist was one of her concerns.

The preacher said, "That, I assure you, will not be a problem. Deacon Grant has a "once in a lifetime" voice. I can't say enough about the quality of his voice. It is, quite frankly, indescribable! You are in for a spiritual thrill!" Dolly relaxed and said, "That is a strong endorsement." She shook his hand, and thanked him for his support.

On Saturday, Robert was more nervous than he had been previously. There was no place for him to go. He worked in the garden, cleaned the buggy, and even groomed the horse. The activity proved to be therapeutic for him. Robert was tired. He was ready for bed, but he took the time to have supper. Nobody was talking, but it was for no special reason. Mom Maggie was in a pensive mood. That explained her quietness.

The new dresses that she and Rachel finished earlier would be worn by the girls to the funeral. Mom Maggie disapproved of all the preparation. She thought it was highly inappropriate, but she did realize that Rachel was completely in the dark. She was too wise to expect a confession from "that jackal" Robert. She would hold her peace and keep her eyes and ears open. "All of my days, I've noticed that things have a way of working themselves out. I'll rely on that."

Sunday came at last, Robert paced back and forth outside. He was ready to explode at any time. He had to exercise more control than he had heretofore. He had to get through Miss Addie's funeral with some dignity. "I must perform this solo without a blemish, even if I break down and scream when it's over, and I'm alone."

He could do it if he could keep his mind on Miss Addie's life, not her death. Robert knew that it would be quite a feat, with her body lying there in the church. He could do it if he managed to get over the guilt he felt and deserved. "I can and I will do it to preserve the reputation that I've tried to build for myself. I can do it! This will be the last act that I can ever perform for her. It has to be excellent!"

Robert hoped that the lecture he'd given himself would be sufficient. He only had one chance to get it right and that was truly scary. "Miss Maggie will be waiting for the slightest sign, but I will disappoint the old bat!"

Robert walked out to the buggy and did something that he loathed. He had to wait for Mom Maggie, Rachel, and the children to get into the buggy. Rachel and Mom Maggie packed the buggy with baskets of food. It was customary to eat after funerals, and they had done their share. Many people came from afar, and they would be hungry. When they were settled in the buggy, Robert flicked the reins.

CHAPTER 7

They arrived at the church a bit early. Mom Maggie and Rachel took the food to the kitchen, and the children helped them. Robert went into the church to view his beloved Addie. He knew it would be easier and wiser if he viewed her alone. Robert approached the coffin with a heavy heart. She lay there looking very sweet, but there was a faint frown on her face. He imagined it to be a troubled expression. "Why wouldn't what she felt at the time show on her face?"

Tears obscured his vision, and he felt his heart leap in his chest! He leaned over and kissed her forehead, then he kissed her cold lips. Robert whispered, "Goodbye. You didn't know it, but I loved you." He slipped out of the side door to be alone and compose himself.

When it was time, Miss Addie's family arrived and entered the church. The church members and friends followed. Robert took his seat on the deacon's bench with the other deacons. The choir sang, and they never sounded better. After a fervent prayer, the minister, Reverend Clyde Bacon, stood and announced his text – "No, Never Alone." No one could paint a picture the way that Reverend Bacon could. When he ended the eulogy, the entire congregation was on fire! Some cried, and some just moaned.

After the cries subsided, Deacon Robert Grant stood. He closed his eyes as the pianist played the introduction. The silence was thick enough to slice, and the anticipation was sky high! Robert began to sing, "Beautiful Dreamer." His voice seemed to soar and take on a life of its own. It filled every corner and crevice in the building, and he stirred souls. He sang as if he were singing to angels in heaven. He sang as though his life was at stake. He ended his solo as he began – sweetly.

The nurses unit was tending the family. The ushers assisted members of the congregation. Slowly order was restored, and the Reverend Bacon gave the benediction. Miss Addie was buried in the cemetery that belonged to the church. Robert didn't go near the grave. It was much too final for him. With a lot of luck, he had managed to weather the storm. Nobody would have guessed that he was the chief mourner, but he was.

Tables were set up in the dining hall and in the church yard. The family was escorted to the dining hall where they were greeted by the members and friends. Robert felt brave enough to go to the dining hall. He nearly fainted when he saw Addie! During the service he couldn't see the family very well. When he stood to sing, his eyes were closed most of the time. Robert was sure that he must be hallucinating, and he began to perspire! His mouth was open and his eyes were wide! He tried to get up, but he couldn't make his limbs move.

The pastor noticed and followed Robert's gaze. He explained that the lady was Miss Addie's sister, Dolly. Robert was somewhat relieved, but he was very uncomfortable with her there. He tried not to stare, but he couldn't take his eyes off her. Rachel and Mom Maggie helped serve, then they took their seats at the table. Miss Addie's family went to Robert and thanked him for singing so beautifully. Dolly took his hand and said, "Reverend Bacon wasn't wrong about your voice. You're tremendously talented! I know my sister would have been pleased."

Robert was speechless! Not only did she look like Miss Addie's carbon copy, but her voice was very similar. Just then, a tall handsome man came over Dolly said, "Mr. Grant, this is my husband – Bill." Robert came back down to earth and shook his hand. Robert saw them exchange loving glances before they moved on. He was impressed.

People were leaving for home now, and Robert was more than ready. Rachel signaled the children, and they climbed into the buggy for the trip home. Mom Maggie was outraged, but she said nothing. "All of that praise." She thought, "What is wrong with the world? My daughter is the innocent one here – not Miss Addie! She took her own life, and they put her on a pedestal. Well, there is a higher authority, thank goodness!"

Rachel said, "That lady was a fine person. She must have felt trapped in some way, to end her own life. She needed someone to confide in and make sense of whatever she saw as a huge problem."

Mom Maggie was tempted to tell all, but she didn't. She said instead, "What she did was wrong, and God will be her judge!" Robert knew what she was implying, and he felt like throwing her out of the window. Instead, he left the room. He wasn't a total fool. Putting his hands on Mom Maggie would have been a tragic mistake for him.

Robert sat outside thinking about Miss Addie. He would never have thought of her as the suicidal type. She was so cheerful and full of life! Knowing that he contributed in a large way to her suicide was too heavy. He buckled under the weight of it. Robert said to himself, "Living without her is my punishment. I won't really be living. I'll just be going through the motions."

The next day was the beginning of another school week. He would do the best he could. The night seemed too long, but, as always, it ended. Robert and the children went to school, and Mom Maggie and Rachel washed clothes. Except for cooking, they practically rested the remainder of the week.

Mom Maggie had to go home and take care of some things there. She had been gone for two weeks. In Robert's opinion, it was two weeks too long. He would take her home after church on Sunday.

⋇ ⋇ ⋇

The week flew by, and Sunday was looking at them. Robert took Mom Maggie and the family to church. As they always did, a meal was served between the morning service and the afternoon service. Reverend Bacon took Mom Maggie aside during the meal to give her good news. "Miss Addie's family wanted to thank Robert, in some way, for singing so beautifully at the funeral. They decided that they could do that by giving his mother-in-law Miss Addie's horse and carriage. I mentioned that you were looking for one. They won't accept any money. What do you say, Miss Maggie?" Of course Mom Maggie was grinning from ear to ear. "I say thank you for thinking about me, and please thank them for their kindness."

Mom Maggie saw that as a two-fold blessing. First, she would be able to come and go wherever she pleased. Secondly, Robert would have the pleasure of seeing her in Miss Addie's carriage and know that he caused her to have it. Yes, she gladly accepted their offer. Reverend Bacon said, "I'll tell Robert, and he can take you there to get it after the afternoon service. I do believe, Miss Maggie, you are most deserving of this." Mom Maggie said, "Please do speak to Robert. Bless you, pastor." To herself she said, "Just another step in his payback."

She watched Robert's face while the pastor was telling him. She saw the shocked expression as his jaw dropped. Mom Maggie watched as he collected himself and nodded. She chuckled, as she viewed the acting ability of her dear son-in-law. Rachel and the children were delighted when they heard the good news. Evelyn said, "Now you can drop in anytime!"

Mom Maggie knew how uncomfortable Robert was, taking her to his dead lover's house, then seeing her take charge of Miss Addie's possessions. With hugs and goodbyes, she got into the carriage and took the reins. She looked at Robert and said, "Thank you for helping me to get this. I'll be able to visit often!" He pulled his eyes away, breaking her gaze. She went down the road, and they went down another. Once again, Robert was commander-in-chief.

The children knew they wouldn't be whipped because it was Sunday. Monday was going to be a big problem, though. It was difficult to unwind after having two whole weeks of freedom and fun. They had almost forgotten their former life, but there it was. It stared them boldly in their faces, once again. They had confided to each other that they wished their father had died instead of Miss Addie. But he didn't, and they were stuck with him.

Little Jim whimpered and wet his pants for the first time in two weeks. Robert heard the soft cries and stopped the buggy. He looked around in Little Jim's direction. "Stop at once, or I'll put you out of the buggy! I'm only going to say this once." Baby Jim swallowed hard and put his hands over his mouth. Robert waited a moment to be sure the little boy had stopped. When he was satisfied, he proceeded down the road. Everyone knew that he would have left the little boy on the road alone and never looked back.

When they arrived home, Robert waited for them to get out of the buggy, then he drove off without a word. Rachel didn't dare ask or want to know where he was going. She prayed that he would stay away forever. Robert hadn't been the same for the past two weeks and she didn't have a clue. Knowing that he would eventually come back prevented her from enjoying his absence.

The children laughed and talked as they prepared for bed. Rachel noticed that even in their laughter, there was a hint of tension. Laughter didn't quite erase the knowledge that their own particular kind of hell would begin when their father came home. Listening for the sound of the horse and buggy was, indeed nerve-wracking for Rachel. She knew that he could burst in the house at any time. Even when he was out, he was in very real sense still there.

CHAPTER 8

When Robert rode off he had no idea what he wanted to do or where he wanted to go. He only knew that he had to leave. He had no love for Rachel or his children. If it were possible, he would have gladly traded all of their lives for Miss Addie's. He would have done that in a heartbeat and never batted an eye. Marrying Rachel had been a big mistake as far as he was concerned. "I need an exciting, adventurous woman like Miss Addie. Rachel's youth and her pretty face attracted me, but I crave much more than that."

Robert found himself near the town saloon. The two churches had been trying to close the place but with very little success. He had never been in there, but something inside of Robert urged him to see what happens in a place like that. He dismounted and went inside. At first, he found the dim lights and the noise disturbing.

He took a seat in a corner and watched the people. There were groups of people laughing and drinking at tables. Robert remembered that he and Miss Addie sometimes sipped a little wine. It had always helped him to loosen up a bit. Sadness threatened to overtake him, but he struggled against it. He almost got up, but he didn't.

A young lady spied him, and she came over to his table. He was about to send her on her way, but on an impulse he decided to see what she wanted. Robert would give it the old college try! He thought, "Nothing ventured – nothing gained." She sat down and gazed at him. "I've never seen you in here before. Are you new in town? Robert nodded. She brightened and said, "I thought so. I'm Bessie." Robert didn't know why, but he said, "I'm Bob."

She asked, "What are we drinking? How about ordering something for us?" She didn't wait for him to answer. She signaled a waitress and ordered a bottle of wine. She said cheerily, "Pour us a drink, Bobby!" He obliged and drank with her. After the third glass she became very appealing to him, and the memory of Miss Addie faded. He leaned over and kissed her, and she responded eagerly. He liked that. She had fire! By the time the bottle was gone, he was completely enchanted by her. He ordered another bottle and took it to her place.

Bessie lived in what appeared to be, a hastily re-constructed carriage house. There was a large room, which she used as a combination bedroom and parlor. There was a tiny kitchen in the back. Two beds were pushed together to make one huge one. Large satin covered pillows were plumped and positioned for comfort.

Bessie said, "Bring the wine to bed, Bobby." She then began to disrobe. This was a brand new experience for Robert, and he was wide-eyed! Bessie helped him to shed his clothing, next. Robert felt his knees buckle, partially from the wine, but also from the excitement.

When their encounter was over, Robert was completely hooked! His position as deacon fled with the treasured memory of his dead love, Miss Addie. He wanted to stay, but Bessie said she wanted to get some rest. Robert had no choice but to go home. He had school the next day. He had to get some sleep if he were to be sharp and on top of his game.

The ride home was the exact opposite of the ride away from the house that he shared with his family. Then, he was down-cast and feeling much sorrow. Now, he was filled with exciting reflections. He had never met a woman like Bessie, and he doubted that he ever would. Her boldness was intoxicating and addicting. Not even Miss Addie could come close to Bessie. Robert had brought this new thing into his life, and he would indulge himself. He knew that it wouldn't be his last visit. Bessie was in his blood! Now, going home to Rachel was a definite downer. He was sickened by the thought of her.

Everyone was in bed when Robert reached home. He went into

the bedroom and looked at his sleeping wife. He thought, "That was my biggest mistake. On a scale from one to ten, she's a minus zero!" He felt that she had trapped him by having children.

Emboldened by the wine that he consumed, Robert snatched the covers off Rachel. She woke up abruptly, and she was confused for a moment. Her confusion turned rapidly to fear when she saw Robert standing over her. She tried to read his facial expression, but she couldn't. His mouth curled in a sneer, and he said, "You don't know how to be real woman. You're just a useless excuse for a red-blooded female. This is what I think of you, stupid!"

Suddenly, he struck her across the face, bloodying her nose. She was too stunned to yell or cry. She curled into a ball in an effort to protect herself from further blows. Robert wasn't finished with her. He dragged her from the bed onto the floor and raped her brutally! Rachel went as limp as a rag. She forced her mind to another place, and she felt nothing!

When Robert tired of her, he left her lying there broken and bitter. Robert got into the bed and was soon snoring loudly. Rachel stayed on the floor until morning. She preferred the floor to lying beside him on a comfortable bed. She didn't know what the morning would bring, but he would go to school. That would bring peace and comfort for awhile.

Rachel blamed herself for Robert's actions. She should have searched harder for the poisonous berries. But then, death was too good for him. She thought, 'Why couldn't he have died, instead of a sweet lady like little Miss Addie? Where is justice?" Rachel didn't know that her children wondered that also. On that, they were in accord.

As she lay there, she saw dawn peeking through the windows. She rose from the floor and heated water to bathe. She pumped enough water to replace what she'd used   and started breakfast. Eventually, she heard the children stirring.

Robert came to the table, acting as if nothing out of the ordinary had happened. Rachel did the one thing that she could do. She spit in the cup before she poured the coffee. He drank it, and she watched without batting an eye. There was, for her, no consolation in what she'd done. It was too small to count. She knew that she would have to become more inventive.

Robert rapped on the table with his spoon to get her attention. "Another cup of coffee!" She answered, "Coming right up." Under her breath she said, "A la Rachel!" Rachel spit in his cup again and gave it to him. He enjoyed it, closing his eyes as he sipped.

The children left for school before Robert. He passed them as they walked. His eyes were focused straight ahead. He didn't acknowledge them, just kept his horse at a steady gait. It did not matter to him that they were all going to the same place. When he was out of range, they talked about him. Fran did a great imitation of him that made the others double over laughing. They changed the subject as other children joined them on the long walk to school.

Mom Maggie enjoyed having transportation again. It was mighty good to be independent! She shocked her sons and their families by visiting them unexpectedly. She brought her famous cookies with her. The children called her their fairy godmother!

Being in their homes was so different from being in Rachel's. There was no tension or feelings of fear, just comfort and love. All of her sons had added a room on their house for their mother. Secretly, each one hoped that she would spend her twilight years with them. Mom Maggie had other ideas. She was still going strong, and she was determined to die in her own bed.

She was thrilled to be wanted. Her daughters-in-law adored her. They spoiled her shamelessly when she visited. Mom Maggie loved all of them, but her heart belonged to her only girl, Rachel. She was the neediest. Fortunately, her sons were neither resentful nor jealous of the time she spent with Rachel. They, too, loved their little sister. Mom Maggie had never talked to them about Rachel's living conditions. They would have broken Robert's knee caps! Although the thought was very tempting, she didn't want to be responsible for their being in prison. Robert would, without a doubt, press charges against them, should such a thing happen. Anyway, she would keep his feet to the fire. Soon, she would pay Robert an unexpected visit. "I know my Rachel is in distress, and he will pay!"

Rachel had more linings to sew. She got several compliments for her work on Miss Addie's coffin. "Maybe I'll use that stitch again. I'll think about it. In the meantime, I have to concentrate on Robert. He's such a pig! How can he abuse me at night and ask for coffee in the morning, as if nothing happened? I'm considering talking to Reverend Bacon about him. On second thought, maybe I won't. He'll never believe anything negative about the good deacon."

She pinned the pieces of material together and started sewing. Rachel wondered where he'd gone last night. "What made him treat me like an old dog?" There was no sensible answer to the questions. Robert was who he was.

The day passed, and it was time for Robert to come home. She had made lamb chops for supper. She put her sewing away and concentrated on the biscuits. Rachel looked at the clock and saw that Robert was running late. The children would be home at any moment.

Robert was no longer the creature of habit she knew. He kept his own hours now. "Now that I think about, Robert had the smell of liquor on his breath last night! He never used to touch alcoholic beverages of any kind. He always had such disdain for those that did, but I distinctly remember the odor of wine. What's going on with him?" Rachel knew that the last thing a cruel man like Robert needed was liquor of any kind. Now, she was really worried about the children.

Robert headed home, but he didn't want to be there. Luckily, his common sense dictated his moves. He couldn't risk someone seeing him go to the saloon in broad daylight. His reputation would surely be at stake. He had spent a lifetime building it. People respected him as a deacon, and one of spotless character. All of that would be torn down in an instant. He couldn't allow that to happen because it was far too important to him. He thought, "What they feel about my singing borders on hero worship. All of that would be torn down in an instant. Most of the people won't tolerate deceit of any kind."

Robert indulged in what had become his favorite past time: reminiscing about Bessie. He longed to be in her bed again. He would wait until the weekend to see her, because he had no choice. He wasn't sure if she went there every week, but he would find her or die trying! "I'm determined to not let the best thing that ever happened to me slip through my fingers. Until the weekend, I'll have to simmer down and endure Rachel and that pack of heathens."

He had a fleeting twinge of guilt about Miss Addie. He was surprised that his love had dwindled so quickly, but it had. "I'm still alive! I know, somehow, that a woman like Bessie would never dream of suicide, ever! She was put on earth to please her man. She knew it, and she enjoyed her role. It took a woman like Bessie, to blot out the terrible feelings I'd had about Miss Addie. The timing was perfect! I was living on the edge before I stumbled into her. If I hadn't met Bessie when I did, Miss Addie would have destroyed my life as well as her own."

CHAPTER 9

Robert drove up to the carriage house and stopped. He took his time because he loathed the people inside. He had convinced himself long ago that his hatred of them was their fault. Certainly, it wasn't his. He'd given them everything, but they didn't appreciate anything. He said to himself, "They're the most ungrateful clowns in the world. They have never missed a meal, and they have clothes on their backs, but they are too short-sighted and stupid." Robert hated the idea of being saddled with them.

His eyes narrowed as he thought, "Rachel will obey me the same way my mother obeyed my father. My dear, departed father was definitely the boss of his home. When I was a child, I remember how fearful and unhappy I was. I hate admitting that, but it's true. When I became an adult, I slowly realized that it was the only way to keep a family intact and respectful."

Robert remembered that he didn't love his father when he was a child. It was only after he became an adult that he could appreciate his father's values. He hoped that, somehow, his father knew he'd changed. He came to admire his father and the total control he was able to maintain. "A firm hand is necessary to keep a woman in line, and your children out of mischief." His father often stated, 'If God wanted a woman to lead, He would have made her first!" Robert couldn't argue with that kind of logic. He was grateful for the pattern he'd set before him. He'd turned out to be upstanding and God fearing. His father, he felt, deserved all of the praise for that. Of course, Robert had added his own touch to the rearing of the children. He pushed them towards perfection with routine beatings. His father had beaten him once with a whip! He still carried the lash marks on his back to remind him. He was soft on his children, in comparison to his father. They don't know how lucky they really are."

Robert couldn't stall any longer. He went into the house, but he was dragging his feet. Supper was ready, and he went directly to the table. The family gathered in the dining room. The lamb chops were cooked just the way he liked, but he would rather die than tell his wife they were good. The children ate in fearful silence.

After supper they would have to line up and be grilled by their father. Evelyn, the oldest child, looked at him as she ate. She wondered if everybody's father was like hers. She and Fran had inherited his talent for singing, but they never sang when he was in the house. He absolutely forbade it. Their teacher had spoken to him about their voices, but he told her to discourage it. The teacher was confused, but she did as he wished.

Robert wanted to stifle them in every way possible. If he allowed them to sing, it could be disastrous for him. "More than likely, I'll be expected to share my space with them. People might ask them to sing and forget about my extraordinary voice. I will not have that!"

Evelyn and Fran were old enough now to do the dishes. That made them feel grown up. Too soon, supper was over. Fran and Evelyn helped Rachel clear the table, and they started to wash the dishes. Robert's voice rang out. "Stop whatever you are doing, and form a line!" Fran was startled, and she dropped a cup. It slipped from her hand, and she prayed silently that her father didn't hear it. She began to tremble with fear.

She walked slowly to the parlor and lined up with the others. Robert called for the whipping chair and removed his belt. "There will be no question and answer period. We will get right to the punishment!" Rachel was glad they were wearing the padded underwear.

Robert started with Evelyn. "You will receive extra lashes for looking at me during supper. You thought I didn't know. You were stupid to do that!" He began to lash her furiously. The padded underwear took the sting out of the blows to the buttocks, but whipping her legs caused her to wiggle and cry pitifully. He never stopped beating them until he reached the danger point. Robert pushed her aside and said "Next!" Fran leaned over the chair. Her eyes rolled wildly, and her body shook violently! Robert lectured her first. "I heard you break something in the kitchen. That will cost you." He struck her viciously and let the pain sink in before he delivered another blow.

He was in his glory as he applied the leather belt to her body. Fran slumped to the floor in a faint. Robert pushed her out of the way with his foot and signaled for the next child. Little Jim was the last one. He had already wet his pants from his extreme fear of his father. He beat him too long, but not as viciously as he normally did. He was getting tired.

Rachel had gone to the kitchen to do the dishes when Robert summoned the children to his "throne room." She heard the sound of every lash. It sent a pain through her heart each time he hit them. Rachel knew only too well that Robert would turn on her if she tried to intervene. She cursed her very existence! Her children needed her, and she needed to kill him, but how?

Spitting in his coffee was not enough. He had to die! God wouldn't do it, so it was all up to her. Robert's voice crashed through her thoughts. "Get up and go to your room, at once!" She heard movement and knew that they were trying to be obedient and get out of his way. If they didn't move fast enough, he would beat them again. Another beating would kill them!

Tears flooded her eyes, and she leaned over the sink. Rachel's body rocked in silent agony. "Dear God, how much longer?" She heard the rustling sound of papers, and she knew that Robert had moved on. He was preparing the next day's lessons and correcting papers. Rachel knew that only a person who was being aided by Satan could make such a fast transition. She wondered what kind of mother and father could have brought such a beast into the world. "It had to have been a curse on them!"

When the kitchen was in order, Rachel went upstairs. She eased the door opened and slipped inside. Quickly, she applied the ointment to their wounds and kissed them. She couldn't stay, and they knew that. He would beat her and them all over again if he caught her in the room.

Rachel picked up some sewing and tried to lose herself in being busy. It didn't work for her. It was impossible to concentrate, so she bathed and went to bed. She said, "I'll go where he can't invade. I'll go to sleep! "He hadn't touched her during the night, and she was greatly relieved. She didn't know that he was becoming obsessed with thoughts of Bessie. It would be accurate to say, he didn't think of much else.

Robert finished what he was doing and sat there. He was reliving his time with Bessie. Robert wondered who was with her at that moment. The thought of anyone else sharing her was revolting. He realized that he had absolutely no claim on her, but that didn't stop him from wanting her for himself.

Robert wondered if he had made any kind of impression on her. Did she think about their time together? "I wonder if she is, even right now, longing to be with me. I want her to think of me as challenging and easy to love. That way, I'll have her all to myself for as long as she pleases me." His thoughts of her were wild, and a bit impossible.

Miss Addie never crossed his mind now, except fleetingly. Her face wasn't clear in his mind when he tried to visualize her. She had been replaced by a lady named Bessie that he barely knew. If he had anything to say about it, he would know her very well, very soon.

Robert dozed in the chair, and he dreamed of Bessie. It seemed so real! He was kissing her full, sensuous lips, and she was kissing him back. She moved away from him, and he followed her. Just as he reached her, he woke up! He was disappointed when he realized where he was. The dream was lost forever,

He went upstairs to the room he shared with Rachel. She was lying there, seemingly asleep. He pulled the covers off her saying,

"I guess I'll have to settle for you."

The next day the children were unusually quiet, even with their mother. Their downcast, defeated expressions affected her deeply. Rachel was afraid that Robert had finally succeeded in breaking their spirits. They didn't respond to her hugs, nor did they talk to each other. Usually, when their father left the house, they came alive. He'd left earlier than usual, and Rachel was looking forward to their chatter. Instead, they were listless and quiet.

She put an extra cinnamon bun in each lunch box. That was one of the few, small ways in which she could show her love. Rachel was painfully aware that they were being scarred for life, but she wasn't equipped to stop the madness. They needed a stable home life. They had lived a hundred lifetimes.

Rachel moaned, "How can they possibly grow up to be sane, happy, healthy adults? I'm certain that this will cause them to be nasty and cruel, or weak and subservient. For them, there is no happy medium. The only things that they can count on are anger, beatings and turbulence. What kind of life is that for them?"

Worry had caused Rachel's head to throb. She tied a tight band around her pain, to relieve the pressure. She'd learned that from Mom Maggie, and it worked. She owed her for so many useful things that she'd taught her. She wished that she had listened and been more obedient when she warned her against Robert. "My children are suffering because I made an unwise choice when I married Robert. Would it have been better if they had not been born? No. They have as much right to live as anyone else. Robert is the one who breathes air to which he has no right." He took pleasure in making their lives a living hell.

In the beginning, Robert had his eye on Rachel. She, like everybody else, was caught up in the spell he cast with his singing. He was incredibly talented. The people of the town held him in high esteem. He was soft-spoken and attentive. Throughout their courtship, he was always a perfect gentleman. Robert dropped his projected image after the marriage. Rachel was engaged to a loving person, but she found herself married to an evil stranger.

In those days, women had virtually few rights. They were almost powerless against their husbands. To ensure a good marriage, the woman had to be very careful in accepting a man's proposal of marriage. She could find herself inextricably bound to a monster. The words, for better or for worse, were considered almost morally binding. Happiness, in a sense, was the luck of the draw.

Rachel did her daily chores, then worked on some of the linings. Her heart was heavy as she worked. From time to time, the tears forced her to stop. Her morale was at an all-time low, because of her children's depression. As difficult as it was, she felt that she could take her lumps, but the children couldn't. They were bewildered, and rightfully so. Robert was missing so much, by treating them like dirt. Rachel thought about Evelyn. "She is intelligent and talented, and so are Mary and Fran. Betty and Mary are vivacious and so loving. Little Jim is comical and lovable. He has a way of creeping into your heart to stay. Robert beats him the same as he would a man! I'm so afraid he's going to kill my baby boy!"

Rachel prayed that they would be in a better mood when they came home. She was afraid that they would hate her one day for permitting this. She would understand, because she blamed herself.

When they did come home, nothing had changed. Rachel kissed and fussed over them, but they were low-key and withdrawn. They were tired of trying to be normal. They went upstairs to get their padded underwear. When they came back downstairs, they started their homework. Rachel didn't know it, but they had discussed their plight among themselves. In the end, they'd decided that nothing would ever change for them until they either gave up or died. They wanted to be cheerful for their mother, but they just couldn't.

Their world was very small. They had never been on a vacation, nor had they ever been away for the weekend or a day. They couldn't remember ever playing outside, except when their grandmother was there. They felt old and beaten down. Their friends at school talked about things that were totally foreign to them. They felt odd when they were around their friends.

Robert came home, but they didn't look at him. There was the line up after supper, and the beating they knew would follow. Without thinking about what she was doing, Rachel asked Robert to stop beating them. That really shocked him, as he thought she was under better control. Her boldness was prompted by the recent change in them.

Robert turned and addressed Rachel. "Line up with those brats!" She didn't move. Robert raised an eyebrow in mock surprise. "Do not make me come to you!" Rachel didn't move because she was unable. Fear gripped her with an iron fist! She was making a feeble stand for her children. Robert said in even tones, "You have defied me in front of your brats, so I must punish you in front of them."

He landed a back-handed blow across her face, and she reeled. He said, "Hmm! You're still standing?" He then began to punch her as if she were another man. She tried to cover her face, and he punched her in the stomach. Rachel bent over, and he chopped her on the back of the neck, with the side of his hand. She fell to the floor unconscious.

He checked her pulse. Satisfied that she was still alive, he turned to the children. Little Jim had wet his pants long ago. They held onto each other for support. "Out of my sight!" he yelled. They tried to decide if they should help their mother, or if they should obey their father. Seeing this, Robert said, "If you want to join her on the floor, you may." They turned reluctantly and climbed the stairs.

Robert was tired of seeing Rachel sprawled on the floor, in his way. Instead of stepping over her leg, he kicked it out of his way. He strolled to the kitchen and pumped a pan of water. He returned with the water and threw it on Rachel! In a moment, she sputtered and moved. Robert crouched down beside her, and held her head up by the hair. "Let's hope that you won't ever be foolish enough to defy me. That is, openly or secretly! Now get up and go to bed, before I decide to make you spend the night on the floor!"

Rachel wanted the children to know she was all right. Otherwise, she would have gladly spent the night on the floor. Robert picked up a stack of papers and sat in a chair. He crossed his legs and never gave her another thought.

Still dazed, she staggered upstairs. Rachel opened the door to the children's room, on a crack. She whispered to them. "I'm all right. Try to get some sleep." Evelyn whispered, "Momma, are you really all right? We thought he had killed you!" Rachel asked, "Are you okay?" They said, "Yes." She knew they weren't, but she did not dare go inside. She tried to reassure them about herself. "I'm fine. We'll talk when we can. Good night, babies!" She closed the door and went to her room.

CHAPTER 10

Robert was exhausted from the beatings he had administered. He sat down to unwind and correct papers. He never gave Rachel a second thought, nor was he concerned that she could be injured. He regarded the beating as a minor interruption in his day. "Every time I think the wench is trained sufficiently, she disappoints me. Will she ever learn?"

He thought about Bessie and Miss Addie, not his wife. He seldom permitted Miss Addie to share the spotlight, in his mind, with Bessie. Tonight, he did. "If I'm truthful, I can't minimize Miss Addie's importance in my life. She was sweet and spicy, and I did love her. We would be together now, if she hadn't chosen to take herself out of existence. I miss her a lot, but I have moved on with my life. That's what I should have done."

Robert shoved Miss Addie from his thoughts, and he focused on Bessie. "Bessie is in a category that only she can occupy!" Since that night, there wasn't a day that his mind had not drifted to her. A new world that he didn't know existed was opened up to him when Bessie sat at his table. That world was steeped in sin and danger, but the good deacon found that it fit him like an old, soft shoe. He had felt quite comfortable and very much at home in that environment.

Robert tried to draw his mind in and get on with his work. That was easier said than done. Trying to concentrate on the next day's lesson was difficult. The need to be with Bessie burned inside of him like a raging fire.

Somehow, he managed to correct the day's papers before he made up his mind to get out of the house. He hitched the buggy and rode off. He couldn't be sure that Bessie would be there, or even if she would want to see him, but he didn't care. He had to see her. He would be satisfied with just a glimpse of Bessie, but a commitment from her for Friday would be ideal.

As he traveled, he saw what appeared to be a child or animal in the road. Robert gave in to the sadistic side of himself. He drove the horse harder and ran over it. He felt a bump, and he heard a little cry as the horse's hooves pounded it into the dirt! He smiled with pleasure at what he had done. Robert looked back and laughed hysterically at the crushed form lying in the road.

Robert was indeed driven by Satan and his imps. The brutal, cowardly act served to heighten his desire to see Bessie. He rode his horse into the wind with no regard for anyone else who might be traveling that road. When he reached the saloon, he was excited and breathless. He almost leaped from the buggy, and he entered the saloon.

He looked around when his eyes became adjusted to the darkness. His heart sank when he didn't see Bessie. He thought, "I'll wait for her. Maybe she'll come." Robert sat at the table in the corner and ordered a glass of wine. He waited over an hour, but she didn't show. Feeling foolish, he got up and left.

Robert walked to his buggy feeling a bit disappointed. As he was climbing into the buggy, he saw her. His heart stood still! She saw Robert, but she didn't recognize him. He called her name, softly, and she looked his way. His face flashed in her memory and she smiled at him. He asked, "Will you take a little ride with me?" Hesitating a minute or so, she said "Yes, I will." The heart that was standing still, beat once more!

He helped her into the buggy, then got in beside her. He flipped the reins, and they rode at a leisurely pace. She sat pressed very close to him, and he loved it. Before very long she said, "Stop a moment." He did, and she put her arms around his neck. Then, she kissed him hungrily. Robert's passion matched hers. She whispered, 'Take me home, honey."

Rachel heard Robert ride away and was super-happy. She started to go to the children's room, but she didn't. "They must be asleep by now," she thought. Her body still ached from the beating Robert had given her. She bathed and rubbed salve on her battered flesh. Rachel thought a sip of hot tea might help, so she made a mug.

Suddenly, Rachel had a nagging kind of feeling that she couldn't explain. It gnawed at her and wouldn't let her rest. She tried to figure out why she was unusually disturbed. "Maybe it's Robert. Maybe the buggy ran off the road, and he's hurt or dead."

Robert came home just before dawn and shattered that theory. Robert hummed as he lay down, which was most unusual.

Rachel feigned sleep, realizing that in less than an hour and a half, they would all be up and about. It pleased her that Robert would get very little sleep. She was unaware that he had already been asleep. A little smile played about Robert's lips. He was the cat that ate the canary.

Rachel got out of bed with the same "tearing at her" kind of feeling. The children came downstairs, but Little Jim wasn't with them. Rachel said, "Will one of you get Mr. Sleepy Head?" They looked at each other, but nobody moved. Rachel had a sinking feeling in the pit of her stomach. She grabbed the back of a chair, to steady her wobbly legs. "Where is the baby?" Fran whispered, "He wasn't here when we woke up. We think he climbed out of the window."

Rachel had to steady herself. To herself she said, "This is not the time to fall apart." To the children she said, 'I'll go upstairs. You know how playful Little Jim is. He's probably hiding under his bed." Rachel was whistling in the dark. She didn't for one minute believe the baby would play tricks when his father was at home. The children knew it, too.

Rachel crossed her fingers, and went up to the room to look around for some kind of clue. On the floor, near the window, was a piece of paper. She stooped to pick it up, and read, "Momma, I'm going to live with Mom Maggie. I love you." Rachel's head spun, and she fought off the awful sickness in her stomach. She took the note downstairs and showed it to the children. They began to cry, and they wrapped themselves around their mother.

She was able, after awhile, to soothe them, but she could do nothing to allay her own fears. She said, "Finish your breakfast, and go to school early. I can't leave you here with your father. I'm going to find Little Jim." They ate hastily, and picked up their lunch bags. "I'll find your brother," she told them. They ran out when they heard their father coming downstairs.

Rachel took the time to put Robert's breakfast on the table. When she started towards the door, Robert bellowed, "Get my coffee! Where do you think you're going?" Rachel looked him in the eye and said, "My baby is missing, and I'm going to find him."

Robert swelled with anger. "Stay right where you are! Don't leave this house, and get my coffee now!" Once again, she looked him in the eye and said, "Get it yourself! My child needs me!"

She turned and walked out of the door. Rachel hoped that he would join her in the search, proving that he wasn't the cold-hearted beast she knew him to be. She knew he wouldn't and that he didn't care. Rachel looked in the barn and carriage house, to no avail. Tears almost blinded her, but she pressed on. She called his name as she searched. She searched the grounds and some of the wooded area behind the house. She noticed that there were no tracks there. It was impossible for her to find him by herself.

She walked to the nearest neighbor's house and knocked at the door. Mr. Barney came to the door, and Mrs. Barney was standing behind him. Rachel was crying, and by now her dress was dirty. He asked "What brings you out here, Mrs. Grant?" Between sobs, she said, "My little boy is missing, and I need help!"

Mr. Barney stepped aside saying, "Come on inside. I'll get my jacket." His wife looked very concerned. She said, "Don't worry, Rachel. You'll find the boy. You'll find him safe and sound. Where is your husband? Is he trying to find the boy? "Rachel for the first time didn't try to defend Robert to others. "He is at home. I don't think he's going to help look for my baby." Mrs. Barney shook her head, sadly. "You'll find him. I'll pray."

Rachel thanked her and left with Mr. Barney. She told him about the contents of the note. He said, "That gives us a starting place. I'll get the horse and carriage. We'll cover more ground that way." They rode, calling Little Jim's name as they went. Looking at the ground, Mr. Barney said, 'There are horse and buggy tracks over here. Looks like they're coming and going. Let's try this road. It runs into the road that leads out of town. Maybe somebody picked your son up. It's possible that they took him to Mom Maggie's place."

Rachel tried to find comfort in his conclusion. They rode about a half mile when they saw something ahead on the road. Mr. Barney could see that it was a human. He glanced at Rachel. She saw it too, and she gasped. She jumped from the carriage before it stopped and started running toward the figure lying there. She was running at a fast pace, but it seemed to her that she was moving in slow motion.

She was positive that it was her baby boy! Yes, it was her youngest child! He was bloodied and crushed! Rachel threw herself on him, trying to will him to live. Little Jim had gone to a safer place. A place where his father could never beat him again. Rachel screamed and screamed! She gathered his broken body in her arms and rocked him.

Her grief was too much for Mr. Barney. He leaned against a tree and cried. There was the sound of an approaching horse and carriage. He wiped his eye to clear his vision. Mom Maggie was pulling up. She looked drained and tortured. Mr. Barney helped her out of the carriage. She leaned against the carriage when she saw Little Jim. For that moment, the great lady was completely defenseless.

Tears ran freely down the weathered face as she knelt there on the road. She took her beloved little grandchild's body from her daughter and carried him to her carriage. Mr. Barney laid him tenderly on the blanket. She prayed for the strength to help her daughter.

Mom Maggie turned to her daughter and took her in her arms. Rachel's sobs tore at her already breaking heart. She had delivered Little Jim at birth. She made a silent vow to find and punish the unfeeling beast who ran over her Little Jim and wouldn't stop to give him aid. Mom Maggie said aloud, "This I promise!"

CHAPTER 11

Rachel rode home in the back of her mother's carriage. She held her baby's crushed body on her lap. She was staring straight ahead, but she saw nothing. Mr. Barney rode behind in his carriage as their escort. Mom Maggie was at the reins. She thought, "This is all wrong! I'm eighty years old, and I'm still alive. My innocent, lovable grandbaby is dead! This is wrong!" She drove the carriage slowly, so as not to jostle Little Jim.

Mom Maggie couldn't help remembering the little things that had endeared them all. She thought about him turning a somersault and waiting for their applause. She remembered his tugging at her skirt to get her attention. She could feel his little arms around her neck. She could hear him say, solemnly, "I love you, Mom Maggie." The memories were tearing her apart!

Tears stung Mom Maggie's eyes, but she refused to make a sound. She had to be strong for Rachel. She could hear Rachel singing to him. She was singing to her dead child. Mom Maggie was sorry that she had not gone to her daughter's house when she first got that warning. She had seen blood on a horse's hoof, twice! She didn't connect it until an hour ago.

Mom Maggie was hard on herself. "I should have known! Why didn't I know? I should have been able to fit the pieces together, long before now! I wasted too much time, waiting for it to make sense, Lord, please show me what to do now!

She tried to get a mental picture of Little Jim's death scene. "Did he try to get out of the way? Was he run over deliberately? Where is this person who is responsible? Have they shown any remorse?"

Mom Maggie could think of a thousand questions. "Asking is easy. I need some answers."

Rachel had stopped singing to Little Jim. Now she was crying. Every time she moaned Mom Maggie wanted to scream, but she bit her lip until the feeling passed. "We will all have a difficult time getting over Little Jim's death. He was the most sensitive one. He would have liked to hug his father, but he knew better. He had a lot of love to give. He was easy to love!"

School was still in session, and that was in their favor. She didn't want the other children to see their baby brother in that condition. "Telling them he's dead will be hard enough." Mom Maggie stopped the carriage and climbed down. Mr. Barney stopped behind her and walked over to be helpful in any way he could.

"Mom Maggie, how can I help you?"

"I'd appreciate it, if you'd inform the funeral director for me."

"I'll be glad to help in any way I can. I'll stop in and tell my wife first."

"Thank you for all you've done for us."

"I'll take the little boy inside for you, Mom Maggie."

"Thank you, Mr. Barney, but I have to do that."

"I understand. My wife and I want to be here for all of you."

"Thanks, and God bless you, Mr. Barney."

Mom Maggie watched Mr. Barney climb into his carriage and ride towards his house. She drew a long breath, then exhaled slowly. She was preparing herself for what she had to do. When she was ready, she walked towards Rachel and her little grandchild.

Gently, she took Little Jim's lifeless body from Rachel and carried him into the house. Rachel followed her, stumbling and crying. Mom Maggie laid him on the bed, and got a pan of warm water. Her hands shook as she bathed him. There were times when she wanted to fall across this sweet child's mangled body and cry her heart out.

She would say to herself when that happened, "I can't afford to fall apart now." She put a clean pair of sleepers on him. It was one of the many that she had made for him. She had done her duty. There was nothing else to do for Little Jim.

Now, Mom Maggie took the time to really look at the child's body. She noted the crushed forehead. She was positive that he was facing the horse. Imagining the horror Little Jim must have felt, as the huge animal bore down on him, was a thought too painful to contemplate. Mom Maggie lovingly placed a sheet over the remains of her grandchild and went to find Rachel. She found her on her knees in the kitchen. Her head was on a chair. She made little gasping sounds, and her eyes were closed.

Mom Maggie crossed the room to hold her only girl in her arms. Just as she reached her, there was a light knock on the door. She turned from Rachel to answer it. It was the funeral director, for whom Rachel sewed. Mom Maggie put her finger to her lips, signaling him to be quiet. He understood and nodded. He followed her to the room where Little Jim lay. He shook his head in disbelief, then carried the child to his carriage.

Leaning against the door for a moment, Mom Maggie then went to comfort Rachel. She helped her to her feet and led her to bed. She brewed tea with peppermint and encouraged Rachel to drink it. The tears flowed constantly.

Then, Mom Maggie braced herself. It was about time for the children to come home. She would face it as well as she could. She sighed heavily as the door opened and the children bounded in. They had seen their grandmother's carriage. They knew that all would be well now. They all started talking at once. Evelyn asked about her little brother. "Is he living with you, now? " Betty said, "He left a letter. He said he was going to live with you. Can we go, too?"

Mom Maggie answered, "There is a snack on the kitchen table for you. After you eat, come back. I want to talk to all of you." They ran out to the kitchen to see what she'd fixed for them. They were back in fifteen minutes. They raced to get the seats beside their grandmother. Mom Maggie said, when they were settled, "Let's join hands and pray."

They bowed their heads, and she asked for the strength to make it through their crisis. She prayed that the children would understand the tragedy that had befallen them. Mom Maggie ended her prayer and said to them, "Our circle has been broken. God has taken one of ours to be with him in heaven. We're sad for awhile, and then we remember that one day, we'll meet again if we live good lives. "

"We remember the times we had, here on earth. We remember the funny times and the sad times. We remember them with love. We remember Little Jim." It took a minute for her words to sink in. Betty asked, "Momma didn't find Little Jim, did she?" Mom Maggie said, "When she found him, his angel spirit was already in the arms of Jesus." Evelyn stood up and screamed, "Little Jim is dead!" They fell on their grandmother and cried. She soothed and encouraged them. "It's all right to cry and be sad. Later, we'll remember only the best."

For awhile, the children were inconsolable. Mom Maggie was patient and understanding. She, too, wanted to fall on her face and cry out to God. She wanted it to be a horrible dream, from which they would awaken. She wanted to fall on her face and cry out to God. She wanted it to be a horrible dream from which they would all awaken.

She wanted him to run to her and climb on her lap, just the way he used to do. However, that was just a wish. "Children, together we will get through this. We aren't made of iron, but flesh and blood. Because we are, we'll cry. One day, when we think about Little Jim, we'll be able to smile. That's what he would want us to do."

Evelyn wiped her eyes and asked for her mother. "She's in bed. I gave her something to help her sleep." Fran said, "I'll miss my brother. He's better off than we are. He'll never be beaten again." Mom Maggie's eyes filled with tears, and she thought about the abuse that dear little fellow must have suffered. She understood why he'd tried to run away. Someone knocked at the door, and she was grateful for the interruption.

She opened the door to Mr. and Mrs. Barney. They had brought chicken and dumplings. Mom Maggie had forgotten about food in her grief. The food was more than welcome. The Barneys had known the family for many years. They stayed, promising to bring supper the next day.

When they left, Mom Maggie went upstairs to see about Rachel. A few minutes after she'd left the room, Robert came home. He was in a very angry mood. "The little brat wasn't in school today, and I want to know why, and where he is!" The children didn't answer because they didn't know what to say to him. They exchanged fearful glances. Evelyn thought, "Little Jim is lucky!"

Robert glared at them, and he clenched his fists. He moved in closer and looked from one to the other. "I'm losing my patience! Get the whipping chair!" Mary moved to get it, and Robert took off his belt. "Line up! First!"

Mom Maggie's voice whipped through the air. "That would be me!" Robert's arm froze in mid-air. Mom Maggie walked across the room and stood first in line. Robert realized that his arm was still raised, and he pulled it down with a jerk. She glared at him with her penetrating eyes. "Well, what are you waiting for? Strike me, if you dare!" Robert backed away, but she kept her eyes locked on his.

Mom Maggie moved out of the line, and stood before Robert, invading his space. "Pay attention to every word I say, Robert. You have struck your last blow in this house. That is, unless you are willing to suffer the consequences. You are a coward and a bully! Soon, and very soon, your faked reputation in this town, will be exposed. You will be known as the low-life snake you really are. Satan is your father, but I am your match!"

She slowed down, saying "Your turn! You may speak now, if you can find your voice." His lips moved, but he was too shaken to make a sound. She said, "Just as I thought, so I'll continue. Little Jim was run over and killed. That's why he wasn't in school. He was killed trying to run away from you! You are not going to attend his funeral. I won't allow you to slap him again by being there! That is what your presence would be — a slap in that innocent child's face! You can pretend to be too grief-stricken to go. Later, I'll decide if the truth is told."

"By the way, you will sleep on the sofa, as long as I am here. My daughter is in deep mourning for her son! You are not! Did I make myself clear? Speak!" Robert looked down at his shoes, and nodded. Mom Maggie was persistent. "What does the head movement mean?" With his eyes still downcast, he said softly, "I understand." She said, briskly, "Good!"

To the children she said, 'If you want to, you may go outside for some air. Do whatever you like doing." They went to her and hugged her. Evelyn said, "Mom Maggie, you are wonderful!" Tears filled her eyes and ran down her cheeks, but she smiled through them. "Your momma and I love you." They grabbed their jackets and went outside. Mom Maggie showed Robert no mercy as she looked at him. "Even an old dog needs air. Your father, Satan, must be very pleased with you."

She didn't have to cook, thanks to the Barneys, so she went up to check on Rachel. She was awake and crying. Mom Maggie sat on the bed and held her. Rachel said, "Mama, you don't have to be so strong for me. You loved him too. His note is here, under the pillow." Rachel felt under the pillow, and found the letter. Mom Maggie read it and held Rachel close. They cried together, for the little boy they both loved so dearly. They cried for the little boy they had loved and lost.

Mom Maggie was the first to pull herself together. She was able to do that because her thoughts were always of Rachel. She felt, "One of us has to be strong, and I guess that's me!" Rachel's tears subsided, and she decided to get up. Mom Maggie told her about the Barney's supper. She said, "It sounds good, Mama, but my stomach is too upset to hold food. I'll come to the table to be with the children. They need both of us so much more, now. They've had such a terrible life."

Just being at the table was painful for everybody. Little Jim's chair was empty. They remembered how much he loved chicken.

They remembered how nervous he became after supper. He knew a beating was coming, and he could never understand why. He knew that wetting his pants made his father more angry, but he couldn't help it. He wouldn't have done it if he could have stopped himself. He was just so scared!

After the grace was said and the plates were filled, Mom Maggie said to her son-in-law, "I find your presence here at this table disturbing and offensive! I, strongly, suggest that you take your plate, elsewhere!" For a brief moment, Robert's face showed his anger, but he quickly re-thought his position, and he left the table with his plate. Mom Maggie didn't care if he climbed a tree to eat. When he left the table, he took an oppressive cloud with him.

Mom Maggie was an awesome force. She made it possible for the family to mourn Little Jim without fear. Robert seemed to be on top, but not for long.

Robert sat in the carriage house, eating his supper. He could have taken his plate to the kitchen, but he didn't want to be around them either. He thought, "That old lady thinks she is the Queen of England. She's going to be one sad biddy, if she continues to push me. She loves the little brat so much, maybe I'll see that she joins him!"

"Where would Rachel be without her pushy mama? The answer is very simple. She would be under my heel, where she belongs. I'll continue to work toward that end. Sooner or later, I'm going to make her mama pay for trying to make me look small. If I'm to maintain control over those fools, in that house, I have to rule with an iron and unwavering hand. They understand nothing else."

Robert wanted to get a second helping and another biscuit, but he would not go in there begging for scraps. "They would love that, those dizzy fools!" That is the way he saw things. Not once did he think about his dead child! He was too focused on himself to do that.

He heard the sound of a horse and buggy nearing the house. He stood in the shadow of the doorway and looked. It was pastor, Reverend Clyde Bacon. He watched him climb out of the buggy, and walked up to house. Mom Maggie opened the door.

He thought, "I must be slipping. I forgot that Reverend Bacon would call. I should be in there to receive him. If I'd eaten in the kitchen, I would have been able to do that. It's too late now. Who knows what that old bat will say? How will I be able to handle this one? How will they explain my absence? The ancient heifer threatened to expose me. Expose what? The fact that I am raising the brats to be steady, productive adults?"

Robert was irate. He had labored hard and long to earn a name for himself. "Before I stand by – while that old lady Maggie ruins me, I'll erase her from the face of the planet! It will be a labor of love. Her interference was the real cause of poor Miss Addie's death. I'll play her game until the opportunity presents itself. She's already lived a long life. If she wants to continue living, she had better give me some respect!"

Robert thought that Mom Maggie had let the pastor in, but it was Evelyn. She looked more like her mother everyday. Evelyn thanked anyone who noticed the resemblance. She thought her mother was pretty. Even the black eye her mother occasionally wore didn't detract from her looks.

Pastor Bacon asked for Deacon Grant, immediately. Evelyn merely said, "He's not here at the moment. The family is in the dining room." Pastor Bacon accepted that and moved into the dining room where they had just finished eating their supper.

He walked over to Rachel and extended his hand. "My dear, you do have my sincere sympathy. I just got word about the unfortunate accident. Little Jim was a bright, lovable child. Certainly, we'll all miss him. Have you thought about funeral arrangements?" Rachel began to cry, and she had to leave the room.

Pastor Bacon addressed Mom Maggie. "I didn't mean to upset

her, Miss Maggie." Mom Maggie said, "No, you didn't mean to upset her, but she just found her baby boy killed on the road. Killed by somebody who didn't care enough about him to stop and give him aid after he was so cruelly run over. Yes, she is upset. What you called an accident, was murder!"

Pastor Bacon listened with widened eyes. When he spoke again, he had dropped his "preacher voice" and become real. "I'm very sorry. I didn't know the facts. I know now that I expected too much of Rachel. I'll wait and speak to Robert." Mom Maggie said, "I'll speak for my daughter. She trusts me to do the right thing. I urge you to forget about talking to Robert. I speak for my daughter, Rachel."

Pastor Bacon took the remark she had made about Robert and filed it in his mind. He would ponder it later. Evidently, there was some kind of misunderstanding here. Mom Maggie had the respect of everyone in the town. Her advice was sought by many people. If she said she was the spokesperson for the family, he had to believe her. He was, also, sure that Robert was in full agreement.

Mom Maggie waited for the children to leave the room before she spoke. Their welfare would always come first with her. Heaving a sigh to release the tension, Mom Maggie spoke to Pastor Bacon. "The service must be brief. My daughter, Rachel, is too fragile to be subjected to a very lengthy service. Will there be a problem with that?" He assured her that it was very possible. Continuing, she said, "one selection by the children's choir will be sufficient. Is that doable?"

Reverend Bacon looked up from the pad on which he was jotting notes. "Yes, so far we are in agreement. We want to please you. This is your service. We'll do whatever makes you comfortable."

Mom Maggie said, "If you would deliver a sermonette, we would like that. This time, the mental health of the family is number one. I know that we can depend on you. Brief, simple, and beautiful. That is all we ask of you." That was over, and she was glad it was. It was, she knew, just another hurdle. The real test was coping.

Reverend Bacon stood up to go. "It's always good to see you, Miss Maggie. All of you are in my prayers. Thank you for making this clear for me. I do understand. Please give Rachel my apologies for being thoughtless. You will have the type of service that you want. Call me if you need anything. I am your servant."   He shook her hand and left.

That being settled, Mom Maggie went to find her daughter. She was in the children's room. She was holding Little Jim's picture and sobbing. When Mom Maggie entered the room, she was struck by the strong sense of Little Jim's presence. Memories were everywhere! The pictures he drew were tacked on the door. His books were stacked on a small table. The horse and buggy that he was trying to make were on top of the books.

Mom Maggie couldn't look at the little, crudely-made horse and buggy without thinking how young Jim died. She thought, "The snake that did it is walking among us. If I'm supposed to know who did it, it will be revealed to me. Until then, I have to force myself to table it. Rachel needs my undivided support."

She put her arms around Rachel, and she put her head on her mother's shoulder. They stayed that way until Rachel was able to leave the room. Being in the room was difficult for Mom Maggie, but she understood that Rachel was drawn there. She knew that losing a child that you've carried for nine months, then suffered to bring into the world, was enough to kill a mother.

Mom Maggie's work was not over. Somehow, she had to get word to the rest of the family. The neighbors, from far and near, came and brought food. Some of them volunteered to contact the family for her. They were good people, who would have done anything for Mom Maggie. She, in turn, would do anything for them.

The children were given permission to cut one of the cakes. Their eyes shone with pleasure at that small privilege. Without being asked, they cut a slice for their mother and grandmother. Rachel didn't want it, but she couldn't hurt them by refusing. Their happiness, as always, was primary.

CHAPTER 12

Robert sat in the carriage house after he'd finished eating. He was tired of being out there, but he wanted everyone to be in bed when he went back to the house. He saw Reverend Bacon leave. "Only the Lord knows what was said in there to damage my character. What will the pastor say if I don't go to the funeral? Can I really convince people of my grief if I don't feel it? I really should go to that funeral and sit on the deacons' bench. If I do that, the old lady might embarrass me during the service. She has more nerve than a bantam rooster. I do believe she's a bona fide witch!"

Robert was understandably upset. He walked back and forth in the carriage house. Ordinarily, he would have beaten everybody in the house, then completed the day's lesson. He didn't like breaking his routine. That is, unless he broke it to see Bessie. Bessie! "This is the first time today that I've thought about her. She is definitely the bright spot in my gray world. I didn't think it was possible, but last night she surpassed all of my expectations."

He decided that he would steal or commit murder to be with her. He'd given her a sizable amount of money when he left her. She didn't ask for it. He wanted her to have it. If she asked him, he would snatch the moon from the sky for her. Aloud he said, " I have to gain more control of myself. I don't want Bessie to know the extent of my feelings for her. I recognize it as an obsession, not really love. However, either one will put me behind the eight ball."

Robert had a bright idea. He would visit Bessie while the others were attending the funeral. "That should give me an extra thrill. Maybe I'll visit her tonight. Maybe, I'll march in the house and tell the old lady to sleep on the sofa herself! Maybe I'll murder everybody in the house. I would never be a suspect. After I kill them, maybe I'll bring Bessie here to live with me."

Robert didn't have a solid plan, but he enjoyed thinking about things that he could make happen. "I'll plan something soon, and I'll work out the details. If it turns out that mass murder is possible, then so be it!" He peered at his pocket watch, then stepped out of the carriage house to check the house. The lights were still burning, he saw. "That means they haven't gone to bed yet. I can't sleep on the sofa if they're in the parlor." Robert was certain Mom Maggie had taken that into consideration when she gave him those instructions.

He muttered, "Well, she's won that round, but the fight isn't over." He made himself as comfortable as he could and settled down in the buggy for the night. His last conscious thought was about slitting his mother-in-law's throat!

One by one, the girls went upstairs to bed. Their grandmother realized they were grieving, also. She didn't want to force them upstairs until they were sleepy. They would have lain awake thinking, and maybe crying. She, however, was prepared to "cat nap" and be available.

It was the longest night of Rachel's life. She would love to go out in the yard and scream as long and as loud as she could. She wanted to howl at the moon like a wolf. Rachel could not bear to think beyond the moment. No words could ease or erase the emptiness she felt. Only time would heal her wounded heart. She knew that every scar is a lasting reminder of a wound. Her life had been altered, forever.

When the dawn dismissed the night, Robert stirred. He was cramped, wrinkled and angry. He felt that he had been treated like a common field hand. "This is the time to go inside. They're all in bed," he thought. Stepping lightly, he entered the house through the back door. To his surprise, his mother-in-law was in the kitchen making coffee. He said nothing, but went upstairs, quickly, and changed his clothes. For the first time in his married life, his clothes weren't laid out for him. He frowned as he selected what he would wear. He muttered, "Dead brat, or no dead brat, if her mama weren't here, I would beat the hell out of her for this!"

Robert gathered some courage and went downstairs. He took a seat at the kitchen table. He didn't see any food, but of course it was too early. He would have coffee and get out of there. Resenting every word he had to utter, he said, "May I have some coffee?" Mom Maggie turned to face him. "Certainly, if you're not too weak to get it yourself. If you are too weak, then I guess you won't have coffee."

Robert's hatred for her boiled over, but he had the good sense to control himself and keep his mouth closed. He kept his face straight, but he cursed her in his heart. He got up and looked for a cup. He had no idea whatsoever where to find one. Mom Maggie watched him, but she didn't help him in any way.

Finally, after opening every cupboard door, Robert found the cups. He poured the coffee and left the kitchen to drink it away from Mom Maggie.

She had been getting disturbing feelings whenever Robert was near. She hadn't been shown what it meant, but she knew it would be revealed at the right time. As always, it would be made plain. When he left he kitchen to drink the coffee, the feeling left with him. Because this was a new feeling, she knew it was an indication that this was a new situation. She didn't waste time or her brain power trying to decipher it, because she didn't have to do that. It would come to her naturally, without that.

Robert left the house without her knowing. She didn't want him to be there a minute longer than he had to be. Little Jim had died in a most violent way, but Robert never breathed a word about him. It was quite clear to all of them that he did not care one way or the other. He could have used the unfortunate tragedy to redeem himself, but he was totally incapable of feeling. Mom Maggie summed it up this way. "Robert is as close to being a monster, as any human I've ever seen or heard about!"

Someone knocked at the door as Mom Maggie was trying to decide what to fix for breakfast. Almost miraculously, two of the neighbors were standing there with breakfast. They'd brought sliced ham, a mountain of pan fried potatoes with onions, and eggs. They even brought freshly squeezed orange juice. Mom Maggie was beaming, and very grateful. She said, "God is so good!" Another neighbor came to take the laundry home. These acts of kindness weren't unusual. Everybody was everybody else's keeper.

Mom Maggie's sons and their wives arrived in time to share breakfast. When Rachel came downstairs, she was pleasantly surprised to see her family. Her brothers became misty eyed when she tearfully told them how she'd found her baby boy, Little Jim, lying mutilated on the road. Her brothers gave her an envelope that contained money. They stayed until after supper. They planned to meet at the church on Sunday for the funeral.

That night, Mom Maggie made her special tea for herself and Rachel. They were able to sleep all night. Robert slept on the sofa, at last! Mom Maggie and Rachel were still heartsick, but the rest was needed and appreciated. They would try to make it through the day. The funeral would be on the following day. It was an uneventful day. Friends and relatives came, bringing more food and comforting words.

They were all a bit shaky on Sunday. They didn't want it to come so quickly. It meant that they would have to put a period after Little Jim's life, and they weren't prepared to do that. Not yet. The services would be held after the usual morning service. They would leave home in time to get there promptly. A neighbor would drive Mom Maggie's horse and carriage for them.

The children were understandably quiet. When they were on their way, Betty looked around and said, "Wait a minute! You forgot Little Jim!" She remembered immediately, and cried aloud. They all understood her confusion, but they all cried anyway.

When they arrived at the church, Rachel's brothers and sisters-in-law were waiting with their children. The relatives on her father's side were well represented. Little Jim's teacher and his classmates were there with Miss Moore. The church yard was full and more were coming. Mom Maggie whispered, "This is a wonderful tribute."

The family formed a line and entered the church. Little Jim's coffin was closed, for obvious reasons. Mom Maggie and Rachel walked up to it. Rachel fell across the coffin, sobbing hysterically. Mom Maggie reeled for a moment, but she steadied herself, as two of her sons reached her side. They led their mother and sister to their seats. Rachel's sobs subsided, and she forced her mind to dwell on nothing.

The church was packed. Extra chairs were placed in the aisles. The dining hall doors were opened, so that people could sit in there. Others were not able to gain entrance, at all. The pastor looked over to see if Robert was sitting with the family, or the other deacons. Not seeing him at all was puzzling.

The children cried very hard when the young people's choir sang. Little Jim had told them he wanted to sing with the group. One of the children read a paper that she had written to honor him. There wasn't a dry eye when the little girl finished.

Reverend Bacon delivered his first sermonette, and it was magnificent. Rachel would not go to the grave site. Two of her sisters-in-law stayed with her. When the burial was over and everyone was seated, Rachel fainted. She had held herself together as long as she could. The children thought she was dead, and they were screaming.

The people had crowded around her in a semi-circle, but they opened up a space for Mom Maggie. She took something from her bag and put it under her daughter's nose. Gradually, Rachel responded. Mom Maggie asked the pastor if he would explain that Rachel had to be at home. Pastor Bacon said, "Of course, but where is Deacon Grant?" Mom Maggie said, "Somewhere, I suppose!" Leaving a bewildered pastor, she and the family carried Rachel to one of the carriages. Most of the family left the church when they did.

When they reached home, they carried Rachel up to bed. Her mother gave her the tea she'd brewed, and she drifted off to sleep. Rachel's brothers and their families went to Mom Maggie's place to spend the night. They would return in the morning. Soon, their friends and the rest of the family members went home.

Mom Maggie didn't give the children time to think about their loss. She let Fran and Evelyn slice pie and pour glasses of milk. With her at the kitchen table, the bond between them became even stronger.

No one wondered where Robert was, and no one cared. Mom Maggie was just glad that he didn't show up at the funeral. She would have been forced to carry out her threat. His awe and fear of her was in her favor. She realized, also, that his hatred ran as deep as his fear, and that she had to be very careful. With her out of the way, he would be free to beat his family to death.

Mom Maggie wanted to take the children, but she didn't want them separated from their mother. The other reason, and the primary one, was her age. She knew she was in the dusk of her life, and that these were bonus years. To leave them through death would be devastating to them. It would result in their being uprooted again, possibly, back to their snake father.

"I'll try to persuade Rachel to come with me for awhile. I want her to stay with me until she has adjusted, somewhat, to our baby Jim's death. I have my own transportation now, and I could get them to school, as well as other places. I have to speak to my daughter about this, at the right time. Meanwhile, I will fight Robert in my own way."

The children talked to each other in hushed tones. This was a habit that was born out of their father's rule of silence. It was a totally unnatural way to live. Little Jim had been the most irrepressible one, primarily because of his youth. Even he was beginning to lose the sparkle and bounce that children have, naturally. His spirit, as well as the others, was being crushed under Robert's heel.

It had made them neither children nor adults. They needed a lot of work if they were to grow up and live in the real world as functioning adults. Mom Maggie knew she would have to start somewhere in rescuing them. She decided, "I know what to do! I will make them a checkerboard tomorrow. They would enjoy something like that. I'll teach them how to play the game."

She watched them struggling to stay up with her. Soon, Betty and Fran began to yawn. They were all tired, but they were trying to stay up because of me. "If you're tired,, maybe it's a good idea to go upstairs."

They admitted they were kind of tired and kissed their grandmother goodnight. She asked, 'Do you think you can handle school tomorrow?" They all agreed that they could. She replied, "Then maybe it's a good idea to be rested when you go." As Evelyn followed the others upstairs, she said to her grandmother, "You're still wonderful. Another day without a beating! I love you." Mom Maggie blew her a kiss and turned away. She didn't want Evelyn to see the tears that flooded her eyes. "Yes, I have to do something about Robert!"

Robert had gone to the saloon to find Bessie. She was there when he arrived. She floated over to his table and kissed him before she sat down. He could feel his heart flutter. She asked the waitress to bring the wine, then she turned her attention to him. He remembered the promise he'd made to himself to gain more control over his feelings. He sat back in the chair and watched her.

Bessie sensed his withdrawal, and she pouted. He thought she looked like an angel, but he maintained his stance. Bessie poured wine in the glasses and sipped from both. He liked that, and his eyes softened. She got up, and sat on his lap. Robert liked that move, also. Bessie put her arms around his neck and whispered in his ear.

She slipped off his lap and picked up the unfinished bottle of wine. He followed her out of the door and into the buggy. He stayed with her until dawn. She'd had the same effect on him, but he was able to check himself, somewhat. He knew that he would rather die than be without Bessie. At the same time, he had to keep their relationship more balanced. Robert didn't know the meaning of the word. What he really wanted from Bessie was the upper hand. He understood nothing else.

CHAPTER 13

Robert bathed before he left Bessie's place. Bessie was far from being the domestic type, so there was no breakfast served. He did, however, have coffee. He didn't mind that she could not boil water. "She has other redeeming qualities and talents. They are more important to me." He kissed her as she slept and tiptoed outside. He didn't want to go home, but he had to pick up a few papers.

It was daylight, but Robert didn't care if he had been seen leaving his paramour's house. He rode along thinking about Bessie and how exciting she was. A little critter dashed across the road in front of him. He tugged at the reins and managed to stop the buggy in time to avoid hitting it. "That was a close call, little fellow," he said, as the animal scampered away.

Robert started to flip the reins when a forgotten incident popped into his mind. Earlier that week, he recalled that he had seen a child or animal in the road. He remembered pushing the horse harder and running over the creature. "That same day, Little Jim had been found crushed on that same road."

Robert pushed his hat back off his forehead. He said, "Well, what do you know? I killed the little brat! He was my son, but he was a sniveling little weakling! The world has lost absolutely nothing! This will remain my secret. There are no witnesses to point the finger at me. So much for that! I wish I could run into that old hag on the road. I would smash her flatter than I did the brat!" He smiled at the mental picture.

It never occurred to Robert that he had shown more compassion for the wild creature than he had for his own flesh and blood. He was evil to the bone. Bessie didn't know who she was entertaining. He flipped the reins and continued on his way. He wore a broad, satisfied smile.

Every now and then, Little Jim's murder scene flashed in his mind. Sometimes, he laughed aloud. Sometimes he just smiled that evil grin. When he approached the spot where he'd killed Little Jim, he stopped. He removed his hat, and held it over his heart. He yelled, "Hey, brat! Did I give you enough respect?" Robert put his hat on and laughed loudly. "One down and a few more to go!"

Mom Maggie and Rachel were having coffee when he arrived home. He didn't speak to them, and they didn't acknowledge his unwanted presence. Robert walked through the room, and a chill brushed Mom Maggie's body! She thought, "There it is again. Another warning! It's something about Robert!"

He took an apple and a banana from the bowl of fruit, picked up his papers, and left for school presumably. He left by the side door to avoid looking at the two people he hated with a passion. He was glad that they hadn't seen him get the fruit. They would have known he hadn't eaten, wherever he'd been. He would have appeared hungry to them. What's more, they would have guessed right. He was hungry enough to eat the banana peeling, but he didn't. He cursed his mother-in-law's presence in his house. He would not forget her scorn, and he would make her pay! "I swear on the head of the dead brat!"

CHAPTER 14

Mom Maggie and Rachel were expecting their relatives. The neighbors had brought enough food to feed an army. They didn't have to go near the stove! Mom Maggie laughed and said to Rachel, "We are going to forget how to cook." Rachel tried hard, but she couldn't answer her mother. She put her head on the table and cried. Mom Maggie waited until she stopped.

"Mama, please excuse me."

"For what? For being human?"

"I'm trying to be brave, but Little Jim's death is too fresh."

"Of course it is! You're a mother, Rachel."

"Sometimes I think I don't want to go on, but I remember my other children, and I get up in the morning and try again.'

"You'll get through this baby girl. We will, with God's help. He'll keep us!"

"I love you, Mama."

Mom Maggie knew that she had no reason to apologize. She thought, "Robert is the one. He hasn't come anywhere near showing sorrow. He's a cold one! The man has two faces. He has a private face that only his family has seen, and he has a public face. Never the twain shall meet."

She shuddered when she thought about what would happen to her daughter and grandchildren, if she weren't there. "I believe they would all be where Little Jim is now. I'm the thorn in Robert's flesh. I'm sure he hates me more than God hates sin!

I'll have to keep that in mind, and walk with caution."

Rachel set the tables in the dining room and in the kitchen. Then she put the food on the back of the stove to keep it warm. While she was doing that, Mom Maggie decided to make a checker game for the children. She found a nice, flat board, and cut out a square. She smoothed the edges, and painted black and red blocks on it – eight down and eight across. She looked in Rachel's button box and found red and black buttons. Voila! The checkerboard game was ready. She said, "The children will have many hours of fun playing checkers. When I go home, I'll make another one for them. I believe it's quite possible that Robert will destroy this one. He doesn't know how to spell the word pleasure!"

They heard the distinct sound of carriages on the gravel path. Mom Maggie's sons and their families had arrived. It was a small reunion. Rachel seldom saw her brothers. They weren't very fond of Robert. His coldness to them had kept them away, but Rachel understood. Her oldest brother, James, after whom she had named Little Jim, loved her so much. She knew that he would deal with Robert if she gave the slightest hint that she was unhappy.

Her brothers' wives loved her like a sister. For years, they had wanted Rachel's children to spend part of the summer with them. They needed to know their cousins, but visits were out of the question. Robert had absolutely forbid it. Rachel had never understood his stand on that. He made it clear that he could not stand his children. Why not allow them to go away for awhile? She had concluded that he merely wanted to keep them from any type of pleasure.

They'd decided long ago that Robert was more than a little difficult, but they didn't know the full extent of his meanness. Few people did! He used people and moved them around like a chess piece. He was a master of deceit. His deacon mask was quite different from his devil mask. Robert, himself, wasn't fully aware of his capacity for evil.

The family brought Mom Maggie and Rachel up to date on the family news. They communicated as much as they possibly could, but poor Rachel was totally out of the loop. Her sister-in-law tried to extract a promise from her to visit. They wanted to help her over the rough places, as they knew her heart was breaking.

Rachel couldn't depend on Robert to understand her grief, or to extend any type of kindness. He wouldn't move his thumb so that she could wiggle out from under it. Her baby boy's death meant absolutely nothing to him. She had to leave the invitation up in the air.

The family decided to wait for the children so they could all eat together. If Mom Maggie had not been there, Rachel would have been on pins and needles. She would surely have been beaten severely for allowing her family to be there. She loved her mother so much, and she was more than grateful for her presence, as well as her protection. Because she was thinking about her mother and what she meant to her, she said, "Momma, I love you so much! I love you more than life!"

Mom Maggie was caught off guard by Rachel's declaration. She almost cried, but she quickly gained control and retorted, "Child, you are about to ruin my reputation!" Her sons laughed at her quip, but they knew she was a very special and extraordinary woman and mother.

Soon the children came home from school. They were so glad to get to know their aunts, cousins, and uncles. While they were enjoying a joke, their father came in the door. He brought the cloud of gloom with him. He'd seen the carriages, but he assumed that they were people from the church. His face fell when he saw who the visitors were. They greeted him warmly and shook his hand.

Robert stayed only because he hadn't eaten anything for two days, except an apple and a banana. Actually, he would rather be anywhere else. He thought, "I detest the entire family. They're all a bunch of blubbering idiots. Because I'm close to starving, I have to be subjected to their foolish conversation. If they knew how much I hate them, they would run!"

The women put the food on the tables. Because Robert was the host and the only deacon present, he was expected to say the grace.

He gave a rare, short version because he was plagued by hunger pangs. He ate greedily and didn't care what any of them thought.

At first they directed their remarks to Robert, but he never looked up. He gave one word answers or he merely shrugged his shoulders. When it became clear that Robert did not want to talk, they ignored him. After he'd eaten some of everything in sight, he left the table. They were all able to relax now, and they certainly didn't miss him.

They had discussed coming back the following weekend for the camp meeting services. Robert's singing and his original religious music would be featured. He hoped they would all get a terminal illness, and he would never have to look at them again in this world or the next.

He'd left the house without saying goodbye. As usual, the gloomy cloud left with him. Mom Maggie was glad to see him go, and Rachel was able to breathe easier.

After dinner, Mom Maggie taught the children how to play checkers and they loved it. Rachel's brothers promised their children that they would get the game for them as soon as they got home. The Grant children had never had so much fun in their entire lives. For now, they were ordinary and loving it.

Mom Maggie and Rachel had made sandwiches for the family's trip back home. They hated to go, and Mom Maggie, Rachel and the children were sorry to see them go. It had been a full day though, and they were all tired. After joining hands in prayer, they departed. Even Rachel slept through the night.

CHAPTER 15

Robert made his way to the saloon to find his Bessie. "After suffering those fools, I need to find comfort in Bessie's arms." The road there seemed to be much longer, because of his anxiety. He said to himself, "I went home hoping that I could work on my music for the camp meeting. But no! The house was running over with nincompoops! Rachel must know that she's in for a well-deserved thrashing when this furor dies down. The old lady won't be there forever. All of this unnecessary disruption because the brat died." Robert laughed. "Correction! All because I killed the brat!"

Robert turned off onto the road that led to the saloon. He never went to her house first. He didn't have a reason for it, he just didn't. When he arrived at the saloon, he saw Bessie talking to a young man. Robert was furious, but he tried not to show it. His imagination was working over-time, though. He imagined Bessie in this man's arms. He wanted to smash her face so that no man would ever hunger for her again!

He forced himself to think over his desire to hurt her. He strolled over to his regular table and sat down to observe her actions. She seemed to be teasing the man. Robert's fists were clenched, and he ground his teeth. Finally, she moved away from the people, then she spied Robert. She smiled and came over to sit with him. He had to fight a major battle for control. Jealously was a feeling that was quite foreign to him.

She said, "This is a wonderful surprise. Let's not waste time. Take me home, Bobby." In spite of himself, he was excited once more, by this woman's earthiness. He kissed her roughly, and she loved it. She whispered the magic words, and he led her to the buggy. When they arrived at her place, he lifted her from the buggy, and carried her inside.

"I have to drive away all thoughts of that other man!" To himself, he rationalized that beating her would only make her refuse to see him anymore. He decided to go the extra mile and be very nice and loving. Robert took his own advice, and it paid off for him. Bessie was putty in his hands, but that worked both ways. He was putty in her hands as well. He stayed all night.

To show him that she appreciated him, Bessie made a clumsy attempt to cook breakfast. The eggs were rubbery, and the ham was burned, but he ate it anyway because she'd tried for him. He never would have tolerated such a meal if Rachel had served it. His mouth curved in a half smile. "I would've beaten Rachel with that same frying pan. She's not Bessie!"

He admitted to himself that his feelings for her had changed dramatically. He had gone beyond excitement. "I love her! I'll keep that a secret. No, I'll never declare my love for her. If I keep that to myself, I'll be able to stay ahead in our relationship. Telling her how much I really love her would not be a good thing for me."

Bessie watched Robert as he struggled to eat the breakfast she'd prepared for him. She knew how tasteless it was. She was certain that he was a man of class and good breeding. Who else would do that? She smiled at him when he looked her way.

"How's breakfast, Bobby?"

"It's very nice, Bessie."

"The truth won't hurt my feelings, Bobby. I'm a lousy cook."

"You did your best. That's what counts."

"Maybe if I do more of it, I'll get better."

"You don't have to do that for me. I don't come here because I'm looking for a cook."

"Lord knows you wouldn't stop here!"

"You're fine just the way you are. We click."

'Bobby, where do you go when you leave my house?"

"I go various places. Don't worry your pretty head about that. There are a lot of other things that should occupy your mind. I'm here when I'm here, am I not?"

"That is very true, Bobby."

"Don't spoil our time with unnecessary questions. I don't need to be a quizzed. Is that a deal?"

"It's a deal, Bobby, and the case is closed."

Robert wished he could be honest with her, but that was not even a remote possibility. "I love the very ground she walks on, but I cannot reveal any part of my life. At least not now. As soon as I find a way to remove Rachel and the others, I will make the change. Until then, everything will have to go along just as they are." Bessie was his heart. He had to be with her.

Robert hoped that Bessie wasn't about to ruin what they had by getting nosy. "For her sake, she'd better not cross the line. I can love her and beat her at the same time." He checked his watch as he stood. He gathered his papers and paraphernalia, then he turned to Bessie. She glided into his arms, and he kissed her. She walked with him to the door, and he kissed her once more. Robert tore himself away and left for school.

The memory of Bessie stayed with him long after he arrived at school. Robert decided that what he had felt for Miss Addie was either a different kind of love, or it wasn't love at all. Bessie was the world's most exciting woman! The thought of another man touching her was infuriating. She had never said she loved him, but in his mind she belonged to him, only! Robert was not the kind of man that would settle for anything less.

With time on his hands, Robert's thoughts turned to Rachel, his wife. He strongly suspected that she was getting uppity by now. "I haven't whipped her in over a week. For now, it can't be helped.

Maybe when I beat her, I won't stop until she's dead. It's a great idea, but it's possible. Her mother is too snoopy to let that happen right now. She'll have to be dealt with before I tackle Rachel."

Robert's pupils worked at their desks while he daydreamed about his twisted life. The web he was weaving, was made of fragile threads. The problem with that was he was standing too close to know. He needed to back away, but his over-sized ego would not allow it. He was being sent false signals.

Bessie had no idea where the man she called Bobby lived, or where he worked. She didn't know if he were a prince or a pauper. He was very careful to keep all information about himself from her. After he left her place, she began to ponder about her mysterious lover. She knew some things just from observing him. "In a sense, he appeared out of the blue. His life and everything about him is cloaked in mystery, and I don't know why. I can tell from the way he speaks, that he is an educated man. That means that he has a good job. Then, maybe he doesn't have to work at all. He could be independently wealthy! His hands are very clean and unblemished, and that is even more proof. I would have to be deaf, dumb and blind to not know that saloons are a new thing for Bobby. He pays too much attention to everything."

Bessie washed the few dishes and made the bed. Nothing stopped her from thinking about Bobby. She thought it might be because her life was the same day in and day out. Seeing a man like Bobby was a departure for her.

She remembered asking him if he were married and had a family. "Bobby changed the subject right away. That was a dead giveaway! I knew that he was very much married, possibly with children. He's away from home a lot, though. That could be one of two things. Either his wife didn't want him, and didn't care where he went, or he was the master of his home." After thinking it over, Bessie was willing to bet that it could be both.

Robert would have been surprised to know how much she had

figured out about him, and with such accuracy. Bessie lived by her wits. Her survival depended, sometimes, on her ability to size up a person or a situation. Reading a man like Robert was, for her, a piece of cake.

Bessie had read Robert correctly, but she didn't see it all. Had she been able to see a little deeper, she would have packed her bag and fled the country. She had never heard that handsome is skin deep, but evil is to the bone! For now, "Bobby", was a wonderful diversion. If the truth be told, she was more than a little fond of him.

Bessie was young and very pretty, but she was seasoned. She majored in life and its experiences. That was what she brought to their relationship, and that was what excited Bobby so much. In his circle, he would never have met someone like her. There was no doubt that he was very glad he did.

Now, Bessie noticed that he had become somewhat possessive of her. There was something recklessly exciting about that. She didn't, however, want what they shared to become dangerous for her. Her experience told her that there was an element of danger lurking beneath the surface. She sensed, too, that beneath Bobby's veneer, lay something that could be too hot for her to handle.

In her short life, she had met all types of men. Bobby, was, by far, the most intriguing man she had ever encountered. Presently, he was not the only man in her life, but she was adept at shuffling and playing her cards just right. On one hand, the challenge that Bobby presented stimulated her. On the other hand, she was a bit frightened. She told herself, "I'll stay in the race until I win, lose or draw."

Bessie sat down to manicure her nails. Her appearance meant a lot to her and her clientele. Robert, above all, appreciated her efforts. She didn't know, but he constantly unfairly compared her to his wife. Bessie didn't want to lose him, but she wished he would stop showing up at the saloon without notice. "To avoid an unpleasant encounter, I'll have to tighten the reins on my other life. That will give Bobby a free hand. I believe it'll work to my advantage. I know that I'm playing with matches, but I can manage him. I'm not in love with him, but I am strongly attracted to the man." Bessie crossed her fingers and said, "To success!"

Robert didn't have much time to visit Bessie because he was extremely busy. After school was over, he had to concentrate on his music. Reverend Bacon depended on him to prepare the people for his sermon at the camp meeting. The word had gone forth, and a huge gathering was expected at the meeting. He had also been asked by the pastor to sing the sermonic hymn on Sunday morning. His services were in demand, and he loved it!

He was working on a new composition. Every year he tried to give the people something that they'd never heard before. Always, he selected a title, then he worked on the verses. He was satisfied with the title he'd chosen and was working on the verses. He wanted them to flow perfectly with the title, "I'm Serving God."

He resented having to work in the carriage house. "I should walk in there and pitch the old bag out of the parlor window. How can I be inspired, sitting here beside a horse! I'm just biding my time. All of them will pay." As busy as Robert was, he would have taken the time to beat Rachel if her mother had not been there. He hadn't forgotten her open defiance when he forbade her to leave the house to look for Little Jim. "She has to be whipped back in line. I'm still sleeping on the sofa, and I resent that. Why, the old hag is taking over my house! Her days are definitely numbered!"

He wanted her out, but Mom Maggie had no intention of leaving until she was ready. When she did leave, she planned to double back the very next day. That would throw a curve into Robert's plans. Rachel and the children were in grave danger now, and Mom Maggie knew it. She couldn't let down her guard for a moment.

Staying around was not a hardship for Mom Maggie. The man who took care of her chickens and garden did a good job. She didn't have to worry about anything when she wasn't there. The man stayed in a room that was built over the carriage house in exchange for doing little chores.

At hog killing time, the neighbors supplied her with meat. Her smoke house was far from being empty. People were good to her because she was good to them. They knew that she would go to them at any hour of the day or night if she were needed. Mom Maggie's mother had told her that medicine grew in the field for every kind of sickness. She would take her to the fields and show her the various things that grew there. Then she'd shown her how to prepare them for usage. Even the doctor sent for Mom Maggie when he was sick!

When the people praised her, she would shake her head and say, "Not me, but God!" Her gift for seeing things that were to come was used to help and not to hinder. Mom Maggie wasn't worshipped, and she didn't want to be. She was held in high esteem and greatly respected by all. The people knew they could trust her with their deepest secrets, and even with their very lives!

She was hated only by Robert. He would have lost all of his fans by speaking one unkind word against Mom Maggie. Robert knew that, and he kept his mouth buttoned. Knowing that added to Robert's frustration. Having to bottle up his hatred made him hate her even more.

One day, Robert sat in the parlor trying to perfect his music. He had to get away from the carriage house, or die! He didn't know why he hadn't seen it before, but he noticed how much Evelyn resembled her mother. At that moment, he began to really hate the child because of it. There was absolutely nothing wrong with either of them. They were both gentle souls. He had created another problem for himself. Now he was really torn. He glared at both of them when Mom Maggie was in another part of the house.

Robert made up his mind to do something about Rachel's "look-alike." "Soon, she'll be as uppity as her brainless mother." It was impossible not to see the affection Evelyn had for Mom Maggie. He played with the idea of destroying Mom Maggie, thereby shattering Evelyn and Rachel at the same time. He thought, "Two birds with one stone. How convenient!"

Robert kicked around his latest idea. "I won't have to tire myself beating Rachel, after that. She couldn't stand up under another close death. She would either die from the shock, or have to be put away in the asylum with the other lunatics. Either way, I would be rid of her for good. If Evelyn survives it all, and I don't see how she could, I'll have her under my heel!"

Robert felt that the idea was worth consideration. "After the camp meeting, I'll devote more time to perfecting and carrying out a plan. In the meantime, I'll concentrate on fine tuning my music. Reverend Bacon and the members are depending on me. I won't fail them, and my voice won't fail me."

He put that to rest and picked up his pen. His intention was to add a note to his music. Just then, Bessie ran through his mind. The image distracted him, and he laid down his pen. Robert was experiencing something new. A woman had never grabbed him the way Bessie had. He didn't relish being made weak by anyone, but there it was. A lady of dubious character had captured him body and soul. He wasn't willing to risk everything for her yet, but he was close.

Robert didn't want to continue meeting Bessie at the saloon. Initially, he was fascinated by the carefree attitudes of the people there. He liked the way the wine made him feel. All he wanted now was to be Bessie's man– her only man. He would not tolerate less from her.

He forced himself to pick up the pen again, but he could not write. He threw the pen on the desk and gave in to the need to be with Bessie. He raced out of the house and hitched the buggy. He didn't care if Mom Maggie was watching. He prayed that Bessie would be there. He only knew he couldn't write another note unless he saw Bessie.

He drove the horse hard! Woe unto anything in his path! Halfway there, his reason returned with a big splash. He had to turn around and go back home. He sat there for twenty minutes, gathering strength and a measure of good sense. Robert had a heart to heart talk with himself.

He said, "If you continue, Bessie would be the victorious one. I would be a defeated man. Is a few moments with her worth giving up my manhood forever, perhaps? I don't think so." Slowly, he was able to understand that he had been about to make a fatal mistake. "Never again!"

At that moment, Bessie was leaving on the arm of a middle aged man. She never knew how close she had come to ruining her times with Bobby. Bessie climbed into the man's carriage, and he assisted her. Her escort climbed in beside her and took her in his arms. He kissed her on the lips, and she faked excitement. She tore herself from his embrace, and he picked up the reins. They took off, in the direction of her house.

Bessie was keeping most of the evenings free for Bobby's visits. She had no idea that he would want to see her during the day. Bessie played a dangerous game, and so did Robert. There could be only one winner. Bessie was in over her head, but she didn't think so.

When Robert returned home, he was refreshed and in control. The wild ride had accomplished that for him. He sat at the desk and composed one of his finest hymns. He stopped long enough to have supper, then went back to the organ. When he was satisfied that he'd removed all of the kinks, he folded the sheets of music and sat back. He imagined the thunderous applause when he introduced his latest music. He thought, "If this doesn't bring souls to repentance, nothing will!"

CHAPTER 16

Sunday finally came, and it was church day. Mom Maggie got into the buggy with Robert and family. She knew he wanted her to drive her own carriage, but fear thickened his tongue, and he kept still. Robert's rule of absolute silence was cast aside. They talked to each other as much as they pleased.

Because of the coming camp meeting, there would be no afternoon service. It would begin that coming Friday. This was Rachel's first service since Little Jim's funeral, and she was tense. The choir touched Rachel's heart with their rendition of an old hymn of the church. She was moved to tears. In her mind's eye, she could see her baby boy's coffin there in the church. She didn't think about what Robert would say or do. Mom Maggie held her hand until she felt better.

Reverend Bacon announced that there would be prayer by Deacon Poe. He said, "Following the prayer, our own Deacon Robert Grant will favor us with a solo." Mom Maggie and Rachel braced themselves, so they could suffer through it, and not leave the church.

When Deacon Poe's prayer ended, Robert rose from his seat and stood near the organ. He closed eyes, as he usually did during the introduction. He knew how to draw your mind in, until you were focused on him.

He began singing, 'Jesus, Lover of My Soul." By the time he began the chorus, people were being overcome. His voice seemed to weave a spell with its golden tones. Fantastic, Marvelous, and Tremendous, the adjectives that were applicable. Robert could sing, and he knew it.

His voice had the power to soften hearts of stone. There were few dry eyes in the church when he ended the solo. The few dry eyes were those of his own family. They knew the real Robert too well to ever enjoy his voice. To them, he was no more than a croaking frog.

He sang the chorus again, almost by popular demand. The ushers were busy tending first one, then the other. After what seemed like a lifetime, people began to quiet down. There was just an occasional "amen" from the congregation. The pastor stood. He was shaken by the solo also. He said, "No one can sing a song of praise like our own Deacon Robert Grant. There is absolutely no doubt in my mind that he is touched by the Master, Himself! Thank you, my brother in Christ!"

When Robert took his seat, he had a look of satisfaction. It went as well as he knew it would. When the service was over, the people practically swarmed around him. They expressed their delight with his voice. They requested that he sing at their funerals, when the time came. Some gathered around him, just to be able to bask in the presence of a man who was gifted by God. Others told him that though the song had ended, the melody was still ringing in their hearts.

That kind of adulation was heady stuff for most people. An egotistical man like Robert needed it like bread and water. After he had milked the people dry of compliments, he told them in quiet, pious tones, "Thanks all of you. You are too kind. I must take my family home, now, as the sick and shut-ins are in need of communion. They look forward to it."

Serving communion was a responsibility that was given to the deacons of the church. That included giving communion to the members that weren't able to attend church service. The people were divided into groups so that each deacon had a fair share. Robert didn't view this as just one of his duties. He saw it as another chance for him to shine. There was a reason behind everything that Robert did. He looked for the slightest opportunity to be thrust into the limelight. He could switch masks quicker than one could say his name. His stage was wherever he chose to be.

He moved away and walked to the buggy. The family was seated and waiting for the show to end. He dropped his religious act when he flipped the reins. The scowl that he wore around them appeared. Robert said nothing but, his attitude spoke volumes. Mom Maggie and the others didn't talk much on the way home. They were thoroughly disgusted with Robert's phony behavior. They didn't understand why the people didn't see him for what he was. Mom Maggie saw his behavior as a mockery. She looked at the back of his head and thought, "No matter how high a bird flies, it has to come down."

When they arrived home, the children jumped out of the buggy. They stood ready to assist Mom Maggie and their mother. Robert, as always, climbed down and walked to the house and never looked back. He would have been pleased if one or both of the women fell. He would only be upset if they weren't seriously hurt.

On communion Sunday, Robert felt very special even at home. He could look forward to dining first and alone. Rachel would give him supper immediately so that he could visit the infirmed. Her secret aim was to get him out of the house as soon as possible. The rest of the family would eat at the regular time and in peace.

Robert ate, then he left the house carrying the communion kit with him. Traveling back and forth to the people's houses would take a long time. It wasn't a chore for him because he loved it. The people were glad to see him, and they showed it. For him, it was one more chance to show off. It would be dark when he finished. He planned to visit Bessie afterwards. She would round out his day,and make it all worthwhile.

At home, the children played checkers while Rachel and their grandmother sat in the kitchen talking.

"Mama, are you ready for camp meeting?"

"It's a lot of work, but I do enjoy it."

"Our family will be here on Friday for the meeting. That's the best part for me. I want the children to be close to their little cousins. They enjoyed being with them so much when they were here."

"Yes, that would be a good thing. Who knows? Things could change for the better. God sees, and God cares!"

"I'll hang onto that, Mama."

Mom Maggie had made a walnut cake for her grandchildren. Rachel thought about her child when Mom Maggie took it out of the oven. Rachel said to her mother, "Little Jim loved cake. Walnut was his favorite. Remember how he would ask, over and over, 'Is it ready now?'" Tears sprang up in her eyes, and she put her hands over her face. Mom Maggie tried to console her, but she was crying, too. They knew that one day things would be better. They also knew that things would never be the same. Little Jim had left a permanent wound in their lives. He was so special.

Robert had served communion to the last person on his list. The people had been happy to see him, especially those who lived by themselves. Gratitude and admiration went a long way with him, but his mind was really on seeing Bessie, by now. He put the communion kit in the back of the buggy and headed toward the road that would lead him to the saloon. He rode at a moderate pace so that he could review the day. A day like this day bolstered his ego and cemented his place in the church and the community. He endured a family that he detested to preserve his standing.

As he rode along, Robert tinkered with the idea of his being "called" to the ministry. He said to himself, "The people would love me even more. Certainly they would respect me in a different way. Reverend Robert Grant has a nice ring to it. I'll give that some serious thought. Maybe I will, and maybe I won't."

He reached the road he wanted to take and turned the horse. He was more calm than usual when he arrived at the saloon. Bessie was the first person he saw when he entered. She was sitting at his table, as if she knew he would come. That made his heart smile. He went to her, walking slowly, determined to give the appearance of having a cool head.

Bessie noticed the difference in him, but she wouldn't let it touch her. He nodded, without speaking, and sat down. She thought, "Oh, have I lost out with him? I can't let that happen! I'll try to fix whatever it is." To Robert she said, "Don't I get a kiss, Bobby?" His heart quickened as he leaned over and kissed her lightly. He was dying to crush her mouth under his, but he had to play the role, at least as long as he possibly could.

Bessie was bewildered. "You can do better than that, Bobby!" He kissed her again, but with more fervor. He liked having her beg. Robert was very good at playing games. His entire life was one huge game. He faked a yawn and said, "This has been a long day for me, Bessie." The roles had been reversed, but she hadn't caught on, yet.

She leaned over and kissed him in as desperate way. "Bobby, will you go home with me, tonight?" His heart was trying to betray him at that point, but he managed to remain cool. Casually, he said, "Okay, Bessie. I'll go home with you." This time he took no wine with him. He wanted to maintain control. The wine, he felt, would have softened him. It was important that he be able to stay the course.

She led him out to the buggy and climbed it. She sat as close to him as she could without sitting on his lap. Robert was able, but only with difficulty, to be reserved. When they rode up to her door, Robert climbed down first, and she slid down into his waiting arms. Bessie tried to cling to him, but he moved away and towards her door.

She followed, pouting. She said, "Bobby, I won't let you forget me. You're too important to me." He felt that it was time to stop the act. He knew it was time to concentrate on the woman called Bessie, and he did! He spent the night because he wanted to be with her as long as he could. Then, too, he didn't look forward to sleeping cramped on the sofa. That was the determining factor.

In the morning, he resumed his former behavior with her. He was cordial, but cool. She made coffee, then kissed him. He returned the kiss because he loved her. He found that he could be distant and still be on fire. It seemed to work well for him. He was much more comfortable, now that he had gotten a measure of control over his emotions. He had an overpowering need to take the lead in everything, including love. He would walk on burning coals for her, but he had to lead! But then, he was just being Robert.

They drank coffee together, but Robert never let down his guard. It was easy to see that Bessie was flustered. His heart screamed, "Hold her!" He squirmed, but he willed himself to sit still.

"Bobby, when will I see you again?"

"I'm not sure, Bessie. I have a lot of things in my life."

"Have I done something wrong, Bobbie?"

"Why?"

"You seem different, and I don't know why."

"Don't worry about whatever you think it is. I'm here!"

"Okay, Bobby."

"I have to go, now. I'll see you soon."

"Will you kiss me, Bobby?"

"I can do that. Come here, Bessie."

When Robert left Bessie to go to school, she cried after he shut the door. She didn't know why she was crying, or even what happened. This was a first for her. She had made men her occupation. "The last thing I wanted was to get sappy over a man. I don't want to fall under the spell of a man like Bobby."

She was always aware of the under-current of danger that flowed through him. Until now, it had been exciting. Bessie felt weird about the odd turn that things had taken.

Now, because of some odd quirk in her own personality, she was falling in love with a dangerous stranger named Bobby. She thought about that. "Maybe his name isn't really Bobby. Maybe it's William or Luther. He could be anybody! What have I gotten myself into? What do I do to get out of it? I'm sure of one thing. I have to make a decision quickly. I have to cut off our relationship while I'm able. I have to pull away immediately! I hope it can be done without hard feelings on his part."

Bessie said that, but she didn't mean it nor did she believe it. She was, she'd come to believe, making a mountain out of a mole hill. It wasn't like her to analyze a thing to death. "Nine times out of ten people who do that, turn out to be pitifully wrong. I'm wrong about Bobby, and he, in all likelihood, is who he said he is. Bobby is no different than any other person. He has off moments, too."

Bessie touched up her makeup and placed a hat on her head at a jaunty angle. "I'm going to shake the dust from my feet and move on. I can't stay here all day and worry. Life is waiting for me!" Bessie threw her head back and walked through the door.

CHAPTER 17

Rachel and Mom Maggie were bone tired when they went to bed at night. The normal day-to-day chores had to be done, and in addition to that, preparation for the camp meeting was underway. Mom Maggie and Rachel were very busy cooking for the gathering. Tents had to be erected, and tables and chairs would be set up. The people would bring their chairs to be certain of having a seat.

On Friday, the family came. Fortunately, they cooked for themselves and were no problem. People came from near and far to be at the camp meeting. Tents and tables were in the process of being set up, and booths were being assembled. Meals were sold at more than reasonable prices. There was homemade root beer and pastries of every sort. You name it, they had it! Choirs and musicians from every part of the country performed.

Everyone was waiting for Nazarene Baptist Church's golden boy to make his appearance. When Robert Grant walked forward, a hush fell over the crowd, because his voice was legendary. There wasn't a sound throughout the song. When he ended with a flourish, the spell he'd cast was broken. The applause was thunderous! Robert had to sing again because the people wouldn't let him leave. The camp meeting was a huge success.

One more day, and it would be over until next year. Robert moved among the people with ease, feeding on their praise. He would sing again before the closing. This time, he would introduce his latest and best composition. Robert had great expectations!

There was a break in the service to give people time to eat and socialize. It was the time to meet with old friends and relatives, some of whom had moved to other states. It was a glorious occasion!

People clamored for Mom Maggie's wares. Her cooking was a big drawing card. When the day ended, everything had been sold. If she and Rachel had more, they could have sold more. They left the grounds tired but happy. Sunday, there would be more of the same thing. The Reverend Clyde Bacon would deliver a sermon after Robert's solo. That would set the tone for the day. Rachel and her household slept soundly all night.

The next day, Robert's new hymn was more than well received. In truth, he had never sung better. Some people fainted, but all were greatly moved by his outstanding voice. He received many offers to sing in faraway places. Robert asked that they get in touch with him by letter. Robert lacked humanity and compassion, but it didn't show in his voice.

Mom Maggie and Rachel were glad to leave when it was over. For the children, it could be called their freedom day. Once more, they had interacted with their cousins and become closer to them. Their parents would bring them over the next day to say goodbye.

Rachel and her mother washed the pans and containers they'd used and went to bed. Robert, who had done nothing more strenuous than sing, took off to be with Bessie. Fortunately, for her, she had finished entertaining someone and was back at the saloon. As always, his heart did a flip flop when he saw her. He yearned to swoop her up in his arms and run away with her.

Robert fought his desires and was able to greet Bessie in a calm manner. Bessie was also battling with her feelings. She scarcely made it, but she put out her hand and said, "Good evening, Bobby." They played the cat and mouse game for a while. Robert had a plan, and he put it into action. He said, "Bessie, order the wine and we'll take it with us." She did, and they went to her place. He poured, but didn't drink. Bessie did! She was nervous and didn't know that she was doing all the drinking.

Eventually, mellowed by the wine, she threw herself at Robert. He softened enough to encourage her. Bessie unbuttoned his shirt and lay her head on his bare chest. She yearned to cry, and he wanted to drop the game, but something held him back. Between sobs, she said, "Bobby, I'm falling in love with you, and I don't want to!"

He loved her with every fiber of his being, but he had to withhold that from her, he thought. "I can't control the relationship if I tell her how much I love her." She kissed him until he weakened and responded to her touch. He was there all night, but he never said he loved her. This was frustrating to Bessie, but it served Robert's purpose. Bessie forgot about ending their relationship. She forgot about the underlying danger. Foolishly, despite all of her savvy, she put her heart in Robert's hands to be crushed.

Mom Maggie's family had gone, and she was free to go home when she wanted to go. She had noticed that Robert stayed away all night, sometimes. Her gut feeling was that he'd found a replacement for Miss Addie. Robert, she knew, could still inflict abuse on Rachel. Her plan was to leave one day and come back the next. She would deal severely with Robert if she ever caught him hitting her child.

After supper, Mom Maggie told Rachel that she was going home the next day. Rachel and the children were sad about that.

"Oh, Mama! I want you to stay a little while longer!"

"I'd like to, baby, but I have to check on things."

"Mama, your tenant takes good care of everything."

"I know, child, but I need to see about some of my business. I will be back sometime soon."

"It's wonderful to have you with us. I hate to see it end!"

"You'll be fine. God will take care of all of you."

"Is there anything that we can do to make you stay longer?"

"I'm afraid not, Rachel. I really do have to go home."

"We'll miss you, Mama!"

"I'm going to miss all of you. You know how close to my heart you are. All of you are special to me!"

Robert was in the parlor, and heard Mom Maggie's plans to leave. He felt like shouting! Already, a devious plot was forming in his mind. "It is time to do away with the old hag. When everybody goes up to bed, I'll put my plan into action." He continued correcting papers as if nothing had occurred. Robert worked on the lesson plan next.

Shortly, the children went upstairs. Rachel and her mother followed in a half hour. Robert waited for two hours, to be certain that everyone was asleep. He quietly opened the door, and went outside. He lit the lantern and went to the carriage house. Mom Maggie's carriage was there beside his buggy. He reached for the file on the shelf. Then he knelt beside his mother-in-law's carriage and began filing the axle.

Robert worked feverishly. His intention was to weaken the axle and render it dangerous to use. To make sure that Mom Maggie would be killed, he loosened the bolts as well. He had left nothing to chance. Robert smiled at the thought of her being hurled from the carriage when she reached the bend in the road. "The old hag will never survive such an accident. Rachel and her daughter won't survive her death. Rachel's brothers will probably offer to raise the others. I'll take a day or two, to think it over, then give in reluctantly. If they don't offer to take them, I'll tactfully suggest it."

He reviewed the scenario once more, to be certain that he had covered all of the bases. He couldn't help chuckling when he visualized the accident scene. When he thought the word "accident", he doubled over with laughter. He was satisfied that he had covered every detail. Robert put the file back on the shelf, and went into the house. For the first time, since he'd been sleeping on the sofa, he didn't mind the small space. He slept like a newborn babe.

The next morning, he sang to himself, in low tones. When he sat down to have breakfast, he was almost cheerful. He smiled at Mom Maggie several times. She noticed and thought he was losing his mind. When he was about to leave for school, he said, "Well, I'm leaving. Have a good day, Miss Maggie. " She looked at him but didn't respond. When he left she said to Rachel, "I wonder what was behind that." Rachel frowned, "I don't know, Mama. We both know he had a reason. There's a reason behind everything he does or says. We'll enjoy his absence, no matter what is running through his mind."

When the children left for school, they were in a sad mood. They knew what they would have to face without her there. Just when they'd begun to feel normal, Mom Maggie was going home. Their father would be in charge again. Mom Maggie said, "That settles it, Rachel. I won't leave until after supper. Those children seem so upset." Rachel perked up a bit. She would enjoy the extra hours with her beloved mama.

Mom Maggie's plan was to double back the next day, but she said nothing. Other than washing dishes, they coasted most of the day. Rachel made a hearty stew for supper from yesterday's meat. The rolls were rising from the night before. They only needed to be popped into the oven. Their day was a well-deserved breeze.

Robert sat at his desk. It was difficult to keep his mind on the lesson. He was excited! He would look appropriately sad when he got the news about his dear mother-in-law's untimely death. He would sing one of her favorite hymns at the service. It would be a huge funeral. She was known and loved by everybody.

He thought, "The exposure will be great for me. Maybe I'll pretend to break down once or twice while I'm singing, but I will continue. That will really impress everyone and push me a notch in the community." He sat there fantasizing, as his students worked. He was so caught up in his dream that he didn't yell at or ridicule any of the students all day. They thought he was coming down with something — some sort of sickness, they believed. Whatever it was, they hoped it would last a long time.

Finally, the school day ended, and Robert rode home at a

leisurely pace. "No need to rush," he said. He looked, but he saw no signs of an accident as he rode, but that didn't deter him. Robert concluded that someone had removed the clutter. He rode along with his head in the clouds. He said, aloud, "This is my real birthday! Today, I begin my life!" He laughed loudly. If anyone had been around, they would have thought he had gone mad. Robert was deliriously happy.

As he neared the house, he saw no signs of a calamity, but he had an excuse for that. "That is the way it would be – no noise." He didn't bother to unhitch the buggy. Had he done so, he would have seen Mom Maggie's carriage where he last saw it. Robert opened the door and walked to the kitchen. There was Mom Maggie with a pan of rolls in her hand!

Robert's eyes bulged, and his mouth became slack. The books he carried fell to the floor with a thud. Mom Maggie put the pan of rolls on the table and stood with her hands on her hips. She stared at him and thought, "This fool has finally snapped!"

Robert seemed to be rooted to the spot. "This must be her ghost! She didn't survive."

Robert backed up against the wall, not daring to look away. He knew that she had powers, but this! Mom Maggie walked over to him, and he screamed. Silently first, then aloud. His heart raced, and his knees were threatening to forsake him. Mom Maggie was swimming crazily before his dimming vision. He fought the toughest battle of his life trying to hold on. Robert felt himself sliding down the wall, but he couldn't stop.

As he lay sprawled on the floor, Mom Maggie nudged him with the toe of her shoe to be sure he wasn't up to his tricks. The children came home, just then, and she asked one of them to get Mr. Barney. Rachel had heard the commotion and came downstairs. She asked her mother why he was on the floor.

Mom Maggie shrugged her shoulders. "He came in and looked at me. Then, wham! He passed out. Evelyn went to get your neighbor, Mr. Barney. We can't lift him."

Rachel said, 'Oh," and stirred the stew.

Robert was out cold. He never moved an inch. Mr. Barney brought Evelyn back in the carriage. He picked Robert up, and carried him to the sofa. Mom Maggie gave Mr. Barney a cloth with ice in it, and he put it on Robert's head. Robert began to stir and mumble. "It's not her!"

Gradually, he came to his senses and wondered why he was lying on the sofa. "Why is Mr. Barney here?" he wondered. Mr. Barney spoke up. "Robert, you passed out in the kitchen. Mom Maggie sent for me to pick you up. Looks like you're all right, so I guess I'll be getting home. My wife was putting supper on the table. Well, so long, everybody." Mom Maggie thanked him for coming, but Robert kept his mouth shut tight.

He was ashamed, but he was more angry than embarrassed. He would have rather jumped into the Grand Canyon than let them see him lying on the floor. Now, it was evident to him, that his mother-in-law hadn't gone yet. He was angry that she was still alive. "No matter. She's no match for me. She'll get hers, sooner than she thinks." Robert knew that they had to be amused by his fainting. There was no way that he could eat with them. He took his plate to the parlor.

Mom Maggie packed after supper and prepared to leave. Rachel and the children cried, but Robert grinned. Robert gladly hitched her horse to the carriage, then he stepped back as she rode away. Under his breath he murmured, "The old hag didn't thank me for hitching her carriage. She didn't have to. I'll get my thanks very soon." Robert watched as she rode out of sight. He thought, "I would go to see Bessie, but I want to be here to receive the wonderful news."

He went inside and picked up his papers. His eyes fairly danced in his head. His heart was light, and he was totally at peace. "My stumbling block is about to be removed – permanently." Ordinarily, he would have lined up the children and beat them. Rachel would have been next on the list. "I feel so good, that I'll give them a break. If things work out the way I expect them to, I might never have to whip them again."

He went to the parlor and worked on his papers. Rachel and the girls went up to bed. They were all uneasy, waiting for the other shoe to drop. Robert looked at the clock. "She should be lying in the road at this point." Robert settled back against the pillows and closed his eyes. He dozed several times, but there was no word. The road was well-traveled that she took, until very late. "Someone must have found her by now. I'll have to be patient. It'll happen!"

CHAPTER 18

Mom Maggie rode away slowly. She didn't know if leaving her family was the right thing to do. It was true that she was coming back the next day, but Robert could beat them badly before she got back. She never knew whether or not the next lashing would be the one that killed one of them. It was upsetting to her to know beyond the shadow of a doubt that her family might be wiped out at any given moment. "That scoundrel is capable of anything and everything!" It was important that she keep a step or two ahead of Robert at all times.

A squealing sound interrupted her thoughts. She listened and decided it was the carriage. She rode a short ways, and the squealing noise became louder. She pulled on the reins and stopped the horse. She climbed down and walked around the carriage looking as she went. She saw that the axle was almost worn in two. Mom Maggie couldn't understand how that happened. The tenant who lived at her place kept it in good condition. She got back into the carriage, but didn't ride further. "It would be foolish for me to try to make it home. I'll wait until somebody comes along and ask for help." She wasn't afraid out there, because everybody knew and respected her.

She closed her eyes to rest them, and she had a flash! She saw Robert kneeling beside a lantern. It was gone in an instant! Mom Maggie had plenty of time on her hands, so she would try to piece together what she had been shown. It might have something to do with her, but what? "What was Robert doing as he knelt? Was he burying something? I don't know. Sooner or later, it will be made plain to me."

Mom Maggie stopped trying to decipher the sign, and closed her eyes once more. "When am I going to learn? It'll all come out in the wash." She didn't feel sleepy, but she dozed a little.

The sound of an approaching carriage woke her. Soon, the carriage drew up beside her, and she recognized Mr. Barney. She said, "The saints be praised! We meet twice on the same day!' Mr. Barney smiled, and asked if she were having a problem. "I noticed you standing still." She nodded, and he climbed out of his carriage.

"What seems to be the trouble, Miss Maggie?"

"I'm not sure, Mr. Barney. I heard a loud noise. I looked at the carriage, and noticed that the axle is badly worn."

"You have any trouble getting here?"

"No. It was clear sailing."

"Okay. I'll get a light and check for you."

"You're a sight for sore eyes. I'm glad you came along."

Mr. Barney got his lantern and checked the horse and the carriage carefully. When he straightened up, he shook his head in disbelief.

"Seems like somebody filed the axle, Miss Maggie. They almost filed it clean in two. All of the bolts are loose, too. I hate to say this, Miss Maggie, but I think this was deliberate!"

"Are you sure, Mr. Barney?"

"I'm really sure. Must be a prank, though. You don't have any enemies. If you'd been going a little faster, you'd be dead."

"Is that a fact, Mr. Barney?"

"You couldn't have made that turn like that."

Mom Maggie said nothing to Mr. Barney, but she knew who did it. She was positive that it was an attempt on her life. She thought about her son-in-law. "I know Robert is evil, but this was a plan that was spawned by the devil, himself."

While the two were talking, another carriage pulled up. It was Mr. Harris, from the other side of town. He recognized Mom Maggie and Mr. Barney. He quickly sized up the situation, and joined Mr. Barney. They unhitched Mom Maggie's horse and hitched him to Mr. Barney's carriage. Then they pushed her carriage to the side of the road. After the men had talked, they decided to meet the next day, with tools and another axle. They would fix the carriage for Mom Maggie. Mr. Harris was glad for the chance to do something for her. She had helped his family many times.

She asked Mr. Barney if she could stay with him and his wife for the night. "My family will be in bed, and I don't want to disturb their sleep." Mr. Barney, of course, was honored that she had chosen his house. What she really wanted was to shock Robert. She now knew the extent to which he would go to be rid of her. "Maybe that was the answer to the chill I get when he enters the room. I'll see."

Mr. Barney helped her into his carriage, and they headed for his house. Mrs. Barney was glad, also, that Mom Maggie was staying with them. She never forgot the time that Mom Maggie helped her. Her daughter was sick and near death. Mom Maggie had taken care of their child, and she lived. Mr. Barney said, "Yes, and you raised me up with your medicine. We owe you plenty. You can stay here as long as you please. You're more than welcome."

She thanked them, and they began to recount instances when she had sat up all night with a loved one. Their compliments made Mom Maggie uneasy. That wasn't what she was about. She said, "You know my answer. Not me, but God! I'll always remember your kindness to me. Bless you, my good friends."

They hustled about, determined to make this great lady comfortable. They showed her to a room upstairs. It was a room that they had fixed up for the company that never came. Mrs. Barney put a pot of hot tea on the night table. There was also a cup and saucer, and a pretty sugar bowl that matched. Mom Maggie was grateful for their hospitality, but she didn't want to be waited on. She would rather serve than be served.

Mom Maggie knew that the Barneys wanted to spend some time with her, but she couldn't. She needed to be alone to sort things. She wondered how her family was doing, and she worried about them. She knelt beside the bed and prayed for her daughter and her grandchildren. "Lord, they're in Your capable hands. Please keep them alive and well. They're precious, but you know that."

She undressed and got into bed. She knew that Robert was responsible for tampering with her carriage. Now, she was absolutely sure about what caused him to faint when he saw her in the kitchen. He didn't know she'd delayed her trip home. He thought he was looking at a ghost. "That also explains my seeing him kneeling by a lantern."

Everything was falling into place, and she didn't like what she concluded. It was painful, but she had to look at it for what it was. There was no doubt about it. Robert was a very dangerous man. She thought, "It's more important now that I stay close." She wanted him to believe she was indeed, indestructible. She wouldn't keep her carriage where he could work on it undercover. She would inspect it thoroughly before she got in it, without fail.

It wouldn't be easy to dethrone him, but she would find a way. He had constructed a flawless reputation. She wouldn't allow herself to sleep, until she'd mapped out tentative plans. She decided to wait until after Robert left for school to go over there. She would ask Mr. Barney to take her.

Robert could barely eat his breakfast. He wondered, "Why haven't they contacted us about the old bag's death? There must be a reason, but what could it be?" They ate as he wished – in silence. Evelyn jumped up to help her mother, and Robert barked, "Sit!" The child went back to her seat. He thought, "The two of them are much too close. They look alike, and they think alike. I will not tolerate two Rachels. Soon, I won't have to."

He looked from one to the other and gloated. "These fools don't know that their world is about to come crashing down around their stupid heads. If I didn't hate them so much, I'd find them almost pitiful. The old hag is dead. Long live the king!"

He wiped his mouth with a napkin and sipped coffee that Rachel had spit into. He finished the coffee and rose from the table. He looked at Rachel, and he almost laughed aloud. He gathered his books and papers, and left the house walking on air! He took the road he knew that Mom Maggie had taken, just to check.

He saw her carriage near the end in the road, but no horse! Robert laughed aloud. "The carriage went off the road, just as I planned. Evidently, Mom Maggie was found later than I'd expected. I'm sure she was taken to the hospital or the funeral home. Either way, she's dead this time. I was wondering why the word hadn't gotten to the house, but I've figured it out. Someone is hesitant about telling Rachel because of the recent death of the little brat. Yes, that's it, I'm sure." Robert flipped the reins and moved on down the road. He felt almost as light as a feather. He began to sing "There's a Bright Side Somewhere."

By the time Robert reached the school, he felt like dancing a jig. He smiled at the students and spoke kindly to them when he called on them. His students were in for another good day. Their teacher was a total stranger, but they would enjoy the ride.

Mr. and Mrs. Barney insisted that Mom Maggie have breakfast with them. She was too concerned about her family to be hungry, but she had to accept. When she sat down, she marveled at the food. Mrs. Barney had cooked ham and sausages. She'd even baked muffins. Mr. Barney swelled with pride. His wife was a good cook, and he knew it. To have the great lady at his table was very special. She gave all, but took nothing.

When Mom Maggie was sure Robert had gone from the house, she asked Mr. Barney to take her to Rachel's. She hugged Mrs. Barney, and thanked them for allowing her to share their home. They were really good people.

Rachel was pleasantly surprised and overjoyed when she saw her mother walk in the door. Mom Maggie staggered a few steps backward when Rachel jumped up and hugged her. They both laughed at that.

"Mama, I'm so glad to see you! And so soon!"

"I'm happy to see you, baby girl."

"What brought you back so soon, Mama?"

"I have a few loose ends that need to be tied."

"I don't know what that means, but I'm glad to see you."

"You and the girls all right?"

"Yes, Mama. We're fine."

"Good! We'll keep it that way."

"We're fine as long as you're here. The children will be so excited when they see you!"

"To be loved feels good. I love them, too. Rachel, I'm really back because I had a little trouble with my carriage. Mr. Barney is going to fix it for me."

"I'm sorry you're having problems, but I'm happy that you're here with us."

Mom Maggie omitted the part about Robert and the role he'd played. She simply didn't want to alarm her daughter. She was still trying to cope with Little Jim's absence. She would tell her, only if she had to do so.

Mom Maggie went out to the carriage house to look around. She saw a wrench on the ground, and she picked it up. She spied a file on a shelf and put that into her pocket as well. "This is what he must have used on the axle. He won't use them again." She looked around, then went back to the house.

The funeral director had brought more satin, and Rachel was sewing. When she lifted her head, there were tears in her eyes. Her mother understood her pain. Rachel said, "I was just remembering." Her mother went to her. When she came back she said, "Time out for tea, baby girl." While her daughter was sipping tea, Mom Maggie went to the garden for vegetables. The cabbages looked nice, so she picked a few heads.

Standing in the garden, Mom Maggie hatched a plan. Robert believed that she was dead. At the right time, she would make an appearance and hope that he would react badly. She would have to have Rachel's cooperation, which meant she had to tell her more. She wouldn't understand without the details.

When she went back to the house with the cabbages, she told Rachel about her suspicions. "Rachel, all I want you to do is sit at the table with your head down. I'll take care of the rest." Rachel agreed to help. She didn't know what her mother had in mind, but she trusted her implicitly.

Mr. Barney came to tell Mom Maggie it would take another day to get another axle. "Don't worry. Mr. Harris and I will get you on the road again." She thanked him, and he left. She said, "Rachel, this is very good. That news is working in our favor. The carriage will still be there when Robert comes home. That will be solid proof for him."

Mom Maggie started supper while Rachel sewed. Soon, Rachel put the sewing aside and played checkers with her mama. It was a relaxing diversion for them, and they played longer than they intended. If Robert didn't make any stops, he would be home very soon. They hid the checkers and waited for the devil's son to make an appearance.

Shortly, they saw him ride up and stop. He didn't go to the carriage house, which meant that he would be leaving again. Mom Maggie gestured, and Rachel took her place at the table. Mom Maggie stepped out of the back door to wait. Robert entered the house and walked through to the dining room, where Rachel sat with her head down.

His eyes glistened with happiness! He threw his head back and laughed. He knew he was on top now! Rachel decided to get dramatic, and she moaned, "Mama." Robert could not be still. He jumped up, clicked his heels and yelled, "Hallelujah!" It was his world now, and he had full control. He calmed down enough to stand over Rachel. "The old hag is dead! Long live the king! Do you hear me? King! Before this day is over, I'm going to beat you until you drip blood! You will pray to join your mama, in hell!"

Just then, Mom Maggie pressed her face against the window. Robert saw her and shook his head to clear it. Mom Maggie moved away, quickly. When he looked again, he saw nothing. His heart slowed down, and he decided, "It had to be the tree branches. I will have to watch myself." He went upstairs to try and pull himself together."

When he went upstairs, Mom Maggie slipped in the back door. She was carrying her shoes. She placed them at the bottom of the stairs. She winked at her daughter and went outside again. The girls came home from school, and Mom Maggie intercepted them. She told them that she was "shaking Robert's tree." They stayed outside and were quiet.

Rachel heard Robert coming downstairs, and she sat up with her eyes half closed. He reached the bottom step and saw the shoes. He thought she was standing there, but he couldn't see her body. A dark stain appeared on the front of his trousers, and spread!

He half yelled, and half croaked, "Get away from me! Get away from me!" He fell backwards on the steps, but the shoes were still there. Robert groped the steps, as he moved up backwards. He screamed as he made his way upstairs. Finally, he reached the top. The sound of the bedroom door slamming was heard. Rachel laughed when she heard dragging sounds coming from upstairs. Robert was barricading himself in the room. It was hilarious!

Mom Maggie and the children came inside laughing. Mom Maggie said, "All I have to do is go to the bedroom and say, "Robert", and he'll jump out the window." They laughed more. She said, "He'll come out eventually. When we hear him opening the door, all of you work on your school papers, and I'll strike a pose. Pay no attention to me. Just look at your work." They weren't quite sure what their grandmother was going to do, but they knew it would be good.

They ate supper and washed the dishes. Robert was trapped in the room the entire time. The girls played checkers for awhile. Evening turned into night. Upstairs, Robert had become tired of being cooped up in the room, as well as hungry. He mumbled to himself. "I can't stay in here forever! It's quite possible that all of it was just a figment of my imagination. I don't know what came over me, but I have to get a grip on my nerves. The old lady is dead, and she can't come back!"

Robert became brave enough to move the furniture away from the bedroom door. The girls heard him and put away the checkers. They became engrossed in their school work. Mom Maggie stood apart from them, with her hands folded across her chest. Her eyes were only half closed so she could peep at Robert.

Hesitantly, he eased his way down the stairs, trying not to make a sound. He was relieved to see that the shoes weren't at the bottom of the stairs. He swallowed hard and crept the rest of the way. Convinced now that it was his imagination, his confidence returned. He stood up straight and walked into the parlor where the girls were doing their homework.

His intention was to give them an overdue beating. He opened his mouth to yell at them, but he realized that he had relaxed too soon. Over in the corner stood Mom Maggie! The girls were doing their work and paying no attention to what he saw. A voice inside of Robert's head screamed at him. "Nobody can see her, but you! She came for you!" He opened his mouth and pointed at her. She, then, turned slowly, and pointed a finger at him!

He found his voice and screamed, "Leave me alone!" He turned and ran from the house, without looking back. They watched as he scrambled into the buggy, and took off for parts unknown. He stirred up a cloud of dust as he fled. Mom Maggie laughed until her sides hurt, and the girls fell against each other laughing. When

Rachel was able to talk, she said, "We'll have peace tonight." They began laughing all over again. Robert had provided plenty of comedy for them.

After everything died down, the girls played a game of checkers, and Mom Maggie played the winner. With all of her heart, she wanted to build a few good memories for them. She often said, "Every child needs something good to look back on when they're old."

After the girls had gone upstairs, and the house was quiet, Mom Maggie sat down to have a talk with Rachel. She began, "All of this has been very funny, but we can't forget with whom we're dealing. Robert is quite capable of murder. That, I think, is about as serious as it can get. We have to be careful. Let me correct that. We must be super-careful at all times. We can never let down our guard. Robert is constantly plotting. I'm sure of that."

Rachel had no doubt that what her mother said was true. What he had attempted to do to her mother was all the proof she needed. She felt responsible for it, in a large way. If she hadn't married him, it never would have happened. Never, at any time did her mother throw it in her face. But then she didn't have to, because her own guilt was sufficient.

Mom Maggie continued. "Before this is over, God will pull the covers off Robert, completely. He will stand naked before the people of this town. In the meantime, we don't want anything terrible to happen before that day comes. By tomorrow, he will find out what really happened to me. He'll be a loose cannon when he learns the truth. This will make him hate us even more, because we have made a fool of him. I'll try to be here as much as I can. When I'm not here, you'll need some kind of weapon. Rachel, if I'm not here, and you think he's going to beat any one of you, get out!"

"I hear every word, Mama. I'll take the children, and go."

"Don't stop to think, Rachel. Go!"

"I will, Mama."

"If you'll leave, I'll take all of you with me whenever I go. Robert is a very dangerous person. I can't stress that enough. You might have peace tonight, but who knows what tomorrow will bring? Use extreme caution!"

"I'll look for a piece of iron to protect myself and the girls. He seems to have an unusual hatred for Evelyn. I don't know why it started or where it came from."

"I've noticed the ugly looks when he thinks we aren't looking."

"That's just one reason to be wary. We must tell Evelyn to be extra careful. If she even faintly suspects that he's going to beat her, she is to run as fast as she can to get to the Barneys' house."

"That's a good idea."

"The Barneys are our best resource. I'll go over tomorrow. We need allies. Is that all right with you, Rachel?"

"I'm in total agreement. Now that I know the dangerous position we're in, I'll do anything."

CHAPTER 19

When Robert jumped into the buggy, he drove crazily up and down the roads. He came very close to overturning the buggy at least twice. The wind beat against his face and calmed him some. Only then was he able to slow down. He was like a man without a country. He had nowhere to go! He couldn't go to Reverend Bacon or to any of the other deacons. Robert had fans, but he had no friends.

He stretched his brain and tried to think of a safe haven. Suddenly, and mercifully, he remembered the saloon. "Yes, I can use a drink of something strong." His hysteria was in check, but he was nervous. He turned the horse around and headed for the saloon. Robert was trying with everything he had not to think about what he'd experienced. Having to handle the horse was helpful.

By the time he got to the saloon, he was feeling better, but he was still in need of a stiff drink. To settle his nerves, Robert thought he should get two bottles of wine, instead of the usual one bottle. Strangely enough, Robert hadn't thought about Bessie. He was much too rattled to think beyond wine. He started to the bar but changed his mind. He sat down and waited to catch the waitress's eye.

Bessie was there, but Robert hadn't seen her. She didn't know he was there until she started to leave. She had been talking to a female when she noticed him. It was obvious to her that he wasn't looking for her, but she went over to his table anyway. His eyes were closed, and he appeared edgy. He was startled when she called his name. Bessie had never seen him in such a state.

She put her arms around him and put his head on her shoulder. She rocked him like a baby. He said, "Bes, I need you tonight." She held him close and told him to come home with her. He waited for the bottles of wine, and then he left with her.

When they arrived at her place, Bessie probed, but she got nowhere. Going home with her didn't mean that he was going to tell her what was wrong. As far as she was concerned, his private life would remain private. He drank a glass of wine and that helped his nerves a little. The second glass of wine accomplished what the first glass started. At last, Robert was able to concentrate on Bessie.

Bessie was happy when she saw his mood change for the better. Because Bessie had unwittingly fallen in love with Bobby, she was greatly affected by his mood. She thought, "I want our time together to be very special to me, as well as to Bobby." She pulled off his shoes and socks and massaged his feet. The wine, combined with the massage, relaxed him completely. Bessie undressed him and gave him a body massage.

Robert was grateful for the attention, and he lapped it up like a lion cub. He reflected on the way she cared for him and how much he loved her. He groaned and pulled her to him. He kissed her with all of the fire he possessed.

He was there all night, but he wouldn't say, "I love you." Bessie wanted to hear him say it, but she knew she wouldn't. She also wanted to know what had put him in such a strange mood, but she knew that she would never know from his lips. She thought, "he's a very strange fellow. That's kind of exciting, I guess. Bobby is, indeed, a man of mystery. I learned at the onset of this relationship that my man disliked curiosity. I conformed to keep him in my life."

In the morning, he drank coffee and kissed Bessie goodbye. For the first time in his teaching career, he went to school totally unprepared. He had corrected no papers, nor had he prepared the lessons for the day. He said, to himself, "What are the students going to do to me? Wag their fingers in my face? Make me stand in the corner? Give me extra work? No! The brats are under my control! I set the pace!"

He put paper and pens on each desk, then took his seat at the desk. He flipped through the pages of a workbook and said to himself, "Today, I'll simply wing it. This will be a review day." He sat back in his chair and waited for his students to arrive. He tried not to think about the incident at home.

Later, when he thought about it, he went to the other classrooms to see if the girls were there. Much to his surprise, they were!

The teachers didn't mention his mother-in-law's death, nor did they offer their sympathy. Under his breath he muttered, "It's true that news travels slower in the country, but not this slow! I certainly tried to leave no stone unturned, so what could possibly be wrong?"

When Robert left home the day before, he hadn't planned to go back to the house. He said to himself, but aloud "I have to go back. I have to take the chance. Surely this can't be part of some elaborate plan to take me down! That old hag had better be dead! If she's not, they'll all pay for this in spades!" This day, Robert stayed at school long enough to correct papers and prepare the next day's lessons. "This will leave me free for whatever the rest of the day holds."

As Robert was riding to the house, he saw the funeral director leaving in his carriage. He was heartened by that. He didn't know the man was only picking up the linings that Rachel had made. Robert pulled on the reins and stopped his horse. He started to turn around and go to Bessie's, but he thought twice about it. He proceeded to the house.

He stopped close enough to leave in a hurry if he had to do so. Robert sat in the buggy a long time. He saw the brats go inside, and still he sat. "I'm sure of what I'm looking for, but I want to watch any and all activity. I have to get to the bottom of this mess."

Robert sat poised and ready for whatever. His horse stood there in silence, too, as if he too had something to gain. Except for a rare flip of the horse's tail, there was no movement in Robert's camp.

Presently, Robert saw Mr. Barney and Mr. Harris come in separate carriages. They went into the house at the same time. They reappeared in about fifteen minutes or less. Then lo and behold! Mom Maggie walked out of the house looking like a picture of health! Robert saw her look at the carriage and smile. She talked to the two men for a few moments. Mr. Harris and Mr. Barney climbed into one of the carriages, and rode away together.

Robert's mind had been clicking the entire time. Now, he knew what had happened that day. He was furious! "The old hag had stopped the carriage in time. The two men saw what happened, and came to the miserable wench's rescue. The ghost thing, at the house, was staged for my benefit! They were trying to make a monkey of me, and I'll make dog meat of them! I'll skin them alive. I hate all of them!"

He stopped the carriage in front of the house and climbed down. Boldly, he went inside. Mom Maggie and Rachel were getting supper ready. Like a bolt from out of the blue, Robert realized how hungry he really was. He'd had nothing but wine and coffee. He hadn't had solid food since breakfast the day before. "I'll sit on my hatred while I eat." The aroma was mouth-watering! They were fine cooks. He knew that Rachel and her mother could make shoe leather taste good. Grudgingly, Robert had to admit that, but never to them.

The platter piled high with pork chops, the fluffy mashed potatoes and gravy, the buttered corn on the cob, and the biscuits, all drew Robert like a magnet. Robert dropped his haughty air and devoured the food. When his enormous appetite had been satisfied and the wrinkles were out of his belly, the ugliness returned. When Mom Maggie wasn't looking, he stared at her with hatred. He left the table, and made everybody glad. They laughed and talked because Mom Maggie was there.

They were hoping that Robert would go wherever he went when he disappeared. That thought crossed his mind a time or two, but he decided to stay. He had plans to formulate and people to murder.

They knew Robert might creep upstairs and murder them in their sleep. If they under-estimated Robert, they would lose.

The next day, they discussed a better plan.

"Mama, I'm a bit tired, but it was worth it. We're still alive."

"Yes, baby girl. One night down, and how many more to go?"

"I think what we're doing will work for us."

"We can't let him out-think us. We have to come up with a fresh plan, all of the time."

"I see where you're going, Mama.'

"That worked for us last night. I'd like to try something else tonight. The girls can push their beds against the door every night. You and I will do the same."

"That's a great idea!"

"He won't stop there. I'll attach a bell to the door knob. That should make us feel reasonably safe at night."

Mom Maggie was fully aware that the plan was not completely fool-proof. She hadn't ruled out the possibility of Robert setting the house on fire at night. She didn't mention that possibility to Rachel. She saw no need to add to her fear. Mom Maggie, herself, would be extra vigilant. She had already thought about it. "I suppose I can always get a nap during the day. I have to out-think Robert at all cost."

Thinking about out-witting Robert made the great lady shake her head in disbelief. "I'm an old lady, but Robert won't give me time to get senile! I guess that's good in some crazy kind of way. Well, I'll use whatever sense the good Lord chooses to hand me."

She had postponed going to the Barney's for help. The walk, she knew, would have been too much for her. Now that she had her carriage back, she would ride over there. She was anxious to check the new axle, anyway. That would really be killing two birds with one stone.

The next day, she paid the Barneys a visit. She was positive that she was doing the right thing because she felt "led" to do it. Mrs. Barney saw her drive up, and she met her at the door. They were more than glad to see her, although they were a bit surprised. Mrs. Barney insisted on fixing her hot lemon tea and cookies. As she sipped the tea, she tried to think of the best way to tell them about their plight. Mr. Barney, without knowing it, made it easier for her.

He said, "Mom Maggie, we're always glad to see you, but is there something in particular that brings you here?" Mom Maggie breathed easier. "Yes, I'm afraid that I need your help again. Actually, we need both of you to just stand by and be watchful with us." They knew this had to be important, and they were honored that she had come to them.

Mom Maggie said, "This is about my son-in-law, Robert. What I am about to tell you, will shock you. Maybe you really won't believe it. He has established a spotless reputation because he sings so well. Talent has absolutely nothing to do with character."

She paused to give them a chance to question, or voice an opinion. Mr. Barney said, "Go on, Mom Maggie. We're with you." Mom Maggie continued. "Robert is vicious and cruel to his family, and I know that he is capable of murder. My family lives in constant fear of him, and I've stayed there so long because he fears me. They are relatively safe, I think, when I'm around. I've come to believe that he is, in an underhanded way, trying to kill me." She stopped once more, to let them absorb all she had said.

Mrs. Barney was visibly upset. She reached for Mom Maggie's hand. "We're so glad you confided in us. We'll help in any way that we can." Mom Maggie smiled warmly at her and said, "I knew that you would."

Mr. Barney had been very quiet, as if he were deep in thought. Mom Maggie was quiet because she felt that he had something important to say. A few moments passed before he looked directly at her. He weighed his words carefully, as he spoke. "It's hard to say this, but I've been thinking about what happened to your carriage. I'd spoken to my wife about it, and we talked. I knew somebody had hacked that axle, deliberately. I started to try to figure out who. Everybody respects you, Mom Maggie, so I had to cross off everybody! Robert was the only one left, and I laid it on him, in my mind. He had every opportunity to do that. I just couldn't figure out why he would. You just gave me a reason. He should be in prison! Too bad we don't have enough proof. It is more likely that he'll trip himself up in the long run. I'll bet my suspenders on it."

Mom Maggie was positive that being open with the Barneys could be a blessing. She asked if they would drop in often and at odd hours. She told them that their presence would prevent beatings for Rachel and her grandchildren. Mom Maggie let them know that Evelyn had been instructed to run there, if it ever became necessary. As expected, they were understanding and cooperative.

They offered to take the girls, or Rachel and the girls. That truly warmed the old lady's heart. To know that they were on her side was uplifting. Mr. Barney helped her in the carriage, and she rode towards Rachel's house.

Mom Maggie made an impressive sight as she traveled down the road. She was large boned and handsome. The years had been very kind to her. Her bearing was like that of a queen, but she was most comfortable when she was serving others. She was always natural and unpretentious. She was to all, Mom Maggie!

Rachel was folding the laundry when she got back. She told her all about the visit with the Barneys. Neither of them felt so alone anymore. That made it all worthwhile. Mom Maggie was tired from the ride and standing guard at night. She skipped lunch and went upstairs for a nap. Rachel could be trusted to call her at the right time.

CHAPTER 20

That same night, they all went up to bed, and Robert prepared the sofa for his sleep. Mom Maggie slept hard the first two hours. She woke up suddenly, as a sharp chill swept over her. She lay there, listening and straining to hear whatever. The step creaked slightly, and she stiffened. "No need to call Rachel," she told herself.

A few minutes later, she heard a bell tinkle and a pushing sound. She got up and pushed the bed quietly away from the door. Just enough to slip through. In the moonlight that shone through the hall window she saw Robert. He seemed to be very determined.

She tipped down the hall, and he didn't look up. He was too absorbed in what he was doing. She waited a few seconds to see if he would sense her presence, but he didn't. She walked closer and stood directly behind him. The bell tinkled as he pushed, but it didn't deter him.

She said, in her Mom Maggie style, "What do you think you are doing?" He froze at the sound of her voice! His heart was pounding wildly in his ears! He fought to keep from emptying his bladder on the spot! He felt trapped, and he was drooling!

Mom Maggie said, in the same tone, "Turn around!" He turned so rapidly, he almost lost his balance. He was trying to hide something that dangled from his arm. Mom Maggie could see clearly by the light of the moon. It was a rope! There was no doubt in her mind what he intended to do with it, once he was in the room. She literally trembled with rage.

Mom Maggie pointed at him, and he shrank. She raised her voice. "You are lower than a snake's belly! You are, also, a fool to think you can get past me! Get downstairs before I ask the spirits to throw you down and break your filthy neck!" Robert turned to go down, but not before she saw the hatred for her in his eyes.

Mom Maggie's hands shook! She wasn't sure if the girls heard what was going on or not. She hoped they had not. She was too upset to go back to the bedroom just yet. She leaned against the wall, and asked God to help her to protect her family from Robert. She thanked Him for the warning. She stayed there until her knees were steady. When she was composed, she went back to the room she was sharing with Rachel. Rachel had heard her mother talking to Robert, and she was fully awake.

"What was Robert doing, Mama?"

"He was trying to force his way into the girls room."

"Did he get in?"

"No, I stopped him in time."

"I'm glad you're here! I slept too soundly."

"No harm done. I woke up."

"Do you think he was after Evelyn?"

"I'm sure of it. Robert is determined to harm this family."

"Sooner or later, one of us will slip, and he'll kill somebody!'

"The Barneys have offered to take Evelyn until this situation is resolved. What do you think, Rachel?"

"Let me think about it for a few days."

"Rachel, we don't have that kind of time. Robert was carrying a rope tonight!"

"Oh no, Mama!"

"He was! I don't like separating the children, but we can't let him kill Evelyn. What is your decision?"

"She has to go to the Barneys at once!"

"Good! I'll take her to their house in the morning."

"We'll keep her whereabouts from everyone. Together, we'll figure a way to get school work for her."

"Then it's settled! She'll be safe, and in good hands."

They lay down and tried to sleep. Mom Maggie knew that Robert wouldn't be stupid enough to come back again tonight. They did manage to doze.

Rachel went to the girls' room in the morning to talk to them about their plans. "You're not to tell anyone where Evelyn is. Please don't worry about anything. We have things under control. This is just a precaution. One of you can take this letter to the teacher."

Robert left the house before anyone got up. He didn't want to face his mother-in-law at breakfast, and the feeling was mutual. Rachel packed some of Evelyn's clothes, and Mom Maggie took her to the Barneys. When Evelyn was out of ear shot, she told them about Robert and the rope. Mr. Barney wanted to challenge him to "fight a man!" Mom Maggie and his wife calmed him and convinced him to let them settle it another way.

Mr. Barney listened, but he was still enraged. "He must be evil through and through! I always liked his singing. You can't help it, because the man can sing. But, there was a smoothness about him that I didn't like. He seemed oily to me, if you know what I mean." Mom Maggie said, "That's a fair description. Most folks never look beyond the surface. You're a smart man, my friend. I don't see him as anything but evil, and a poor excuse for a man. Breath and britches! The Lord knows he meant to strangle Evelyn with that rope. His own child! That, my friends, is lower than low."

Mrs. Barney assured Mom Maggie that they would take good care of Evelyn. Mr. Barney promised to start dropping in immediately. He said, "This is urgent. We will work with your granddaughter." Mom Maggie went to tell Evelyn that she was leaving. Evelyn knew she was there for safety reasons, but she hadn't been told about the rope.

She kissed her grandmother and said, "I'll be okay. I like the Barneys. Tell Mama I love her, too." Mom Maggie pushed back the tears and left. She headed towards what had become her home away from home.

She didn't know how Robert would face her again, but she knew he not only could, but would. He would stay away tonight, but as always, he'd come back to eat the very next day. Hunger had always driven him back. Mom Maggie smiled slightly. The ride had been good for her. It cleared the cob webs and stimulated her mind.

She thought about Robert. She didn't believe that monsters, such as Robert were born evil. "They were, simply born a baby. I believe something happened, or somebody did or said something that caused them to change. Whatever it was changed them from their innocence to evil. I have no way of knowing what the influence was in Robert's life. At this point, it really ain't important. We have to deal with what he's become. We have to deal with what he is today."

Mom Maggie waved and smiled, occasionally, at the familiar faces she met along the way. Some pulled up beside her to talk a bit, or to ask about a particular remedy for their sickness. As always, she gave them her best advice.

She moved along, and her thoughts turned once more to Robert. She wasn't anxious to have him dominate her thoughts and her every move, but that was the way it had to be. She thought, "He's a walking bomb, waiting to explode. That excuse for a man is totally without conscience. That makes him very dangerous. It's mind-boggling to me that he's able to sit at the table and eat with people he planned to murder, and feel absolutely nothing! I don't believe too many people could do that. He's lined up with his father, Satan, and he's going to spend eternity with him. Remorse is a word that he knows nothing about. Murder is his only aim. I'm thankful that Evelyn is safely tucked away. She's one less that we have to worry about."

Mom Maggie knew that she or Rachel would be the logical ones for Robert to attempt to get next. However, she knew that you could not tell where he would strike. They were, therefore, all in danger.

When she reached the house, she had decided to not unhitch the carriage. She left it in plain sight, just in case. Rachel had just hung the last piece on the clothes line. They went inside to talk and have a cup of tea. Rachel was full of questions, but she waited for her mother to catch her breath. Over tea, she told Rachel that Evelyn was settled. The Barneys had turned out to be extra special people.

Mom Maggie said, "Rachel, we both know that Robert is cocky enough to come back here, probably by tomorrow."

"You're right about that, Mama."

"He'll be too hungry and too determined to kill us to stay away."

"Have you thought about putting your herbs in the coffee or tea to make him sleep?"

"Baby girl, you're getting good! That was going to be my next statement. What I use is harmless. I'm not about to join Robert in doing the devil's work."

"You don't have to tell me that. I know you, Mama."

"I'll start using it as soon as he comes back."

"How long will it hold him?"

"He'll sleep all night, and so will we."

"Good!"

"Sooner or later, he'll suspect something, but by that time we will have another plan. We'll face obstacles as they come at us. Now that Robert isn't here, I think I'll bake sweet potato pies, for us. I'll get one over to the Barneys.

"That's a good idea, Mama. I'll help you."

"Thank you, baby girl."

The girls brought Evelyn's homework and a note from her teacher. The note stated that everything would be handled with discretion, and that Robert would not be told anything. Rachel took the homework and one of the pies to the Barneys' place. Mom Maggie was surprised that Rachel wanted to go. It was a good move. If Robert decided to come back unexpectedly, it would be far better if she were there, and not Rachel.

It turned out to be a mini-reunion. Mr. and Mrs. Barney were happy to see Rachel. They assured her that their house would be a comfortable home for Evelyn. Mr. Barney said, "If, at some time the rest of you need to, this house is yours, for as long as you need it." Their warmth was refreshing to Rachel and most appreciated. She said, "Thank you for your kindness. We have grown to love both of you. Either Mama, or I , will get homework to Evelyn."

Mr. Barney said, "I've been driving past to check. I'll come in from time to time." Rachel hugged them and kissed her daughter. She enjoyed the rare ride home. She was home in time for supper with the family.

CHAPTER 21

After school, Robert went to the saloon to find Bessie. As usual, she was there. This time, however, she was laughing with a good looking young man. The man leaned closer to her. Robert couldn't be sure if he kissed her or not. His blood boiled! The scene he was witnessing pushed him to the limit.

Without thinking about the possible consequences of his actions, Robert walked over to them, and the smile froze on Bessie's face. He was too angry to speak, but he gave her an icy stare. Robert was struggling to remember where he was, and who he was. He wanted to reach out and wring her pretty neck. After a few minutes, he was able to gain control. He turned and walked out of the saloon.

Bessie came back to life and ran after him. When she caught up to him, she tried to explain. Robert was in no mood to listen to her babbling. He walked away from her, but she followed him. When he reached the buggy, he picked Bessie up and threw her into it. She struck her knee and cried out in pain, but he paid no attention to her. She tried again to clear herself, but in vain. She didn't know Robert.

They rode at a fast clip to Bessie's place. She was afraid to get out of the buggy, but she knew she had no choice. She slid down and into his arms. He carried her into the house. She wasn't foolish enough to think that everything was all right until he threw her on the bed. Bessie tried to beguile him with her best smile, but the effort was wasted. She was in deep trouble!

Robert stood over her and yelled, "Explain!" Tearfully, Bessie said, "Oh, Bobby, I'm in love with you. We were just talking. He's just a casual friend!" Robert stood Bessie on her feet. She was about to smile when he struck her with his fist. She fell backwards, but she landed on the bed. Frantically, she tried to crawl away from him. With a look of sadistic pleasure on his face, he followed her and yanked her to her knees. He looked into her eyes, enjoying the fright he saw there. A bruise was forming under her left eye, and her body trembled with fear.

Robert's favorite game was cat and mouse. He asked her, in quiet tones, "What were you and your friend planning to do?" Bessie attempted to respond, but her voice failed her. Robert slapped her as hard as he could, and her head snapped back. She opened her mouth to scream, but Robert grasped her neck in his hands, and squeezed. Her eyes widened, and she gurgled!

Slowly, he released her neck, then he kissed her hungrily. She was in too much distress to respond. Bessie had always suspected that Robert had a dark side, and she'd found it exciting and thrilling. She was learning first hand what it meant to deal with Robert's dark thrilling side. Bessie was in over her head, and she knew it.

Robert never thought that he would ever be forced to beat Bessie. She was the exact opposite of Rachel, who needed to be thrashed periodically. He was almost sure that Miss Addie wouldn't have required beating. She was sensual, but she was a lady.

Bessie could tell that Bobby was distracted. She glanced around the room, hoping to see something that she could use as a weapon. She saw nothing. There was no way to escape, because he was closer to the door. Robert picked her up, and he said quietly, "Do you still love me?" Bessie's throat was sore and scratchy, but she said, "Yes, I love you, Bobby. I promise to never talk to another man. Please don't hurt me again. Do you love me, Bobby? Why, don't you ever say that to me?"

His answer was to take her in his arms and kiss her. Now he was tender with her. His anger had been spent, and he wanted to make it up to her. "Bessie, I don't plan to share you with anyone. You belong to me. If you don't think you can be true to me, tell me. I'll walk out of your life the way I walked into it."

Bessie was sure, from his humble words, he would never hit her again. She was quiet and didn't answer immediately. Robert folded her in his arms and kissed her. He moaned and she responded to him. He said, "Sweetheart, forgive me. I love you."

At his words, all of her defenses were shattered. Bobby had told her he loved her. She had waited for what seemed like forever to hear him say that. Bessie turned her bruised face to him and claimed his lips. Robert smiled to himself. She had been conquered! Three little words had turned the tide. Robert had peeped at her whole card! He played her like an organ!

The large bruise on Bessie's face didn't touch his heart in any way. He totally ignored it, except to hope that it would serve as a reminder for her. "Step out of line, and you will pay!" Bessie didn't know he felt that way, and she couldn't read his mind. She slept in his arms all night. In the morning she sang a popular tune through her swollen lips. Robert looked at her and at the damage he had done to her pretty face. He felt absolutely nothing! The love he had for her hadn't changed. He thought, "I was forced to chastise her. Love had nothing to do with it. She had to be taught a lesson. That is what it took to teach her."

When Robert's coffee was ready, Bessie called him to the table. She had put a few buns on a plate for him. He looked at it, and shook his head. He knew what he was missing at home. "Well, it certainly is not Rachel's breakfast, but it'll have to do." He sipped in silence, but Bessie chattered away. She was still riding on his confession of love.

When he finished the meager breakfast, he wiped his mouth and left the table. That was Bessie's signal. She walked to the door with him and kissed him goodbye. She said, "Bobby, I'll be here when you get back." Robert could not help saying, "Where else would you be? Your face will curb your extra-curricular activities." The remark stung, but Bessie smiled and waved anyway.

She went inside and closed the door. Bessie touched her face, gingerly. "What just happened here? Bobby beat the living daylights out of me, and I forgave him. I forgave him before the bruises disappeared, or stopped hurting! Why have I given him so much power over me? What kind of man is he, and what kind of woman am I? Do I need him to love me that badly? If the answer is yes, then why? I just gave up, no, I just lost a big chunk of my self."

Bessie was upset and frustrated. She lay on the bed, and sobbed her heart out. After a while she sat up and put a cold compress on her mouth. As best she could, Bessie concealed the facial bruise with makeup. "I'll get back at Bobby in the only way I know." She went to the saloon, and picked up four men in rapid succession. In the afternoon, she bathed and waited for Bobby, but he never came.

Robert had a small problem to solve. He tried to decide if he should go to Bessie's, or eat crow and go home. He weighed his options. If he wanted to eat, he would have to take food to Bessie's place. "The old hag is still there trying to thwart my plans, but they have food!" His stomach decided for him. He'd go home! So much for seeing Bessie.

He solved the problem of to eat or not to eat. As he rode towards home, he tried to formulate a plan. "After supper, I'll work on my papers, then pretend to be asleep. I'll wait to be sure that the old bag is asleep. When I'm sure she's sleeping soundly, I'll climb up to their bedroom and drop a torch in the window. If they wake up, it'll be too late. Either the fire or the smoke will get them. The girls will have to be sacrificed with Miss Maggie and Rachel. I'll be able to endure eating with them because I know this will be their last night on earth. Contrary to common belief, I know my ugly mother-in-law does not have nine lives, and I will prove it –tonight!"

Knowing that his plot to murder his family would go off without a hitch, he rode home. He rode up to the house like a man in charge. He dropped his haughtiness when he felt Mom Maggie's fierce eyes on him. She was setting the table, and Rachel was bringing in the food. They sat down, and Robert took his seat as usual. When he did, Mom Maggie said, "Robert, trade places with Fran! You are no longer the head of this family. You have lost that right!"

Robert was furious! He blurted out, "That is not for————." One look at the great lady's cloudy countenance, and he cut off, abruptly, what he was about to say. He wanted to get up and storm away from the table, but he was much too hungry. He traded seats with Fran. He thought, "I'll put up with this, because this is your last night to shine!"

Robert bowed his head, but Mom Maggie spoke up, again. "I'll talk to God! He doesn't know you!" She said the grace, and the meal began.

Robert wanted to toss the hot gravy in her face, but he knew that would have been disastrous for him. Suddenly, he was aware of Evelyn's absence, but he pretended to not notice. He drank two cups of coffee, this time a la Mom Maggie! Rachel and the children conversed about school, while Mom Maggie kept an eye on Sir Robert!

Rachel cleared the table, and Robert sat there yawning. Finally, he got up and went into the parlor. He took out his papers and yawned. Every time he yawned, they smiled. By the time the dishes were done, Robert was fast asleep. Rachel breathed a sigh of relief, and the children finished their homework. Afterwards, they played a couple of games of checkers.

Bedtime came, and they went to their room. Mom Maggie went to the parlor to check on Robert. He was snoring softly. She looked down on the man who, just two days ago, had tried to strangle his own child with a rope. He lay helpless before her. She could have easily smothered him, or drove a knife through his heart. Someone else might have done so, but not Mom Maggie. That kind of thought would never enter her mind. She only wanted to protect her family against him. That she would do by prayer and by planning.

Mom Maggie felt a chill as she stood over Robert. She hugged herself for warmth and turned away from Robert. She'd only taken a few steps when she saw the image of Little Jim appear in the air!

He was crying! The picture faded quickly. Mom Maggie clutched her heart, and the tears threatened to flow freely. She said aloud, "Lord, what does it mean? Am I being tricked by my grief?"

Mom Maggie turned back to Robert. His mouth was slack, and saliva had gathered in the corners. She asked aloud, "Is there some type of connection? I've been given a mystery that must be solved. Well, it's one day at a time."

Mom Maggie followed Rachel upstairs. As a precaution, they had the girls push their beds against the door again. Mom Maggie tied the bells to the door knobs. With Robert safely in dreamland, they were well rested in the morning.

Robert woke up, certain that he was dreaming. 'No! I'm awake." He had, much to his dismay, fallen asleep and hadn't followed through with his plan to torch the house. He was disgusted with himself. "The place and everybody in it, should be nothing but ashes! Of all the rotten luck! I've had too many setbacks, but I will overcome in the end."

At breakfast, he took Fran's seat, just as he had been told to do by the one he called the old hag. "The old hag has debased me in every conceivable way. This is the final straw! I am a man with a mission. That, sometimes, requires patience." Robert had no doubt that in the end he would be the victor.

"The old hag has weakened my position as master of the house. It is just one more strike against her. She has done enough in one day to make me kill her. Old lady Maggie is definitely skating on very thin ice."

Robert ate his breakfast quickly. He had to get away. His mother-in-law and Rachel had to die, and he needed solitude to plan their deaths. He left the table and went to school earlier than usual to meditate.

CHAPTER 22

Rachel and Mom Maggie talked about Robert when they were alone. It seemed that their entire lives were centered around surviving Robert's attempts on their lives. They were growing weary of trying to stay at least one jump ahead of him. Every other facet of their lives had become, of necessity, secondary. Where and when will it all end?

Mom Maggie and Rachel decided to prepare dinner for the Barney family and Evelyn. That was one way to show their gratitude to them. They set about this. When everything was ready, they got into the carriage and rode over there. Evelyn was happy for the time with her grandmother and her mother. Mrs. Barney appreciated not to have to cook. They spent a couple of hours there, and it was home sweet home.

When they arrived home, a woman was waiting for Mom Maggie. Mom Maggie recognized Maude Lewis, who lived on the other side of town. Her face was tear-stained, and she was quite upset. She clutched Mom Maggie's arm, frantically. "Thank God! I found you. My mother is very sick and the doctor isn't home. Will you please help her? She has a very high fever, and I can't break it!"

Mom Maggie's heart went out to her, but she knew she couldn't leave Rachel at Robert's mercy. She told Maude this, and she began to beg. Rachel said, "Mama, you can go. Remember, Robert always stays away the first night? He's very predictable in that way. We are safe. Besides, Mr. Barney does check on us." Mom Maggie reluctantly agreed to leave her daughter. Her heart was torn in two, but she and Maude got into the carriage and left.

For the first time in ages, Rachel and the girls were alone. They played checkers with their mother, as dinner had been prepared earlier. Rachel thought, after awhile, they should do their homework. They would delay supper as long as possible to give Mom Maggie time to get back. When it was apparent that she had been detained longer than expected, they sat down to eat.

They were having dessert when the door opened, and Robert came in! He sat at the table to be served. He said, "I see the old crone has finally gone home!" No one answered, and he continued. "Get that food in here! Now, we will pick up where we left off. When I'm finished eating, line up! You're out of practice!"

Robert ate like a starved pig. Mom Maggie wasn't there to doctor his coffee, and things looked bleak! He pushed the chair away from the table, and stood up. He said, "Line up, now.' As he spoke Fran brought the chair in. Tears were streaming down her face. She'd begun to think that this portion of their lives was over.

They had stopped wearing the padded underwear because it hadn't been necessary. They were under their grandmother's watchful eye and protection. He beat all three girls until they were bloody! They fell to the floor screaming when he stopped.

Betty had a seizure as she lay there. It was probably brought on by a combination of pain and extreme fear. Robert beat her as she writhed on the floor. Rachel rushed to her aid, but Robert whacked her across the shoulders with his belt, then kicked her! Rachel shook off the blow, and continued to run to her child. She fell to the floor, but she started back again. Robert kicked her away once more, then he jumped on her.

Fran and Mary were scared stiff! Robert yelled, "I'll kill you, bitch!" He began pummeling Rachel with his fist, and she grew still. Robert had worked himself up to the danger point. As Rachel lay there unconscious, he put his hands around her throat and applied pressure. Just then, the door opened!

Mr. Barney was standing there with his rifle, and it was pointed at Robert! "Get away from her!" he barked. It took a few seconds for

Mr. Barney's voice to penetrate and break the spell. Robert let his hands fall away from Rachel's throat. Mr. Barney struck him with the butt of the rifle, and he fell to the floor.

Mr. Barney looked down at him with disgust. He said, "You miserable dog! It must take a lot of courage to beat a woman and children. Get up, and go to the corner. I dare you to move a muscle!"

Just then, Fran said hysterically, "Mama's not moving! I think Mama's dead!" Mr. Barney left Robert and directed his attention to Rachel. He told Fran to bring some cold water. Betty lay on the floor next to her mother. She was no longer seizing, but she was dazed. Fran brought the water, and Mr. Barney dipped some napkins. He placed them on Rachel's forehead. He directed Fran to massage her wrists.

Mary entered the room holding a bottle. She said, "Mom Maggie puts this under people's noses." Mr. Barney tried it. Soon Rachel stirred and tried to speak. While Mr. Barney was focused on Rachel and Betty, Robert slipped away. Mr. Barney put Rachel on the sofa in the parlor. He put Betty in the big lounge chair. Fran helped him to make hot tea for Betty and Rachel.

Rachel's throat was sore, and she was very badly bruised. It was obvious to Mr. Barney that she needed attention. Nobody knew if Mom Maggie would make it back that night. He decide to bundle them up and take them to his house. They could leave a note for Mom Maggie. There was a slim chance that Robert would come back that night. If he saw that there was no carriage around, he could finish killing them or burn the house down.

The girls helped, and they made it out to Mr. Barney's carriage. Fran left a note for her grandmother. It read, "We are, you know where." That was code, in case Robert came back and read it.

Mr. Barney put Rachel and Betty in the same bed, to make tending them easy. Evelyn and Betty were together. Evelyn was having such a good time at the Barneys that she had forgotten how it was at home. She felt guilty because she was so comfortable.

The Barneys didn't go to bed until everybody was settled. Mrs. Barney was up early to help the girls. They didn't go to school. They weren't sure what their father would do when he saw them. There was no doubt that he would be there.

In the afternoon, Mom Maggie rode up worried and afraid. "I got the note, and I understood what it meant. What happened at home?" Mr. Barney spoke. "I went over to check, and I decided to go inside. I didn't have a good feeling about Robert. When I walked inside, I saw him choking Rachel. Betty was on the floor, too. I was glad I'd carried a rifle. I had a feeling that I might need it, and I did. Robert slipped away while I was tending to Rachel. I thought it would be best to bring everybody here, just in case."

Mom Maggie said, "God bless you, Mr. Barney. I'm in your debt. You saved my family and I'll never forget that!"

"The girls didn't go to school. Under the circumstances, it was, I think the best thing to do," said Mr. Barney.

"I fully agree with you. You and your wife couldn't be better friends. I love you both!"

"Shucks, Mom Maggie. Tsk! Don't thank us for doing our duty."

"I must, Mr. Barney, because I'm so grateful."

Mom Maggie wanted to see her daughter and grandchildren. They had a close call. Rachel's face looked awful, her throat was very sore, and her shoulder had been kicked out of place. She had painful bruises on her back and side. Her mother bathed her carefully. She said, "Baby girl, I'm going to have to set your shoulder." She then, expertly, set her daughter's shoulder, then made a sling.

Next, she moved to the bed where Betty was. After checking her thoroughly, she told her it was all right for her to get up. Betty didn't know what a seizure was, and her grandmother didn't tell her too much. She only knew that she was glad to be up and about.

Mrs. Barney made coffee for Mom Maggie, and she sat down to enjoy it. She explained, "Maude Lewis' mother was very sick, but I shouldn't have gone. My family needed me."

"I believe you did the right thing, Mom Maggie. Besides, you had no way of knowing that Robert would double back the same day," Mr. Barney said.

"I feel so responsible for my family. If my carriage had been there, he wouldn't have had the guts to go inside."

"That's true, Mom Maggie, but your family is still alive."

"No thanks to me, Mrs. Barney."

"My husband was in time to keep Robert from killing them. He was there because you asked him to help you protect your family. So if you look at it that way, you didn't let your family down, at all. If you hadn't gone to see the lady, you would have been worried. Everything worked out."

"Bless you, Mrs. Barney. I have to admit that it did work out."

Mom Maggie had to admit that it had, indeed, worked out. She was certain, though, that had she been there, nothing would have happened. Robert was becoming more demented every day. She owed the very lives of her family to the vigilance of Mr. Barney. She thought, "Whatever they believe they owe me has been erased. The slate was wiped clean!"

Robert smiled and said, "They would probably have to ask what a one is!" Robert continued to ride around, not knowing if he could ever go back to his home.

He remembered Evelyn, and he wondered where she was, and why she wasn't home. "I hope she's lying somewhere at the point of death! She turned out to be Rachel's number two! God, how I despise both of them! They were smart to keep her out of my way."

Robert knew he could always go to Bessie's when he had no place to go. "I cannot let her know that I'm practically without a home of my own. That bit of information could give her the upper hand, and that will never do. No, I'll have to watch what I say and do to avoid tipping her off."

When he was tired of wandering around, he headed for Bessie's place. He needed Bessie in so many ways. He had made an error in judgment, and he was paying for it. Robert knew now that going home tonight was the worse thing he could have done. He had thrown aside carefully laid plans and allowed his emotions to run rampant. Heretofore, his control was the one thing of which he was most proud. Tonight, he'd lost it totally.

He kicked himself for allowing himself to throw away his own script and play it by ear. He thought, "I am an educated, careful player. Any numbskull could have done it that way! I don't know why I let them get under my skin. It's over now, and I can only hope to learn from this experience."

Bessie's house was just around the bend. He moved his horse a little faster. Her place was a safe harbor, and he couldn't get there fast enough. Bessie was asleep when he arrived. She had waited for him, but he didn't come. She felt that she had entertained enough for the day, so she did what she seldom did – she went to bed early. She heard a light knock and peeped out of the window. She saw Bobby standing there, looking very agitated.

The first thing she noticed, when he stepped inside, was the huge knot on his head. Bessie wisely decided not to mention it. She had been with him long enough to know how to overlook certain things. She accepted that he was secretive. If he didn't mention it, she wouldn't. Robert didn't kiss her, or greet her in any way. Bessie didn't push it.

Without a word, Robert undressed and got into bed. Bessie tried to snuggle, but he was pre-occupied. "Not now, Bessie!" she scurried to her side of the bed, hurt and puzzled. From that moment on, she took her cue from his actions. She, who viewed herself an expert on men, didn't know how to handle or please one temperamental guy named Robert. Bessie wondered if anyone did.

Robert was annoyed with Bessie. He was deep in thought and did not want any intrusions. The situation had changed so dramatically that he was being forced to either give up his plans to kill the entire family or come up with a more foolproof plan. Robert chose to do the latter.

He had two more snags to iron out. Until he found out where Evelyn was hiding, there was no chance to kill her. The other, and the most important, was Mr. Barney. Unfortunately, he had witnessed his brutality. That further complicated things. Robert couldn't allow the trail to lead to himself. There had to be more doubt than proof.

Robert began to think about timing. He wasn't so sure if he should make a move now, or not. "Perhaps", he thought, "I should allow some time to elapse before I put another plan into action. When old lady Maggie and Rachel have been lulled into a false sense of security, I'll strike!"

He favored fire, at this juncture, because it was swift and effective. However, he didn't rule out other means. Meanwhile, he would keep a low profile and wait. He was positive that something would develop. Physically and mentally drained, Robert invited sleep to come.

Bessie watched him as he slept. She wondered where he was when he wasn't with her. She wondered if there was a woman out there who loved him. She wondered if that woman were sad or glad when he stayed away at night. Has she seen his dark side? Probably. Bessie believed that one day her relationship with him would end. She wondered when! In her heart, she believed that she would be the loser.

Rachel had nightmares on her first night home. In her dreams, Robert was hiding under the table. She was at the sink washing dishes. He crawled from under the table and cut off both her legs. She fell on the floor and screamed. Her cries were muffled, and couldn't be heard by Mom Maggie, who was in the next room.

She screamed and thrashed about on the bed, until Mom Maggie shook her gently. Rachel's gown was drenched with perspiration, and she clung to her mother. Mom Maggie understood what was going on. She had survived a very brutal beating. It wasn't easily forgotten. She needed more time. Rachel cried with relief when she realized it was all a dream. Robert wasn't really cutting her up alive!

Mom Maggie soothed her. "It takes time, baby girl. It will get better. I'm more than sure of that. Rainbows don't come before the rain." She got up and lit the lamp. Just as when Rachel was a child, she didn't want her to be in the dark with her terror. She slept the rest of the night.

In the morning, Mom Maggie gave the girls keys to use. The doors would be locked at all times as a precaution. She told them to stay away from their father. Under no circumstances were they to go to him, even if he demanded that they do so. They were not to obey any orders he might give them. Mom Maggie didn't know when or where Robert would strike, so she tried to prepare the girls. Mr. Barney checked faithfully everyday.

Robert was in church on Sunday, sitting with his fellow deacons. "He has enough nerve to supply the whole town." Mom Maggie muttered. He glared at them, but he dropped his eyes quickly when he saw Mom Maggie watching him. In the open, he was no match for his mother-in-law. In the dark, he had been losing badly.

Rachel had not recuperated enough to go with them, so Mom Maggie took the girls. Mr. Barney stayed at home with Rachel, just in case. He mused, "Rachel must be in bad shape. She would have been dead in five more seconds. I'm surprised that the old hag would leave her alone."

Pastor Bacon's voice cut through Robert's thoughts. "I'm going to ask our own Deacon Grant if he will bless us with a solo." Robert hadn't been prepared for it, but he rose to the occasion. He took his place near the organ. He cleared his throat and said, "I'm going to attempt to sing, "I'm On the Battlefield." I would like to dedicate it to my dear family." The organist began to play the introduction, and Robert closed his eyes.

Mom Maggie said to the girls, "Come on. We're leaving!" When they got up, all eyes were on them. She marched her grandchildren down the aisle, with her head held high. She thought, "People won't understand what I just did, but they will one day. I refuse to sit there, after that hypocritical announcement. When he opens his eyes after the solo, he'll be surprised to see our seats empty!"

Fran took her grandmother's hand. "I understand why we left. Daddy is letting us know that he's in a war with us." Lovingly, Mom Maggie pinched Fran's cheek, and they climbed into the carriage. Life and living had made her grandchildren wise beyond their years.

Rachel was surprised to see them back so soon. She said, "Mama, I hope your carriage didn't break down. You're early."

"No, baby girl, the carriage is fine, but I'm not."

"You don't feel well, Mama?"

"Nothing like that, Rachel. Robert has become even more daring. This morning, he sang, 'I'm On the Battlefield', and he had the nerve to dedicate it to his family. I couldn't sit there through his hypocrisy. His warning wasn't lost on me. We'll be ready for him, too."

"He's so sure of himself! I wish I could erase the day that I married him. I wish I could erase Robert!"

"What's done is done, Rachel. We can't afford to waste time looking back. There's too much ahead of us that bears watchin'."

Later, the Barneys brought Evelyn over to visit her family. They had begun to think of her as their daughter, and she had bonded with them. Rachel saw what was going on, and she wasn't happy about it. She hoped it wouldn't cause problems in the future. They stayed for supper and socialized with each other. The girls missed their sister so much! Evelyn seemed to enjoy being with her sisters, but she was just as eager to leave with the Barneys.

Rachel cried when the Barneys took Evelyn with them. Mom Maggie saw, and she knew why she was crying. She didn't talk about it to her daughter. She knew only too well that Evelyn's attachment to Mr. and Mrs. Barney was the least of their problems.

She walked into the kitchen where the girls were sitting, looking very lost and miserable. "Who thinks they can beat me in a game of checkers?" That was the medicine they needed. Smiles replace frowns, and they rushed to the table for a game. Once again, Mom Maggie had saved the day.

When Robert finished his solo, he swaggered to his seat with the roar of the crowd in his ears. A little smile played about his lips, and he closed his eyes for a second or two. He looked over to see the look on his mother-in-law's face, but she wasn't there. He guessed accurately that they had walked out on him. He muttered under his breath, "It's another move to embarrass me!' He discounted, entirely, what he'd said before the solo, as well as the motive behind his bold announcement.

Robert was sure that everybody was talking about how his family had walked out just as he was about to sing. He felt everyone's eyes were watching him, to see how he was taking his latest humiliation. He wasn't able to see beyond his own ego.

After the service, Reverend Bacon went over to Robert. He said,

"I saw the family leave before your solo, and Rachel wasn't with them today. Is there a problem?" Robert stammered, but he managed to say, "Rachel's not really sick, but she is nursing a cold. You know how she is. She wouldn't want to expose anyone to her cold. Miss Maggie must have forgotten something important and had to leave." The reverend replied, "I suppose that could be the answer, but I'm concerned." Robert was able to dig down into a bag of lies and say, "I'm going home now, to check. If there's something wrong, we'll get in touch with you. If you don't hear from me, you'll know that everything is okay."

Reverend Bacon nodded, and moved on. Robert was very pleased with himself. He felt that he had handled it superbly. He left soon for Bessie's house. He had been sleeping at school in the cloakroom, now and then. He didn't want Bessie to know he was in a sense homeless.

Robert just missed running into one of Bessie's male friends, by a hair! She expected Robert to stay for the afternoon service. When Robert walked in, he sniffed the air. He asked, without a hello, "Do I smell tobacco?" Bessie tried to invent an answer. "Yes, you do smell tobacco. I had a cigar. You know I have a few pimples. I was going to make a poultice, but the odor was so disagreeable that I threw it away."

Robert walked up close to her, and she trembled with fear. She remembered the last time. He saw her fear, and he asked, "Why are you shaking? I only asked a simple question. Bessie, you dance very well, but I'm not convinced." She fell to the floor before him, and wrapped her arms around his legs. "Bobby, please believe I love you. I would never betray you!"

Robert was angry, but he was, also, caught up in her groveling. It seemed to please his sadistic nature. "How can I be sure of your love, Bessie?" Bessie thought he was beginning to weaken, but she held onto his legs even tighter. "I'll do anything for you, Bobby. Haven't I given myself to you totally? I only want you honey. I love you!"

Robert reached down and pried her from his legs. When he did that, Bessie cried. He stooped and picked her up. She stood before him, searching his eyes for a shred of forgiveness. What she saw there instead was mockery. Robert caught her off guard and struck her in the face. Bessie attempted to hit him back, and that infuriated him. He beat her until he was tired.

She lay on the floor, battered, bleeding, and humiliated. Robert sat on the bed watching her. He didn't love her less, but she had to learn to respect him. "Maybe you'll think twice before you bring another man in here," he said softly. Bessie moaned and tried to raise her head. Robert went to her and picked her up tenderly. He was now as sweet as he had been cruel.

Bessie was sure that he was mad. She was afraid to stay in his life, but she was fearful of leaving him. She knew she had to give up the kind of life she was living, or he would make mince meat of her. It was glaringly clear that he was someone she should have never met.

Robert undressed Bessie and bathed her bruises. His dog had become his queen again. He pulled the covers over her, and kissed her passionately. She was afraid to not respond, so she put her arms around his neck and kissed him back. Robert moved his mouth from hers and put his hands around her neck. Her heart did a somersault, and she was afraid to breathe. Robert's hand tightened, but not enough to rob her of air.

"I love you, Bessie. I love you more than I thought I could love a woman. You are exciting to me, and I love every inch of you. I'm positive that you love me as well." His hands gripped her throat a little tighter and fear danced in her eyes. Getting enough air was beginning to be a problem. Bessie's mind began to race. "He's killing me slowly! Oh, God!" She tried to think of a prayer, but she couldn't. She tried to remember the rest of 'Now I lay me down to sleep', but she couldn't. She tried to remove his hands, but she couldn't.

He kissed her and she grasped for air. He allowed her to breathe, then tightened his grip again. "Yes, Bessie, I do love you, but I will kill you if I ever suspect that you've been with another man. Trust me!" He released her, abruptly, and she reached for her throat. She couldn't be sure that he wouldn't kill her on the spot, even now.

Robert said, "All right, Bes. It's your turn to talk." Bessie swallowed hard before she could speak. "Bobby, I don't like being afraid, because I do love you. I belong to you —- only you. Bobby, please don't beat me any more! Please! Please don't beat me, Bobby!" Bessie began to weep loudly.

The cruel side of Robert had been fed and satisfied. He took her in his arms and rocked her. "Hush, sweetheart! The beatings are all up to you. Don't cry. You'll ruin our time together." He wiped her face and kissed her. Bessie knew what was expected of her. She put her arms around his neck and kissed him. Twisted Robert was still in charge!

CHAPTER 24

Robert spent the next three nights sleeping in the cloak room. He could have rented a room, but he didn't want the people to know what was going on at home. He bought a pillow and some blankets. He rolled them up and tucked them into a corner before school started. He missed the comforts of home, but this arrangement served his purpose.

Robert had begun to ride past his house after dark to see what was going on there. He would take advantage of the slightest slip-up. He noticed that the house was freshly painted, and there seemed to be some sign of building going on in the rear of he house. Rachel, without his knowledge, had saved a substantial sum of money. Mr. Barney and Mr. Harris volunteered to provide the labor.

At first, looking at the changes that were taking place without his permission, rankled him. On second thought, he realized that they were doing him a favor. After his plan to kill them succeeded, her would have a bigger and better house! Robert laughed out loudly as he rode away from the house. "No need to burn that down. I'll get them one by one."

Mom Maggie made the girls swings and a monkey bar. They played outside now, before it became dark. Rachel or Mom Maggie were always standing guard at the window. They had been told to run in the house if they ever heard or saw a buggy coming. They were not to wait to see who it was. They were very happy about the changes in their lives. An extra bedroom was one of the changes.

When Mom Maggie went home, she took all of them with her.

Most of the time, they stayed the weekend. They would go to church on Sunday, then go back home after the service. The girls had never known freedom before and this was exciting and wonderful. They knew that their grandmother was responsible for every good thing in their lives. They couldn't love her more! Rachel, aside from the low moments she had about Little Jim, was thriving. Mom Maggie had to remind them constantly that danger still lurked.

It was hog killing time, and Mom Maggie and Rachel knew the pig was ready for the slaughter. Mr. Barney promised to take care of it for them. There was a lot of activity preparing the meat for the smoke house. The girls played while the adults worked.

Betty was tossing a ball in the air. She threw it too far, and it landed in the wooded area behind the house. She ran to the spot where she was sure it landed, but it wasn't there. She walked a little deeper in the woods, looking around for her ball.

She decided to go back to tell her mother about the ball. She turned, and suddenly her father was there blocking her path! Robert had left the buggy a good distance away and walked. Betty opened her mouth to scream, but he clapped his hand over it! He was carrying a little pail of beautiful berries. Before he removed his hand, he said, "Baby, I'm not going to hurt you. I love you, but you never realized it. You were my favorite, but I couldn't show it. The others would've been jealous of you. I'll prove it to you. Take some berries! They are delicious!" Betty nodded, and he moved his hand from her mouth. "Take as many as you like," he said.

He smiled at her. She had never seen him smile before, but he didn't look mean anymore. Betty took a handful, and she ate some. She smiled at her father because they were delicious, just like he said. He urged, "Take some more, sweetie. I'm leaving now. Don't tell them you saw me. I love you, baby." He kissed her cheek and left.

Betty looked around a little for the ball, while she was eating the berries. She realized that she wouldn't find the ball because it was lost. She started back home. When she reached the edge of the woods, her stomach cramped terribly. She put the rest of the berries in her pocket. She walked on, trying to get home, but her legs became weak. She thought, "I'll sit down, and my stomach might stop hurting." The abdominal cramping worsened, and she had difficulty breathing. She called, "Mom Maggie!" She had to lay on the ground. Betty was sicker that she had ever been in her life.

She tried to crawl towards home, but she fell on her side. She heard loud noises in her head, and she couldn't see very well. Blood oozed from her mouth, and she called "Mama! Mom Maggie!" Very soon, she couldn't see at all. The noises in her head and ears became louder and louder, then stopped. Betty was dead!

At that moment, Mom Maggie dropped the knife she was using and stood deathly still! An eerie chill had washed over her body. She clutched her throat and cried, "Oh, not again!" Rachel went to her mother and helped her to a stool. Mom Maggie rocked back and forth wailing! She drew Rachel to her and said, "Baby, we have to be strong! We have to be strong! We have to be strong!" Rachel didn't understand, but she believed her mother had felt or seen something.

Fran got off the swing and looked around for Betty. She took Mary by the hand and walked to the carriage house, thinking that she might be hiding. When she couldn't find her, she and Mary went to get Mom Maggie and their mother. Fran hoped they wouldn't be upset with them, because she didn't see Betty leave. She couldn't be very far.

Mom Maggie saw them coming, and she knew! She stared straight ahead as Fran told them about Betty chasing her ball and how she had disappeared. They had looked for her with no luck. Rachel asked if they had seen or heard a buggy, and Fran said no. Rachel was relieved, but Mom Maggie wasn't. She knew, but she said nothing. She knew what she knew!

Mr. Barney heard what Fran was saying and came over to them. "Stay here. I'll search." Mr. Barney and his wife had grown close to the Grants, and they thought of them as family. He was always ready to help where he could. Mom Maggie, Rachel and the girls went into the house to wait.

Mr. Barney scanned the grounds quickly. He prayed silently, then started towards the wooded area. He hadn't gone far, when he saw Betty lying on the ground. He rushed to her, calling her name. Her eyes were open, but she didn't move. Mr. Barney felt for a pulse, then checked her pupils. Out of desperation, he began to breathe into her mouth, but Betty was gone!

He started out believing that he would find Betty bouncing her ball somewhere. Instead, she was dead! He noticed a berry in her hand. He removed it to get a closer look. 'Oh, Father in heaven! These are poisonous!" He cried quietly as he put the berry in his pocket. He wiped his eyes, knowing that he couldn't prolong the sadness much longer. He picked up the child and carried her home.

Mr. Barney cried as he walked. He remembered that not too long ago, he had carried another one of Rachel's children. "How much can poor Rachel take?"

Rachel had been waiting in the yard for them to return. She was certain that Mr. Barney would find her little girl and bring her home. When she saw him coming, she went to meet him. She asked, "What's wrong with her? Did she hurt her leg? Can't she walk?" Mr. Barney said nothing, because he had no voice, but the look on his face told the whole story.

Rachel screamed and fell to the ground. She lay there screaming and pounding the earth with her fists. Mom Maggie came out of the house to help her child. She wanted to hurry, but her feet felt like lead. She got down on the knees beside her baby girl and wrapped her in loving arms. Rachel wanted and needed her mother.

Rachel gasped for breath and clawed the air. She screamed, "Mama, what's going on? I've lost another child!" Mom Maggie said quietly, as she rocked Rachel, "We have to find strength. I'm here, and so is God!" Rachel moaned, "Where is God? Does He know what's going on? Does He care? I need Him now!" Mom Maggie held her tighter. "Child, He sees and He cares for us. Let's go in the house."

She helped Rachel up and she staggered as if she had been dealt a blow. Mom Maggie steadied her and got her into the house. She knew that she had to put her grief and mourning on hold, for her daughter's sake. She brewed her special tea for Rachel and coaxed her to sip it. She helped her to bed, and she slept.

Mr. Barney had placed Betty on the bed in her room. Mom Maggie undressed her and bathed her with a tender touch. Her tears fell on her dead grandchild. Mom Maggie put fresh underwear and a gown on Betty. She prayed for strength to do that for the child. Fran and Mary wanted to see Betty, and Mom Maggie permitted them.

Fran rubbed her sister's face and cried. Mary shook her, crying, "Get up, Betty! Get up!" When she was sure that Betty could not get up, she climbed in the bed beside her sister and cried. The scene was almost too much for Mom Maggie to bear. When the girls had quieted down, she convinced them to go downstairs.

Mr. Barney had contacted the funeral director for them. He was their right arm in time of trouble. Mom Maggie knew it was best for the director to come while Rachel was asleep. She asked Fran if she would fix something for the two of them to eat. They weren't hungry, but they managed to eat a slice of cake with a glass of milk.

Mr. Barney returned with his wife and Evelyn. Evelyn went upstairs to see her little sister. She stayed a long time, so Mom Maggie went to check on her. She was lying on the floor, in a faint. Mom Maggie got her salts, and put it under Evelyn's nose. A few seconds later, Evelyn shook a little, then opened her eyes. She began crying, immediately. She said, "She should have been with me. Everybody should be there."

Someone knocked on the door, and Mr. Barney got up to answer it. The funeral director had arrived. Mrs. Barney took the children in the kitchen so they wouldn't see what was going on. Their grandmother excused herself and went upstairs. When they carried her grandchild downstairs, she leaned against the wall because her heart was breaking. She called on her maker for strength to go on and wiped her eyes. She held her head high as she joined the others downstairs.

Mr. Barney had his suspicions. He planned to go back to the place where he found Betty and look around. He wasn't sure that he would find anything significant, but he wouldn't rest until he looked. He decided that he would go the next day.

Mom Maggie knew that Rachel would sleep through the night. "The Lord knows she'll need one good night's rest. We all have to get through the days ahead. How could this have happened to Betty? Was Evelyn right? Should we send the other children to the Barneys? Should the entire family move in with them? If only temporarily?"

She closed her eyes to shut out everything. It didn't work for her. She continued to think and wonder. "Betty did eat the poisonous berries. I saw them in her pocket. I'm not really comfortable with the explanation, and I wonder why? There is no doubt in my mind that she did ingest them. First, Little Jim, and now Betty! We put locks on the doors, but Betty died on the outside." Mom Maggie closed her eyes again. "Why is death stalking our family?"

Mr. and Mrs. Barney were in the kitchen with the children. That gave her a breather. She was the strong one, but like every mortal, she had weak moments. This was one of them. Rachel's children were very dear to her. She remembered that they were preparing pork. She rose from her seat slowly and went outside to continue her task. She needed to be busy, and it would be dark soon.

The Barneys followed her, and pitched in when they saw she was determined to work. Each was lost in his own thoughts, so they labored in silence. They made the deadline. The last piece of meat was hung in the smoke house as darkness threatened to envelop them. Mom Maggie couldn't thank them enough for their help. They would have stayed the night, but Mom Maggie assured them that they'd be all right. Evelyn wanted to stay, but her grandmother encouraged her to go with them.

Mom Maggie kissed Mrs. Barney's cheek. Mrs. Barney promised to bring the breakfast and lunch in the morning. She and her husband took a lot of the pressure off Mom Maggie. Their thoughtfulness was incredible. Taking Evelyn with them meant that there was one less child to worry about. In Mom Maggie's mind, they'd become as dear as any family member.

Fran and Mary wanted to sleep in the room with their grandmother and mother. She understood, and let them do that. They'd been introduced to death when Little Jim was taken from them. It was natural for them to be fearful. They needed extra love and lots of reassurance. Their grandmother understood that, too.

Rachel woke early in the morning. Her body was rested, but her mind was in turmoil. The death of her child hit her with full force! She sat up in the bed and screamed! The children were startled. They jumped up and went to her. Rachel wailed, "Tell me it's not true! Tell me it's all a bad dream!" She gathered Fran and Mary to her bosom and cried, hysterically. "I won't let you out of my sight! I can't lose either of you!"

Rachel held the children so tightly that they were uncomfortable. Her mother gently pulled the children from her tight grasp. She gave Rachel a small sip of the herbal tea. It was just enough to take the edge off. She sat beside her until she calmed down a bit. Mom Maggie couldn't ask her child not to grieve. It was a natural response to death.

Almost as if on cue, the Barneys came with food for breakfast and lunch. Evelyn went upstairs to be with her mother. Mrs. Barney warmed the food and set the table. Every now and then, she cried for the family's loss. It was so tragic!

Mom Maggie was carrying a tray up to Rachel when she saw before her her dead grandson, Little Jim, and Betty. Tears were streaming down their faces. The picture faded as quickly as it had come. "Oh, Father God! They don't seem to be at peace!" She was shaken by what she saw. The answer was slow in coming, but it would come.

Rachel was hollowed-eyed but calmer. Mom Maggie fed her like a baby. She didn't want to see people, and her mother would make sure she didn't have to do that. Mom Maggie left Evelyn with her mother and went back downstairs.

CHAPTER 25

Mr. Barney announced that he was going to search the area where he'd found Betty. He believed that something was terribly wrong with the picture. For starters, he didn't believe that the type of berry that Betty had in her hand, could be found in that particular area. A careful search of the grounds proved him right. Those berries grew much deeper in the woods.

When he was satisfied that his suspicions had merit, he started back home. It was clear to Mr. Barney that someone had given Betty those berries. At the edge of the woods, a shiny object caught his eye. Out of curiosity, he walked over and looked. It turned out to be a small pail. There were a few berries in the pail and some were scattered on the ground. Someone, he believed, had thrown it there. He wondered, "Why would someone buy a new pail, then throw it away?"

To be certain, he took the pail back to show Mom Maggie. She would know if it belonged to Betty or to one of the other girls. Their next move would depend on the children's answer.

As soon as he arrived at the Grant's house, he took Mom Maggie aside to talk about what he had discovered. As he suspected, Mom Maggie had never seen the pail before. To double check, she showed it to the girls. They confirmed that it wasn't Betty's, nor theirs.

When Mr. Barney and Mom Maggie were alone again, they discussed the new turn of events. Mom Maggie said, "I see where you're going with this. Someone followed Betty and gave her those berries to eat! They had no further use for the pail, so they threw it away."

Mr. Barney nodded. "Although, we can't prove it, at least not yet, this has Robert written all over it!"

Mom Maggie shivered and said, "I'm afraid you are right. He must be stopped!"

"Mom Maggie, I think that all of you should move in with us."

"It's a good idea. I'll talk it over with Rachel."

"I don't think you can move too soon."

"I agree, Mr. Barney, but I can't talk about this to Rachel, yet. She's dealing with enough."

"You're right again. She shouldn't be told until she can handle it."

"In the meantime, we will protect my family. I think it's time I got a gun."

"I think that would be a good thing. I'll bring you a rifle."

"I don't like guns, but this is out of hand. I don't have a choice."

Robert went to his make-shift bedroom at school. He felt better now than he had in ages. His plan had begun to gel. He laughed when he remembered how gullible Betty was. "Why would she be stupid enough to believe I had ever loved her? She was ready to forgive me, and I was ready to kill her! Stupid, just like her stupid mother!"

Robert laughed again and thought he was very clever and persuasive. He was sure that he would sleep well tonight. He smelled success, and it was wonderful. He tried to decide if he should go to the funeral or not. "Maybe I should go, to keep tongues from wagging. People will surely wonder."

He unfolded the blankets and spread them on the cloak room floor. His sleeping quarters were cramped, but the inconvenience would be worth it in the end. He visualized himself living in his house. He would decide at that time if he should take Bessie there.

"Rachel is probably hysterical, and the old crone is strutting around trying to be a big-time comforter. The brat's death would be a blow to her, also, and that's good! I'll destroy her one way or another. Soon, I'll be able to move back home in style and in peace."

Robert settled down for the night with a clear conscience. He truly believed that the child's death was justified. Robert's father had shaped his life, but he had gone down a path that his father never would have traveled. The pupil had surpassed the teacher! Robert closed his eyes and slept like a baby.

In the morning, he bathed and dressed, then prepared for the day. The water was cold, but he couldn't do any better. He remembered to roll up his blankets and make them as inconspicuous as possible. So far, so good.

"The news of the brat's death would have gotten around, by this time." He would say, if asked why he'd come to school, "I have to be busy. It seems to help." He would keep his answer simple. That was always best.

His pupils began to straggle in the room. They looked at him wide-eyed. They didn't expect to see him at his post. They liked Betty a lot, but they feared her father. The children had counted on having a substitute teacher. They settled down quickly, to avoid Mr. Grant's wrath. Robert said to thm, "Open your books to page seventy." The school day had begun.

Bessie felt confident that Bobby was on his job, whatever that was. She couldn't sit home all day, so she went to the saloon. She came alive when she stepped inside. She wanted to be with the people she knew. The men were fond of her, and so were the women.

Bessie felt brave enough to confide in one of the men. She'd tried to keep her fears bottled up, but it was becoming harmful to her. After listening to Bessie, the young man offered to confront Bobby for her. She begged him not to, but she promised to seek his help when she needed him. She knew he could be counted on to help her.

She went home alone after a few hours. Bessie had always been a free spirit, but Bobby had beaten all of the vim and vitality out of her. She hated the person she'd become. Bessie hated that she had her head in the lion's mouth and couldn't get it out. She didn't know how to do that.

Robert wrapped up things at school and went to Bessie's. He didn't go to the saloon, because he expected her to be home waiting for him. She hadn't done any entertaining. The beating was still too fresh in her mind. Robert was walking on air! Bessie was home, and he had eliminated one more brat. He felt that nothing could bring him down or spoil his mood.

Bessie had bought ham and macaroni from a store that sold a few cooked items as well. Robert thought about the sumptuous meals served at the house. For one brief moment, he was very sorry he couldn't go there. Bessie didn't try to figure out the huge change in his mood.

When the meal was over, Robert pulled her down on his lap. He kissed her, but it was hard for her to respond to him, genuinely. Bobby kissed her one moment, and choked the next! This see-saw existence was too much for her. With him, there was no in between. He was either terrific or a terror. Only after he continued to kiss and pet her, did she relax and return his fire.

Pastor Bacon rode up to the house to pay his respect to the family. He asked to speak to Rachel or Robert. Mom Maggie said, "I'm sorry, pastor, but Rachel isn't able to see anyone, and Deacon Grant does not live here. You are welcome to stay, and I will be glad to speak for my daughter." The pastor's jaw dropped and he gasped! "I had no idea. Where can I find Robert?" She answered, "He didn't leave a forwarding address. Your guess is as good as mine. If you'll sit down, I'd like to make arrangements for my grandchild. My daughter has permitted me to speak for her."

Pastor Bacon felt that things were moving too fast. He was still dealing with the news about Robert. He cleared his throat and took a seat, but he hadn't lost his stunned look. Mom Maggie began. "Naturally, we'd like the service to be on Sunday. I'm not sure if my daughter will be able to attend. She has lost two children, tragically, in a matter of months."

Pastor Bacon said, "I feel terrible about this senseless loss. I am sure Robert is grief-stricken, too." Mom Maggie replied, "He is not the man you think he is, Reverend. That's all I'll say about that. Is it possible for the children's choir to render a selection? We'd like a short service. You know we favor a sermonette. Will that be possible? We're not inflexible, pastor." He looked up from his notes and answered. "Your wishes will be carried out, Miss Maggie. Is there anything else that I can do?"

Mom Maggie stood as she said, "I think that will be all. We do appreciate your coming. We were very pleased with the service for our baby boy. I know the services for Betty will equal that." That was music to his ears. He lingered a few moments, then left.

Mr. Barney and Mr. Harris took on the job of contacting the family for Mom Maggie. Neighbors came and went, always bringing food. Mrs. Barney was her right arm – always there. Family began to arrive, and, as usual, they used Mom Maggie's place as the guest house.

Rachel had not left her bed. For her, this seemed to be the last straw. Sometimes she would remember how Robert had beaten poor Betty while she was having a seizure. She would tell her mother about Robert's extreme cruelty to Betty, then dissolve in tears.Rachel wanted to go downstairs, but she felt that she couldn't.

Sunday arrived much too quickly. Evelyn helped Rachel get ready for the funeral. When they arrived at the church, Mom Maggie scanned the crowd for some sign of Robert. She didn't see him. That meant they could go inside. She steeled herself, and put her mind on what was before them. Rachel's brothers were on either side of her for support.

Betty lay there in a white coffin. She had a pink ribbon in her hair to match her pink dress. Rachel's brothers steered her to the coffin. She trembled as she leaned over and kissed her child. She moaned and tried to turn, but she fainted. Her brothers took her home when she'd been revived. The girls cried constantly. Mom Maggie held up, even though her heart was breaking. Helping her family was uppermost in her mind. "I'll cry later."

True to his word, Reverend Bacon kept the services brief. He could see that the state of the family was precarious. He saw, too, Robert Grant was not present. He didn't want to rush to judgment, but certainly things weren't as he thought. He decided to be watchful, as well as prayerful.

Friends and neighbors went to the house, but they left early. Rachel's fragile condition was obvious to all. Mom Maggie brewed the tea, but she waited until Rachel was in bed before she gave it to her. She was crying as she drifted off to sleep.

The girls stood in the center of the room, holding on to each other. They cried for each other, and they cried for their sister, Betty. They didn't know which one would be next! They no longer felt like children. How were they supposed to cope with the awful things that were happening? The Barneys stayed the night, so that Evelyn could be with her family. It was important that they be together, tonight of all nights.

Mom Maggie was able to hold back her grief until everyone was asleep. She sat in the kitchen, with her head on the table and sobbed. She said, "Lord, I know you aren't taking these children. Robert is! Please strengthen me and make things right." She sat awhile in meditation, then she sipped a little of the herbal tea. Only then, did she go to bed.

There was heavy sadness over, through, and around the house. Another light had gone out and would be missed forever. Hearts had been broken unnecessarily. Mom Maggie thought, as she climbed into bed, "And after this, comes the dawn. With His help, we will meet it head on!"

The night passed quietly, and the family arrived after breakfast. They weren't staying this time. The uncles wanted the girls to spend part of the summer with them. Mom Maggie told them she was almost positive they could. She promised to visit them as soon as she could. The girls talked to their cousins, but they didn't laugh or play checkers, as they had before. After speaking with Rachel, their family left for home.

Mom Maggie asked Rachel if she felt like going downstairs, but she didn't push. She would try again the next day. The Barneys continued their work, along with Mr. Harris. The building was going remarkably well. Mrs. Barney fixed lunch for everybody.

The next day, which was Tuesday, Mom Maggie shooed the girls off to school. Mr. Harris picked them up after school was over. The grown-ups had decided that one of them would pick the children up after school everyday. This was part of their protection plan. They had been instructed to never go near their father, even if he ordered them to do so. If he approached them, they were to scream and run. Never were they to stand still and listen to him. Mom Maggie knew their lives depended on it.

Next, she went to Rachel's room. Without saying a word, she laid her clothes on the bed. She waited a moment, then spoke, "Rachel baby, you're getting up today. You have to see how the work is progressing, and we need you with us." Mom Maggie knew that every day she allowed Rachel to stay in bed made it easier for her to retreat completely. Very soon, it would become a way of life, and she would be a recluse.

Rachel heard the determination in her mother's tone. She opened her mouth to decline, but Mom Maggie gave her the familiar "no nonsense" look. Rachel closed her mouth, and threw back the covers. She dressed and went downstairs. No one understood her grief more than Mom Maggie, for she was grieving, too. She was doing what was best for her child.

CHAPTER 26

Robert was preoccupied these days. He was trying to formulate a plan to kill another child. He decided, finally, that he would be guided by the circumstances, as they were presented. He wasn't sure which one he would catch with the pail of berries, but he was certain to catch one of them. "It happened to be Betty. The next brat might have to be killed with my bare hands. I most certainly will be prepared to do that, too."

He came up with what he thought was a brilliant idea. "I'll lure one of them, or maybe both, after school." Robert smiled at the idea of catching and crushing two at the same time. 'If I can kill the rest of the brats right away, it would be very effective. That would be the final blow for Rachel. She would be a permanent basket case. I'll shoot for today!"

Robert had reached the peak of his madness! He had the cunning of one whose every move was orchestrated by the devil himself. He thought, "The house will be all mine, and the old girl, if she survives this, will have to vacate!" Robert couldn't help laughing aloud, as he pictured the scene. Robert's pupils looked at him, but he didn't notice.

Robert was anxious to put his idea to work. One of his pupils gave a wrong answer, but he was too pumped up to care. His eyes were on the clock. Now that he had settled on a plan of action, the day was dragging its feet. He rustled papers and shifted in his seat.

He couldn't stand it any longer. He gave the class their homework assignment, and dismissed them early. Robert opened the desk drawer and took out a jar of coins. He'd been saving a long time, and the jar was full. He would use the coins to entice the two girls. He peered out of the window when it was time. When he saw the children's classmates leaving the building, he closed his door and left. There they were!

He glanced at the coins and rushed outside. Instead of walking, as they always did without fail, they were climbing into a carriage! Robert shook with frustration and rage! "Of all the rotten luck! This should have worked! It was a simple, uncomplicated plan." He reminded himself that this was just a minor annoyance, not the end of his scheme.

Robert took the coins back to the classroom and put then in the drawer. It turned out to be a bad day. After his disappointment, he needed to be with Bessie. He closed down and left the building. The ride and the soft breeze blowing in his face accomplished what they were supposed to. They refreshed him.

When he reached Bessie's house he was only mildly perturbed. She came home moments after he arrived with a bag of food. Bessie was glad about the timing. She'd rushed to get there. She'd had a feeling that he would show, and she was right. It was clear where she had been. Robert saw the sack of food, but he wondered, for a moment, if the bag were a cover for her.

Because he was crafty, he assumed that she was, too. He relented and decided to take things at face value. She kissed him, and he welcomed the intimacy. Being with Bessie was what he needed. Whenever he'd been dealt a blow, such as he had today, he needed to find solace somewhere. Bessie was keenly aware of this needs and his mood. She was eager to please her man and fulfill his fantasies.

Robert crushed her to him, and she melted in his arms. This was the Bobby she loved! Bessie would enjoy this side of him while it lasted. She never forgot his manic side. It lurked there and could be summoned at a moment's notice. That sad fact clouded the relationship. Bessie was miserable most of the time. She thought, "For now, I'll try to shut out all my fears and enjoy being with Bobby."

Fran and Mary never knew the danger they had escaped. Riding home from school was new and a lot of fun. Mr. Harris sang songs for them, and they laughed at the comical lyrics. Their father had always rode past them, but they were used to it. They were finding out, now, how much fun riding was.

The girls didn't know that Mr. Harris had gotten a glimpse of Robert looking at them from the steps. He understood, fully, why it was necessary to guard the children. He hadn't known Robert very well, but he always enjoyed his singing. Mr. Harris wondered how one so gifted could at the same time be so totally evil.

They arrived home safe and sound. Rachel was relieved, and her mother said a silent prayer. The first chance he had, Mr. Harris told Mom Maggie about observing Robert.

"Mom Maggie, you were right to have me pick up the children."

"Mr. Harris, did anything happen today?"

"No, but it could've been bad for the children. I saw Robert standing on the school steps. The girls were getting in the carriage. He seemed to be really mad!"

"The Master is keeping us a step ahead of him. I'm grateful to you, Mr. Harris. We can't win without you and our friend, Mr. Barney."

"I couldn't live with myself if anything happened to the children, and I could've helped, but didn't."

"You think that way because you're a fine person. I think it's probably a good idea to escort them to school, too. I'll do my share."

This was a bad day for Rachel. They were packing Betty's clothes to donate to needy children. Mom Maggie would put an article in a box, and Rachel would take it out! Her mother was patient. Packing took much longer than it should have. Mom Maggie said,

"We're giving these things to children who need them. The orphanage is always asking for donations. Betty would like that. This doesn't move her out of our lives. She will remain in our hearts forever. She'll always be a lovely memory." Rachel knew she was right, but she cried anyway.

Mom Maggie suggested that they visit Evelyn. Rachel jumped at the idea. They gathered food for dinner, plopped the girls in the carriage, and headed for the Barneys. The visit was a dose of medicine for everyone, until Mrs. Barney suggested that Evelyn remain with them permanently.

Rachel was taken aback! "I will not let another child go! I don't know how you can ask such a thing!" Mrs. Barney apologized immediately for appearing insensitive. "Evelyn has become a big part of our lives. I know now that I shouldn't have mentioned that to you. I'm really sorry." Rachel softened a bit, and said, "Certainly Evelyn will be allowed to visit you often. I don't mind that at all." Mom Maggie didn't see the problem and saw no need to discuss it. Evelyn would go home with her mother when this mess was over, and that was that!

All was forgiven and forgotten by the time supper was on the table. They were all good friends who had gotten together. They had a great visit. They were home before dark. Mom Maggie checked the windows and doors before she was able to relax. Rachel tried to be cheerful, but her pain was hard to cover up. The night was especially difficult. The family hoped that in time, she would be better. Never the same, but better.

That night, Mom Maggie dreamed about Little Jim. When she awoke, she saw Little Jim's image. He was pointing at Robert! To keep from crying out, Mom Maggie had to put her hand over her mouth. Now, at last, she knew. She knew beyond a shadow of a doubt, that Robert was responsible for Little Jim's death! Mom Maggie had a pain in her chest, and she prayed that it wasn't a heart attack. She lay back against the pillows and forced her mind to become neutral. Gradually, the pain subsided, and she allowed herself to remember.

Robert was the one who ran over her grandchild! "He crushed his little body as if he were no more than an animal, then left him lying in the road. He must have known what he'd done, but he did not care." In the darkened room, she let the tears cascade down her weathered cheeks.

Mom Maggie felt foolish for crying. She wiped her face and tried to make sense of what she knew. Learning what she had, was not going to put Robert in prison. Her premonitions were not hard evidence to anyone but her. Still, this sign was confirmation for Mom Maggie. Robert had killed two of his own children and tried to strangle another with a rope. That made him a fiend of the worse kind! He didn't deserve to dwell among the human race. "His very existence is an insult!"

Mom Maggie was fully aware of her helplessness. She said to herself, "As sure as I'm sitting here, Robert will meet his doom. I won't have to lift a finger. He cannot die a peaceful death. Meanwhile, I'll do what I've been doing. I'll protect my family with my life, if need be."

Mom Maggie heard the sound of a horse and buggy approaching. It was too late for visitors. She rose quietly and looked out of the window. The rider stopped in front of the house but did not get out of the buggy. She tiptoed to the place where she had hidden the rifle and loaded it. She went back to the window and waited. She was almost sure it was Robert.

She went downstairs and looked out of the parlor window. She could see, in the moonlight that it definitely was Robert. He sat in the buggy. She supposed he was waiting for what he thought would be the right time for him to strike. Eventually, Robert started climbing out of the buggy, and she opened the door. Mom Maggie pointed the rifle at him and said, "If you think you can run faster than this bullet, come on in!"

Robert was shocked to see her awake and alert at that hour! He believed that he would catch them asleep. He tried to leap into the buggy, but he slipped and fell. Mom Maggie stepped outside with the rifle cocked. Robert jumped up, with the grace of an elephant, and vaulted into the buggy. He turned the horse and rode away, very glad to be alive!

A couple of minutes later, another man rode up, but it was their friend, Mr. Barney. He was surprised to see her standing outside with a rifle at her side.

"Miss Maggie! Having problems?"

"That fiend just left. I heard him ride up, thank goodness. He high-tailed it out of here when I raised the rifle. He's determined, and so am I."

"He's disgusting! I was riding by to check the house. I'm too late to deal with Robert, but you go back to bed. I'll hang around for awhile."

"Thank you."

She knew that sleep would come now, and she was more than ready. She would deal with tomorrow on tomorrow! Rachel seemed to be sleeping peacefully, and that was what it was all about, for her.

CHAPTER 27

Robert drove his horse at a fast pace and didn't slow down until he reached the school building. He went inside and leaned against the wall. "That old crone was going to shoot me!" he said. "She's more dangerous than I thought! She just made a costly mistake. I'll file that under revenge!"

Robert collected his wits and prepared his pallet on the floor. He mused, "Maybe I should have stayed with Bessie. This encounter with that ugly old crow never would've happened." Robert wasn't the type to cry over spilled milk. He tried to have plan B waiting in the wings.

Robert Grant stretched out on his bed and closed his eyes. He wanted to sleep, but he couldn't. He forced himself to stay there in bed. He was, after all, in a school building. What would he do if he got up? He used the time awake to bolster his spirits. Aloud he said, "It doesn't matter to me, how many battles I lose. There is no way that I can lose the war."

Evelyn popped into his mind. Robert tried to figure out where she was staying. He concluded that she might not be in the area, since she no longer attended school. It was possible that she was living with one of her uncles. If that were so, there was little chance of getting to her. "I realize now that I should've killed her first. I hate to think it, but I might have to write her off."

He had plenty of time on his hands, and he was facing a sleepless night. He used the time to plot. His thoughts turned to Fran and Mary. He mumbled, "I'll get them if the carriage rides turn out to be a temporary thing. If the coins don't do it, something else will."

Now, he'd had enough of thinking about the family he didn't want. He visualized himself claiming the house. That brought a big smile, and very soon he slept.

The next day, Robert waited with the coins. He hadn't caught them going, but he would snare them coming. He was almost stunned when he saw Mom Maggie arriving with Fran and Mary. "The old lady brought them!" After school, someone in a carriage picked them up. Robert was thrown a little, but he had anticipated that happening. He watched for three days to be positive. He was not easily discouraged.

In one week, school would be over for the summer. He would put plan B in action. Robert planned to watch them carefully the final week of school. Somebody might let down their guard. He would be on them like white on rice. The smallest slip might be a golden opportunity for him to strike.

He said to himself, "All is not lost. There's several things that I can do. I can abduct them from the church yard while their mother and Miss Maggie are helping with the food. I can blend into the background and never be noticed. The jar of coins will be irresistible."

Naked hatred motivated Robert, and revenge pushed and fed him. People would have snatched their children out of his classroom if they knew the extent of the evil that lurked inside of him. He wore his two faces and managed to keep them straight. No one knew that the grieving father had caused the death of the very ones that he pretended to grieve. He thoroughly understood how to blend in with well-intentioned people. Skillfully, he used his talent to mesmerize and gain popularity. Robert was a master of deceit.

Robert planned to keep the house under surveillance, as much as he possibly could. Next time, he would be more careful. "Riding so close to the house was a big mistake, and I've learned from that. I'll be sure to walk. The old bat's hearing is as sharp as an animal's."

On Sunday, Robert went to church. His suit was slightly rumpled, and his shirt collar wasn't starched. He sat with the other deacons, as he expected to do. Mom Maggie, Rachel, and the girls were already there. This was Communion Sunday, and the deacons assisted the pastor in serving the congregation. Robert was assigned to serve the area where his family sat.

Mom Maggie said to the family, "Don't take it!" She sat with her head held high. Actually, Robert was afraid to go near his mother-in-law, but he had no choice. He served the pew in front of the family, then moved to the one on which they sat. His hand shook visibly as he leaned over with the tray.

Mom Maggie stood on her feet, and the children and Rachel looked straight ahead. They were ignoring Robert's presence. The pastor said, "Yes, Miss Maggie." Robert looked like a trapped rabbit. He didn't know what his mother-in-law was going to say or do. He wished for the power to disappear, knowing that it could not happen.

Mom Maggie said, "Pastor Bacon, my family and I will accept communion from any deacon other than Robert Grant." Pastor Bacon didn't know how to address this very odd request. It had never happened before. Mom Maggie had put him on the spot, and he was not sure how to handle it. He had the utmost respect for her, but his deacon was his right hand man. How could he disregard his feelings? He waited a few minutes, hoping that she would explain, but she said nothing. He asked, "May I ask why? This is highly unusual." Mom Maggie said, "Robert Grant is not fit to be a deacon in any church!" She turned to Robert. "Shall I go on, father of the year?" Her stare was unwavering.

Robert wanted to beat her to a bloody pulp, then strangle her with his bare hands! He had never been so enraged. He pulled himself together enough to look at the congregation. He saw that every eye was fixed on him. He, quickly, decided to give the communion tray to another deacon, and took his seat on the bench. Mom Maggie sat down, and the deacon served her and the others.

There was a low murmuring running through the congregation. The stand-off between Mom Maggie and Deacon Grant was puzzling. Mom Maggie's word carried a lot of weight in the community. The people knew that there was something very shady going on.

The pastor restored order, and the communion service continued.

Robert knew that going to church after what happened had been a colossal mistake. As he sat there thinking about the fiasco, his hatred grew by leaps and bounds, until he was nearly consumed by it. Wisely, Pastor Bacon decided not to ask Robert to sing the sermonic hymn. He suspected that Mom Maggie and her family would've walked out. At that point, Robert would have declined, saying that he had a cold or sore throat. He noticed that the people who were thrilled by his singing were looking at him differently.

He wasn't aware that Mom Maggie, or anyone else, knew he killed the children. Had he known that Mom Maggie was wise to him, he never would've appeared in public. It would have been out of the question.

The service was finally over, and Robert lingered on the fringes of the gathering. He was waiting for the chance to kidnap the girls. His wait would be in vain. Mom Maggie and Rachel brought food, but they didn't stay. They couldn't wait to get home.

Neither was in the mood to fend off questions or endure the buzzing atmosphere that was certain to follow. What Mom Maggie said in there was a bold step! She had opened Pandora's Box and she would have to deal with it, but not in a crowd. Sensationalism was definitely not her style.

She knew that Robert might, after this, become more reckless. Certainly, he would be more determined to destroy them. Aloud, she said, "With God's help, I'll be prepared." Rachel, thinking her mother was talking to her, asked "Prepared for what, Mama?" Mom Maggie had tried to shield her daughter from most of the unpleasantness. She didn't want to explain in front of the children. She merely said, "Prepared for Robert's shenanigans."

Rachel pressed her for an answer. "What do you think he'll do?" Mom Maggie fished for words. "We all know he's capable of anything. He is unscrupulous and dangerous!" Rachel had a lot to digest, so she didn't respond to her mother's last remark. She became so quiet that her mother began to worry about her.

Mom Maggie had not wanted to pile misery on top of misery. Her daughter was mourning her children's death, and she was fragile. On the one hand, she had no choice. The line had to be drawn.

Suddenly, Rachel said, "Mama, when we get home, I want you to tell me what you're holding back. I'm grateful for your protection, but I need to know whatever it is. Will you do that?" Mom Maggie didn't answer until she'd pondered the situation. She felt Rachel's eyes on her, but she had to think. Finally she said, "We'll see." Mom Maggie wanted to know for sure that it was the right thing to do. That particular truth would be difficult for a strong man to swallow. She noticed that the girls were quiet. It was apparent that they could hear and were listening. The subject was closed.

They rode up to the house and stopped. Fran said, "Our house is pretty!" Rachel had been paying attention to very little around her since Betty's death. She looked at the house for the first time and saw what Fran meant. She had to agree. "It really is! Mr. Barney and Mr. Harris did a great job. I'll have to get new beds for you."

They went into the house, but this time Rachel checked. Her mother was impressed. She knew what she was doing. Rachel was trying to prove that she was able to handle whatever. She went to the kitchen to find something for supper. They had taken their food to the church. The children liked fried chicken on Sunday, but sliced ham would have to do. Rachel wouldn't let her mother help. In no time, she had a good meal on the table.

Fran helped with the dishes, before they got out the checkers. Playing with Mary was fun because Fran won every game. Rachel and her mother went to the parlor to chat. Mom Maggie skated all around the one thing that Rachel was anxious about. When Rachel couldn't stand it a minute longer, she put her hand on her mother's arm. "Now, Mama!"

Mom Maggie drew a deep breath and took the plunge, but gently. "Baby girl, this won't be easy for me to tell, and it won't be easy for you to hear." Rachel closed her eyes and said, "That's all right,

Mama. I'm ready!" When Rachel opened her eyes, her mother began.

"We, Mr. Barney and I, believe strongly, that Robert gave Betty poisonous berries that day. Some were in her pocket, and one was in her hand." She paused to let Rachel catch her breath. Tears flowed down her face, but she motioned for her mother to proceed. She was holding on!

"Mr. Barney searched the place where she was found. The poisonous berries grew much deeper in the woods. He found a new pail at the edge of the woods that contained some of the berries. He brought the pail back to see it any of us could identify it. We couldn't of course. The girls hadn't seen it before."

"It was clear to Mr. Barney and me that somebody gave her the berries, then threw away the pail." Rachel said, through her tears, "Robert!" Mom Maggie took her hand. "That's what we believe, too." Rachel leaned back against the settee. "Is there more, Mama?" Her mother peered at her to see if she were able to hear the rest. Satisfied that she was, Mom Maggie continued.

"Yes, I'm afraid there is. Whenever Robert was near me, I had an eerie kind of chill. The other night, it became clear to me. I saw an image of Little Jim. He was pointing at Robert. This might be flimsy to some, but I know what was revealed to me."

Rachel sat with her eyes closed, trying to make sense of what her mother had said. She struggled with what she'd heard for awhile. Suddenly, things began to fall into place, and her eyes flew open.

"Mama! He did it!"

"Baby girl, what's going on with you?"

"Mama, I know Robert did it! Robert left the house that night, shortly after Little Jim climbed out of the window! Oh, dear God! Robert has killed two of my children! He killed his own children! What kind of monster is he? He did it without batting and eye. Afterwards, it was business as usual!"

Mom Maggie reached out and held her in her arms. It was

rough, but she knew that her daughter was doing well. She was so proud of the strength she showed. Living with Robert had been one long nightmare. One day, she would look back at her life and see her growth. Mom Maggie felt in her spirit that the end would surely come. A weight had been lifted off her, just by telling.

"Mama, we'll face this together. It's a big mess, but we will be here for each other."

"I hear you, honey. We're family. That means everything."

"He can't snatch another child away from me, Mama! I won't let him!"

"No, we will protect our own."

"Mama, while I was blinded by my grief, I couldn't see what you had to bear, or how you lost sleep to protect your family. I see now, Mama. Over and over, you give me more reason to love you!"

Mom Maggie smiled, and her face seemed to glow! Any inconvenience she'd had was worth it. Serving was all she knew, and what she did best. Her baby girl's protection was her only focus. She kissed Rachel's cheek, and Rachel kissed hers in return. The bond was very strong. It was unbreakable.

Now that Rachel's eyes had been opened, she wanted to know everything. She asked, "Mama, have you left out anything?" Mom Maggie said, "Just one more thing. I caught Robert sitting in his buggy in front of the house. When he climbed down, I intercepted him. He was persuaded to leave in a hurry, when he saw the rifle cocked at him. It was actually a comical sight. He slipped and fell before he was able to get back into the buggy. He took off, at the speed of lightning." Rachel laughed at her mother's funny account. Mom Maggie was please with that. She knew that laughter could be as effective as her special herbal tea.

Rachel said, "Mama, we'll have to double our precautions in some way. Robert will be hell bent on getting revenge now. Her mother agreed with her. She said, "We will have to stay together. All of us must move as a unit. The carriage should be checked with a fine tooth comb before we use it. I'll put the rifle in the carriage whenever we have to go out. Robert is not above waylaying us on the road. We will never be away from the house after dark."

Rachel asked, " Are all of the bases covered?" Mom Maggie thought for a moment. "I'll ask Mr. Barney to get a dog for us. We'll need one that we can keep in the house. We don't want Robert to be able to toss it a chunk of poisoned meat. When we've done all that we can do, God will take up our cause and go the rest of the way for us. Robert will not, and he cannot, win!"

Rachel was very impressed with her mother's evidently well thought out plans. She said, "You've covered almost everything. The girls can't be outside alone for any reason. They won't be allowed to wander away, ever! It's best, really, that they stay inside, period!"

Mom Maggie had to agree with her logic. The girls were far more mature in some areas, than other children their age because of their experiences with Robert. They would understand why they couldn't go outside and make the best of a bad situation. They were aware of the peril that would place them in, and they would be co-operative.

Rachel added, "When school is over this week, we can ask our trusted friend, Mr. Barney, to take them to one of their uncles. They were going anyway. They'll just be going earlier than we planned. If Mr. Barney can't go, we'll ask Mr. Harris." Mom Maggie said, "Brilliant! It's settled. Now, let's cut the cake!"

CHAPTER 28

Robert had a lot riding on the last week of school. It could end for the old crow and her off-spring at that time. "The brats are too well protected going to and from school. I believe I know how to get around that. I can snatch them before they leave the building. I'll cast a spell over them with the help of the coins. They're just as stupid as Betty and Little Jim."

Robert's patience was wearing just a tad thin. If he succeeded, he could move into the house as early as next week. Now, with school closing, it would be rather difficult to sleep there. If he could move into the house, he wouldn't have to depend on his lover's, Bessie's, kindness. He was determined to not stay at her place everyday. That would ruin his image.

He thought about what he called the spectacle at church. "It'll take a lot to erase the damage she did. She tore down in one minute what took me years to build! Pastor Bacon was between the devil and the deep blue sea. He didn't know what or who to believe. More than ever, they must be removed. Things will subside, once I've destroyed them. I'm sure of it!"

To be sure that he would catch "the brats", he dismissed his class fifteen minutes early and waited outside their classroom. The door opened, and the children filed out. Fran saw him first. She yanked Mary's arm, and they fled for their lives! He started after them, but the other children were in his way, and they slowed him down. He cursed them, but it didn't help. The girls were running as fast as their legs could carry them!

The carriage was waiting for them. They climbed up into the carriage and looked back after their father. Robert watched from the door as they road away out of his sight. Breathlessly, Fran told Mr. Harris what happened. He assured them that they had done the correct thing. They were anxious to get home. Fran was aware that they had narrowly escaped something awful!

After hearing about what had happened, Mom Maggie and Rachel decided to keep them home the rest of the week. Mr. Barney arranged with the school to pick up their assignments and report cards at the end of the week. A few more days at school wasn't worth the risk. The other teachers had kept the secret thus far, but it wasn't enough. They would soon travel to their uncles' homes.

Mr. Barney brought them a great watchdog named King. Fran and Mary fell in love with him. Mom Maggie and Rachel could sleep, knowing that King would wake them up with his loud barking. If anyone dared to approach the house, King was on the job! Faithful Mr. Barney continued to make his rounds. They were more than ready for Deacon Robert Grant.

Robert waited and watched until Wednesday to snare the children. Finally, he understood that they weren't coming back to school. He had frightened them away! "So much for plan B. Now, I'll have to work out another strategy."

Robert would not allow himself to entertain thoughts of failure. He consoled himself by calling them mere set-backs. He maintained that set backs did not spell failure. "At least not in my book. I can see victory, and it's almost within my grasp." When he reached it and the timing was right, viola!

Disheartened, he rode to Bessie's place. Bessie greeted him, but she merely grunted. Her heartbeat quickened, as she feared what might follow. He was obviously distracted. Bessie didn't initiate conversation. She assumed that something had gone wrong for him and hoped he wouldn't take it out on her.

She would end the relationship, if she could find a way to do it smoothly. If she could avoid having him beat the daylights out of her, she would. She had begun to feel like a prisoner in her own home, and she was tired of it. Often, she thought, "Bobby is more strict than my parents were."

She glanced at him. He sat with his eyes closed, but she knew he wasn't asleep. She watched him, while building a case for herself. She thought, "Here I sit, with a man who has never told me his last name. He beats me for his sport, and he expects me to be here for him, at all times. Maybe, I'll get some of my male friends to teach him a much needed lesson. I want my freedom back!"

Robert hadn't mentioned food, and Bessie was getting hungry. Robert was plotting, but Bessie couldn't know that. She could only pray that she would escape without being beaten. It was getting dark, and he still hadn't spoken. Suddenly, he stood up and walked out of the door without uttering a word. Bessie heard the horse and buggy leave, and she breathed easier. She sat there for awhile. "Why am I still here? He's gone!"

She decided that Bobby wasn't coming back. She couldn't really figure out why he had come. He acted as if he hadn't seen her and he hadn't said anything. "He didn't even grunt!" She applied makeup and headed for her favorite spot.

When Bessie walked into the saloon, it seemed like ages since she had seen her buddies. Everyone asked about the man who used to pick her up there. He hadn't been there lately, and they were curious. To some, she told the truth. "I'm trying to find a way to get rid of him without being beaten to death. I have a love-hate relationship with this man, and it's wearing thin!"

Bessie stayed awhile, and she left with a male companion. She entertained the gentleman at home, then sent him away. Bessie felt good. She was getting her groove back! This was her life before Bobby entered it and ruined everything. She whistled as she bathed and prepared for bed.

❖ ❖ ❖

Robert left Bessie's with the outlandish notion that he should try to get into the house. If he could do it quickly and quietly, he would be able to slaughter the entire family at one time. He would make sure they were asleep and approach the house on foot. He would pry open a window and enter that way.

Robert waited until after midnight before he walked up to the house. He raised the crow bar he carried and started to force the kitchen window open. Suddenly, a dog started barking from inside the house. Robert was startled! He backed away from the window instinctively. Before he could clear his head and react with some dignity, the door opened, and Mom Maggie was outside with a rifle. King ran towards Robert, and he fled.

His hat fell off, as he ran to the buggy, but he didn't have time to think about it, or pick it up. He leaped up into the buggy, but not before King tore the seat of his pants. King jumped up and down, trying to get hold of Robert! He flipped the reins and zigzagged away. He didn't stop until he reached Bessie's.

During the wild ride over, he hadn't had time to think about what just happened. Between Mom Maggie and the dog, he felt that his life was about to end abruptly. He had no doubt that his mother-in-law would shoot to kill. As he climbed down from the buggy, he panted, "That crazy old coot!"

He practically fell in the door. He made so much noise, that Bessie sat up in bed. She asked, "Are you all right, Bobby?"

"Shut up!", he snarled.

She thought, "Like I really care." Bessie longed for the day when he would leave and not come back, ever!

When she turned around, she could see that his pants were missing a large chunk out of the seat. Also, when he left, he was wearing a hat. It seemed to be missing. Bessie had to pretend not to notice, for fear of a beating. Robert removed his clothing and studied the torn pants. He threw them across the room and cursed! That was the first time Bessie had ever heard him swear.

Robert couldn't tell Bessie, but he had been out-witted again. "Those stupid fools are as determined to live, as I am to kill them. Maybe, I'm trying too hard to save the house. I'm missing something small. I'll go to bed. When I stop trying, the perfect plan will come to me. This is probably a case of not being able to see the forest for the trees. I'll let the right idea come without forcing it."

Robert got into bed and held out his arms to Bessie. She hated him, but the old excitement was still there. Maybe it was there to stay! On some level she enjoyed playing his game, and Bobby knew that only too well. However, nothing could convince her to not leave him the first chance she got. She was involved in something that was too hot for her to handle. She knew that better than anybody.

CHAPTER 29

School closed the next day. Time was nudging Robert once again. Just as he had predicted, Robert came up with a plan that was a masterpiece. It would be played out on Monday. That would give him time to set everything in motion.

He would pay someone to lure Mom Maggie on the pretense that someone who was deathly ill needed her. "The old hag won't be able to say no, even though she's no more than a glorified witch doctor. I'm not impressed because the doctor sends for her when he's sick. He's a fool too!"

The next step in his plan was rather iffy. Robert would waylay her and kill her if necessary. "I'll probably decide to kill the ugly old bag. When that's over, I'll go to the house and kill the others. I'll make it look like a robbery in both cases. The finger of guilt must not be pointed at me, but at some nebulous character."

Robert was positive that he was a genius after all. Somehow, he got through the school day, but it wasn't easy. The possibility of success at last had him on a high. He even dared to look beyond his plan for mass murder to make long range plans for himself.

On Saturday, he refined the plans he had made. He found the woman who was a new-comer in town, and she agreed to entice Mom Maggie to leave the house, for a price. With the dog there, he felt that she would be more apt to do this.

He decided that he would not kill Mom Maggie unless it became absolutely necessary. She had no claim to his house, so he could afford to let her live. As for the dog, a nice chuck of meat would take care of him.

Robert had the woman, whose name was Janet, rehearse her lines over and over. When she had perfected them, Robert was satisfied. He would pay her well after Mom Maggie left the house. How well, depended on how convincing she was. Robert rubbed his hands together.

Robert got up on Monday morning to make a dry run. He needed to know how much time it would take to overtake Mom Maggie's carriage. He had to be sure that she was on the road. Also, he needed to know how much time it would take to get from there to the house. It all had to be perfectly timed to work the way he intended.

Bessie smiled to herself when he left the house. She had plenty of time to entertain her beaus, she figured. Bessie didn't know that Robert was a teacher and that school was over for the summer months. She threw caution to the wind and went to her favorite haunt.

Bessie's depressed mood changed dramatically when she entered the bar. Familiar faces smiled when she looked their way. She felt like a caught fish that had been taken off the hook and thrown back into the water. She was born to be a free spirit. That lifestyle fit her like a comfortable old shoe. Anything less was foreign to her and totally unacceptable. Robert's somber face faded quickly from her memory. This was her home away from home, and she was the golden girl!

On Saturday, Mom Maggie and Rachel had an early morning visitor. Their pastor, Reverend Clyde Bacon dropped by. He'd never come so early before. They could tell by his fidgeting that he was on a mission. When he found a comfortable moment, he said, "The incident at church has been troubling me. I need to talk with Mom Maggie. I take great store in whatever you say. Can you clear this up for me?"

Mom Maggie knew it was time. She and Rachel sat together and faced Pastor Bacon. He perched on the edge of his chair. He knew, instinctively, that something was about to be revealed to him. He had come looking for answers, but now he wasn't sure that he wanted to hear what Mom Maggie was about to tell him. To back out at this point, however, was unthinkable. He steeled himself and focused on the two women. He could tell that this was very difficult for them as well.

Mom Maggie looked directly into his eyes as she spoke. "I will come right to the point. Robert Grant is a wolf in sheep's clothing! We are positive that he is responsible for Little Jim's and Betty's death. He ran over Little Jim, deliberately, and he fed poisoned berries to Betty! We have proof of that!" The pastor opened his mouth and couldn't seem to close it.

Mom Maggie continued to speak. "Robert attempted to strangle Evelyn with a rope when he thought we were asleep. We had to send her away to protect her from him. In the beginning, he tried to kill me by hacking the carriage axle almost in two and loosening the bolts. In addition to that, he's tried to get into the house twice."

"Robert is a child of Satan! We have been fighting for our very lives! We have been blessed to have Mr. Barney and Mr. Harris assisting us. We owe them a great deal. Whenever we need them, they are here. Believe me, we need them often! Mrs. Barney was good enough to take Evelyn into her home. That information is for your ears only, Pastor. Any leak could jeopardize Evelyn's safety!"

He said, "My lips are sealed!"

Rachel added, "Pastor Bacon, Mama has spoken the truth. We are still living in danger. My girls are leaving this morning, for their safety. This upheaval is Robert's doing. We are prisoners in our own home. You will never know, nor can you ever imagine the horror we have experienced living with that madman. Without my mother, we could not have survived!"

Pastor Bacon shook his head throughout their testimonies. When he did speak, it was with deep respect. "Robert has deceived everybody in this town. He is a disgrace to the church and to the human race. I understand why you felt that neither of you could come to me. I was completely taken in by the man! I was blinded by his great talent. Satan used him and his talent for his own purpose. What a waste! He should be in prison! Ladies, Robert will be removed from the Board of Deacons. We will not tolerate his actions! From this moment on, you can count on my full support." He stayed awhile longer, then left to confer with the board about Robert.

Soon it was time for the girls to leave. When Mr. Barney came to take them, Rachel and the girls cried. Mom Maggie was too relieved to cry. Fran and Mary waved until they were out of sight. Rachel said, "Mama, they're gone, but this time it's different. They're still alive!"

The girls were safe, but part of the problem still existed. They were mindful of that. Mom Maggie said, "Telling the pastor was the right thing to do. Robert should be exposed, not protected. When he discovers that he's been removed from the board, he will probably speed up his plans. Maybe his anger will cause him to make a costly mistake. We'll stay on top of things."

Rachel squeezed her mother's hand in a rush of love for her. She just could not imagine life without her. Mom Maggie sensed her mood and gave her a peck on the cheek. "You'll be happy very soon. This can't last much longer. When it's over, this house will burst at the seams from so much love and laughter. You'll see!"

Robert had made his practice run and worked out the kinks in his plans. He would go to Bessie's and relax until it was time to make his move. His plans were taking shape, and he was in a very good mood. He rode back, knowing it would soon be over. He would take his rightful place as occupant and master of his home.

As he drew near Bessie's place he noticed a carriage parked there, but he paid little attention to it. Robert drove up behind the carriage. Suddenly, the door opened and Bessie was standing there dressed in a robe. A man stepped out of the house, turned and kissed Bessie. As he walked to the parked carriage, Bessie waved and blew him a kiss. Robert was so angry, he was feverish!

Too late, Bessie saw him and tried to close the door. Alas, Bessie was too slow. He pushed his way inside and faced the trembling woman. Bessie knew she had been caught, red-handed, but she attempted to lie her way out of it. "Bobby, it's not the way it looked! He really is my cousin! My favorite aunt's son. I never told you about my Aunt Bessie. I was taking a nap when he came. That's why I'm wearing my robe."

Robert watched her squirm and enjoyed every minute. Bessie tried again to explain her way out of the predicament she was obviously trapped in. "You believe me, don't you? I wanted him to wait to meet you, but he had to go home. You wouldn't know, but my Aunt Sadie is very sick. Bobby, please don't be mean to me! You really can trust me!"

Bessie fell to her knees and sobbed. Robert kicked her, and she slid across the floor! He walked over to her and kicked her again. Bessie screamed and tried to get up. He said, "Which is it, Bessie? Your old Aunt Bessie, or your old Aunt Sadie?"

Robert watched her struggling. She made it to her feet, and staggered to the bed. She sat there shaking and whimpering. Robert said coolly, "I warned you about being with other men, didn't I, Bessie?" He expected an answer, and Bessie knew that. She nodded and looked at him pitifully. She was trying to read his expression, but it was too difficult.

He hissed, "You are a liar and a no good tramp! I hate your guts. I'm going to kill you for making a fool out of me, Miss Bessie!" She crawled, rapidly, to the far corner of the bed, knowing that she couldn't escape. She knew that foolish action was better than no action at all.

Robert roared, "Come here, Bessie!" She crawled to him, crying as she did. He ordered, "Kiss me the same way you kissed your boyfriend!" Nervously, she gave him a little peck on the cheek. Wrong! Robert was so angry that he punched her in the face! Blood dripped from her mouth, and spurted from her nose. "Tell me how much you love me, Bessie." Bessie tried to wipe her bleeding nose. "I do love you, Bobby. Please give me another chance. I'll prove it to you. Please!"

Frantically, she wrapped her arms around him, but he put his hands around her throat. He squeezed until she gurgled and wet herself! Bessie pulled and clawed at his hands, but he held her neck in an iron grip. He had toyed with her long enough!

She opened her mouth wide, in an effort to scream. Her eyes darted back and forth. She was too weak to fight for air, and everything was fading. Bessie slumped, and Robert threw her on the bed. He had loved her, and this was how she loved him back! He felt that she deserved what she got.

Robert looked at Bessie for the last time, then went outside for some air. The encounter with Bessie had been exhausting. He leaned against his carriage to rest a bit. He whispered, to nobody in particular, "Why is there a flaw in every woman I meet? Bessie came very close to being worthy of my love, but not close enough. She was exciting, but she is a worthless tramp!"

He knew that he couldn't permit that murder to interfere with his plans to murder the others. He decided to ride to a spot where he could see Mom Maggie as she passed. That would be his cue to go to the house.

Janet went to the house to see Mom Maggie, as Robert had directed her to do. She related the rehearsed story.

"Miss Maggie, my mother is extremely ill. You don't know me, because I am new in town. I heard so much about you!"

"Doc Freeman lives not too far from where you say you live. You should talk to him. He's a good doctor."

"I tried, but he didn't answer the door. He must be out on a case."

"Please Miss. I'm sure he'll be there by the time you get back."

"Miss Maggie, my mother will die if you don't come!'

"What seems to be the problem?"

"She has a high fever and terrible cramps. I'm afraid for her!"

Mom Maggie listened, but she wasn't convinced of her sincerity. The girl wavered under the great lady's piercing eyes. Something inside made her not trust this woman who she didn't know. She suspected that she was part of one of Robert's elaborate schemes. Mom Maggie could not be moved, but she gave the young lady medicine with specific instructions. She had to trust her instincts as usual.

※　※　※

After several hours passed, Robert knew the woman had failed. "This has been a rotten day," he observed. He would have to rethink his plans, but he had no place to go. Finally, he decided to go back to Bessie's. "I'll have to spend the night with her corpse. I don't have any other solution, but it won't present a problem. Things always look better in the morning." He turned the horse in that direction.

He forced his mind to think of nothing that would depress him. He was in an almost hopeless place, but he couldn't afford to dwell on it and remain sane. He had to believe that he would take possession of his house. Killing Bessie was just a necessary incidental.

He was tired when he arrived at Bessie's place. He opened the door and went inside. He knew instantly that something was wrong. He didn't see Bessie's body! "She didn't walk away, because she was dead. Who could have removed her body so soon? How would anyone know?" Robert knew he had left her on the bed, dead! He couldn't make heads or tails of the crazy situation.

Very soon, it occurred to Robert that whoever had removed Bessie might come back. He gathered his belongings, knowing he couldn't stay there any longer. The entire day had been one failure after the other. He was not going to give up. Setbacks had always made him more sharp. He would look forward to a brighter day tomorrow. That upbeat thought didn't alter the fact that he would be reduced to sleeping in his buggy along some lonely road. Almost immediately he brightened a bit and said to himself, "Tomorrow I'll find more suitable lodging in another town. Certainly I can manage to endure a little hardship. Things always look better in the morning." Satisfied that he'd settled the problem, he picked up his bags and started towards the door. He reached for the door knob, but the door opened suddenly. Robert was totally unprepared for the sudden turn of events, and he stopped in his tracks.

Three men walked inside and planted themselves in front of Robert. He peered anxiously at their faces, hoping to find some sign of friendliness. He only saw naked hatred, and he couldn't fathom why. He felt sweat forming in his armpits, and his mouth began to quiver uncontrollably. His hands opened without his help, and the packed bags fell to the floor with a muffled sounding noise. He thought, "I've always been able to think on my feet, but these men seem to be driven. Who are they? Is this a case of mistaken identity?" He struggled without success to come up with a plan.

Robert couldn't walk forward, so he backed against a wall. At that point, one of the men spoke. "You seem surprised to see us. For your information, we know what you did to Bessie. No thanks to you, Bessie was able to crawl out of the house after you left. A passerby saw her and took her to the hospital. We went to her as soon as we heard the news. She said that you would come back, and we've been waiting for you. Bessie didn't die, dog, but you will!"

At that point, Robert felt and looked like a trapped animal. He was desperate, but he could see no way out. He wanted to live, but his brain had stopped functioning. He could not think of a way out of his predicament. His eyes moved swiftly from one man's face to the other. He saw only that their stony expressions remained intact. At one point, he thought, "I'll offer them money! Everybody loves money!" The thought left as quickly as it came. "Whatever I have in my wallet they can take after they murder me."

Robert desperately wanted to live. Death was something that he seldom thought about. When he did, he visualized himself dying a very dignified death in his old age. As a respected member of the community and top notch deacon of his church, he knew there would be standing room only at his funeral. Someone would sing some of the hymns he'd composed, and there wouldn't be a dry eye in the church. He would look down from the special place in heaven and smile indulgently. Then he would nod and say, "I did it my way, and I did it well." Only then would he be ready to take charge of whatever God had chosen for him to do.

Now the tables had turned, and nothing was as he'd expected. For the second time in his adult life, Robert cried. He was about to meet his death at the hands of strangers, and he was far from being prepared for such an end. He still sought a way out.

At that moment, Little Jim's and Betty's face flashed before his eyes! He screamed, "No! No!" Robert's arms beat the air, and he slid along the wall in an attempt to get away from the images of the children he'd murdered. He covered his eyes, but it didn't help. He could still see them. He beat at the air with his hands, but they were still there – mocking him. The men were forgotten as Robert screamed and ran around the room in circles. Finally, he backed himself into a corner and held out his hands to them. "Please leave me! Please give me a little peace! I'm sorry that I killed you! Can't you see how sorry I am? Stop haunting me!"

Robert attempted to escape their faces, but he fell over his packed bags. He lay on the floor in an awkward position screaming. His once handsome features were twisted and spittle oozed from the corner of his mouth. He'd forgotten that his life was in peril.

The three men had watched his antics with amusement for awhile. They believed that he was pretending to be mentally ill to avoid whatever he'd have to face from them. They couldn't know, because only Robert could see the faces of his dead children. The children he'd murdered in cold blood.

Very soon the men's amused facial expressions changed to disgust. They had grown tired of Robert and his dramatics. One nodded slightly to the others, and they moved in for the kill. Nothing short of Robert's blood would satisfy them.

Robert's shoulders heaved as he lay spent on the floor. For awhile he had almost forgotten the danger he faced. Now he heard the sound of feet moving towards him, and it all came rushing back.

The faces of his children faded as the muffled sounds came closer and closer. Robert knew it was time. He scrambled to his feet and stood there swaying for a second, before falling heavily to his knees. He pleaded with the men to spare his life. "Give me a chance! Please don't hurt me! I'll leave the country immediately! Bessie will never hear from me again! I'll arrange to send her enough money to make her rich! I swear on the head of my dead mother! I'll do whatever you want me to do! Please! I don't want to die! You said that Bessie is all right. I'm glad about that! I really am! I lost my head! I didn't mean to hurt her! I love her with all my heart! I do! Don't kill me! Please! Please let me live!"

The men ignored his cries, and the saliva that dripped from his open mouth. Robert wet his pants, and they ignored that as well. It was clear to Robert that the end of his life was certain, but he was too distraught to compose himself. The dignified death he'd dreamed of was not to be. His mouth was open wide when one man seized his head and held it back. One of the others took out a large gleaming knife and slit Robert's throat from ear to ear! As the knife slid across his throat, he let out a blood-curdling scream! Robert's eyes danced crazily in his head.

Now Robert's spirit was poised, ready to take flight into the depths of hell. The man moved the knife from Robert's throat and plunged it into his heart! His reign of terror was finally over. Robert was dead!

The men weren't satisfied. They took turns kicking Robert's body a few times before they carried him to his buggy. They threw him into the back of the buggy, then climbed in themselves. To keep their friend Bessie's name clear, they rode away from her home. At a safe distance, they parked and climbed out of his buggy and went into the bar. They'd decided to mingle there awhile to establish an alibi should it become necessary. They were reasonably sure that they hadn't been seen, but they had to be sure. In the morning they would take the good news to Bessie, and she would be able to rest easier. She could resume her life without fear of "Mr. Bobby."

Robert lay in a twisted position in the back of his own buggy. Oddly, he had planned to spend the night there when the strangers intercepted him at Bessie's place. The difference was that he'd also planned to get up at dawn. Now and then another buggy passed, but no one bothered to investigate the seemingly empty buggy.

✧ ✧ ✧

At the precise time that Robert met his death, Mom Maggie felt something in the air! She stood still as the feeling washed over her. In a moment the images of her dead grandchildren appeared before her, and they were smiling. When the images faded she said, "I'm almost afraid to interpret that. I believe it meant that justice has been served! I wonder how, when and where!"

Mom Maggie left the room where she'd seen the vision and went to the kitchen to be with Rachel. She wanted to be near her child after the experience she'd had. She thought, "The house seems so lonely and empty without the children. Rachel will never get used to this. She's been a mother too long."

Because Mom Maggie had promised to share everything with her daughter, she told her about the disturbing vision. "It shook me to the core, Rachel. I can't be positive, but I know it means something. Whatever it is, we'll know at the proper time. Things have a way of working themselves out. Sometimes it's what we want, but sometimes it's not. Either way, it's always what we need. I believe that with all of my heart." Rachel hugged her mother and said, "Mama, I believe in your gift. I would be crazy to not believe. I'll try to be patient. We'll wait and see."

They talked awhile longer, then they decided, jointly, that they would not relax their precautions. King was still at his post, and he would stay there for the duration.

✧ ✧ ✧

The next day they rose refreshed and went about their usual routine. The vision, however, was never very far from their minds. Rachel suggested that they should write letters to the children after lunch. That' what they were doing when they saw their pastor coming up the driveway. They met him at the door and invited him inside. It seemed to be a social call, and they were pleased. Rachel brought him a cool glass of tea. After a bit of small talk, he cleared his throat and told them why he was really there.

"I thought it would be better coming from me. I'm afraid the news is not good. This morning, Robert was found lying in the buggy. He had been butchered to death! It probably occurred sometime last night. There were witnesses, I gather. That's what old Doc Freeman said." Pastor Bacon held his breath and waited for the fallout that he felt was sure to come.

Rachel stiffened and closed her eyes for a moment. Mom Maggie stepped in. "Pastor, we won't drink a toast to the occasion, but God allowed this to happen this way. He has brought peace and closure to our lives. For that I am grateful to my God." She was sorry that the children were sacrificed before Robert met his end, but she didn't say it. That she kept to herself.

Rachel was quiet. She was remembering all the bad times. She thought about how she tried to find the poisonous berries, but couldn't. She thought, "If I'd found them, my children would have been spared. Robert would have been stopped in his tracks long before his fiendish mind concocted their deaths."

Rachel's memory stretched back even further. "My first mistake, I must admit, was not listening to Mom Maggie's warnings about Robert. I, too, had misgivings, but Robert's charm effectively muddied the waters. All of my friends had been envious when the marvelous singer chose me. I began to believe that my mother was being old-fashioned and wrong. I thought she didn't understand such a man as Robert."

All of those things she thought about, but she kept it to herself. She had, with the arrogance and stupidity of youth, stepped into Robert's trap. She realized now that she really wasn't responsible for his satanic nature. She decided at that moment to stop blaming herself so much because she really wasn't responsible for the things he did. She refused to kick herself because it was just a waste of time. Now at last, Rachel was clear on that. She thought, "I'm finally clear on that. I refuse to let Robert control me from the grave. It's all over for him. He merely reaped what he sowed."

Rachel looked over at her mother and vowed silently to spend the rest of her life loving and cherishing her mother and her beloved children. She would do everything in her power to erase every vestige of evil and turmoil from their precious lives. She acknowledged that the debt was hers alone, and she would pay it.

Now that Rachel had uncluttered her mind, she turned her attention to the pastor and his mission. "Reverend Bacon, we won't have a service of any kind for Robert. He doesn't deserve one, and we don't want one for him. The funeral director can dispose of his body as soon as possible and in his own way. If he can be buried for a dollar, we'll go for that. I believe that's the way it should be done, under the circumstances."

Pastor Bacon was in total agreement with her. "I'll speak to the funeral director for you, ladies. His place is on the way. It won't be a problem for me. If you think of something else that I can do, I'll be here in a flash. Your family will be in my prayer."

He stood slowly and retrieved his hat. He extended his hand and Mom Maggie and Rachel extended theirs. It had all been a bit too much for him as well. His shoulders sagged a bit, but just for a moment. He thought, "These ladies have risen above it all, and I must do the same." Having said that to himself, he squared his shoulders and stood more erect. He bade them both goodbye, and walked out of the house to his buggy.

Rachel and Mom Maggie stood side by side watching the pastor ride out of sight. They had been in the storm so long that is was hard to believe it was finally over. Innocent blood had been spilled so needlessly, but three children had been saved. They had to remember it that way if they were to preserve their sanity.

Mom Maggie was the first to move. She opened the windows, letting in the fresh air for the first time in ages. Rachel followed her lead. Together Mom Maggie and Rachel removed all traces of Robert. Everything was discarded in the trash cans, including his portrait. They checked carefully to be sure that nothing was left. The house seemed to sparkle with a new kind of brightness.

When they had finished, Mom Maggie turned to her baby girl with a broad smile on her face. "Rachel, it's out with the old! In with the new!" Rachel kissed Mom Maggie's cheek, and Mom Maggie patted her baby girl's hand. They said nothing. They didn't need words because love is really more than telling.

The great lady's mission was over!

COMING IN 2010 FROM THE ELEVATOR GROUP
Cousin Myrtle, a novel, by P. J. McCalla (August)
*Creativity for Christians: How to Tell Your Story and Stories of Overcoming
by the Members of One Special Church*
by Sheilah Vance with Rev. Felicia Howard (June)
*Mr. and Mrs. Grassroots: How Barack Obama, Two Bookstore Owners,
and 300 Volunteers Did It*
by John Presta (January)
Dining with the $ Diva by Betty Fisher (March)

ALSO AVAILABLE FROM THE ELEVATOR GROUP
Land Mines, a novel, by Sheilah Vance
Journaling Through the Land Mines by Sheilah Vance
Chasing the 400, a novel, by Sheilah Vance
Soul Poems: Life as Fertile Ground by Melodye Micëre Van Putten
Obamatyme: Election Poetry by Melodye Micëre Van Putten
A Student's Guide to Being Happy in Argentina by Hope Lewis

AND FROM THE ELEVATOR GROUP FAITH
*A Christian Woman's Journal to Weight Loss:
A 52 Week Guide to Losing Weight With the Word*
by Patricia Thomas

For more information about the books above,
see www.TheElevatorGroup.com or contact us at:

ELEVATOR GROUP
* PUBLISHING *

Helping People Rise Above™

The Elevator Group,
PO Box 207 • Paoli, PA 19301
610-296-4966
info@TheElevatorGroup.com